Praise for TRUE VOWS

"What better way is there to prove romance really exists than to read these books?"
—**Carly Phillips**, *New York Times* bestselling author

"Memoir meets romance! In the twenty years I've been penning romances, this is one of the most novel and exciting ideas I've encountered in the genre. Take a Vow. It rocks!"
—**Tara Janzen**, *New York Times* bestselling author of *Loose and Easy*

"An irresistible combination of romantic fantasy and reality that begins where our beloved romance novels end: TRUE VOWS. What a scrumptious slice of life!"
—**Suzanne Forster**, *New York Times* bestselling author

"The marriage of real-life stories with classic, fictional romance—an amazing concept."
—**Peggy Webb**, award-winning author of sixty romance novels

THE ICING ON THE CAKE

THE FIRST REALITY-BASED ROMANCE™

Alison Kent
THE ICING ON THE CAKE

Health Communications, Inc.
Deerfield Beach, Florida

www.hcibooks.com

Library of Congress Cataloging-in-Publication Data

Kent, Alison.
   The icing on the cake / Alison Kent.
      p.   cm.
   ISBN-13: 978-0-7573-1535-0
   ISBN-10: 0-7573-1535-6
   1. Online dating—Fiction. I. Title.
PS3561.E5155I25 2010
813'.54—dc22

                                                          2010025707

Publisher: Health Communications, Inc.
           3201 S.W. 15th Street
           Deerfield Beach, FL 33442–8190

TRUE VOWS Series Developer: Olivia Rupprecht
Cover photo ©Dreamstime
Cover design by Larissa Hise Henoch
Interior design and formatting by Lawna Patterson Oldfield

To Walt

If you had canceled your

Internet subscription in December '96

as you'd thought you might do,

I would've missed out on a life spent with

the best man I've ever known.

I love you. Forever.

Or at least for forty years.

Dear Reader

WHEN I FIRST LEARNED THAT HCI BOOKS would be publishing Reality-Based Romance, I wondered why no one had thought of doing so before! Just look at the popularity of TV shows like *Survivor, The Bachelor, The Real Housewives* franchise, and *America's Next Top Model.* We love reality programming. RB Romance™ made perfect sense, giving readers the same glimpse into real people's lives with the "happily ever after" the romance genre delivers so beautifully. Kudos to TRUE VOWS Series Creator Michele Matrisciani for her vision.

Working on the launch of TRUE VOWS with authors Judith Arnold (check out *Meet Me in Manhattan,* one of the first three TRUE VOWS books) and Julie Leto (*Hard to Hold*), and Series Developer Olivia Rupprecht, has been one of the best writing adventures of my career. So many combined years of experience and such talent all in one place made for incredible brainstorming e-mails and conference calls. My undying appreciation goes to Judith, Julie, and Olivia for their talent and insight, and a special thank you to Julie for suggesting me for the gig. Also, a shout out to Veronica Blake for suggesting to her HCI colleagues to enter the romance genre, and to HCI's president and publisher

Peter Vegso for his open-mindedness and encouragement surrounding the new concept of "reality-based romance."

Reading the *Washington Post's* feature on Michelle Snow and Todd Bracken sparked my creative juices even before I got to the end. The photos of their cupcakes had my imagination—not to mention my taste buds—running wild. I'm humbled to be able to bring their story to life, and I thank them for being forthcoming, receptive, and patient, and for Ben Folds's *The Luckiest*.

The Brackens's relationship is the epitome of what makes romance the most popular form of genre fiction. True love, as William Goldman tells us, doesn't happen every day, but what Todd and Michelle share will happen for a lifetime. It was a pleasure to work with them and to watch their dream—Frosting, A Cupcakery—come to life. Now to get to Chevy Chase, Maryland, and sample their wares . . .

I encourage you to visit the official TRUE VOWS site: www.truevowsbooks.com, to interact with the couples and novelists, learn the latest news on the TRUE VOWS line, read about the upcoming books in the series, and even have the opportunity to tell HCI BOOKS your true love story for a chance to be the subject of a future TRUE VOWS book.

Happy reading . . . and happy cupcakes!

Alison Kent

One

*Snowflake: coconut bottom with coconut
vanilla buttercream top

"MICHELLE! DANA'S HERE!"

Elbowing open her bedroom door while fastening the clasp on her necklace, Michelle Snow called out, "Be right there!" in response to Christina's update. Liz, one of the foursome, was already in the tiny kitchen, brewing coffee and mixing a pitcher of mimosas for the weekend brunch. Dana, not surprisingly, was the last to arrive. She'd marched to a different drummer—and kept time to a different clock—as long as the four Alpha Phi sisters had been friends.

It had been too long since the group had gotten together, and Michelle was thrilled to be the one playing hostess this time. Yes, they'd be doing a lot of stepping around one another in her pint-sized condo, but she knew not a one of them cared. They had food, drink, and the best of company with whom to share the afternoon—not to mention months' worth of gossip to catch up on. And her place, well, if nothing else, it offered an intimacy no Friendship Heights venue could.

Taking one last look at her reflection, Michelle smoothed the skirt of the dress she'd changed into after making sure the table was set and the food ready. She loved dressing up as much as she loved cooking and entertaining—all joys instilled by her mother through the years. If she turned out to be half the hostess Ann Snow was, Michelle would consider it one of her life's greatest accomplishments.

With that thought came a smile that warmed her all the way to her toes. She really had hit the jackpot with her friends as well as her family, and counting herself both lucky and blessed, she headed for the front room. There, she held her arms wide in welcome, greeting her Sunday guests. "You guys look great! All of you! I'm so glad you're here!"

"Are you kidding?" Dana set her purse on the chest beneath the flat screen TV just inside the front door, her gaze never leaving Michelle's as she pushed a riot of coffee-black curls from her face. "Look at you! I love that dress!"

Laughing, Michelle spun once where she stood, the periwinkle fabric flowing softly against her skin. "I do, too. I don't know why I don't wear it more often."

Dana took in the table set with Waterford crystal and Royal Tara china, then frowned down at her penny loafers, khakis, and chino vest. "I feel decidedly underdressed. And plain. And I know Oxford casual does nothing for my eyes. But then again, there's not a lot to be done with brown, is there?"

"You're anything but plain, silly!" The other woman's complexion was perfect for the earth tones Michelle had never been able to pull off. "You're chocolate cake and iced tea and Portobello mushrooms rolled up into one."

"And mud. Don't forget mud." Dana wrapped an arm around Michelle's shoulder and hugged. "Actually, all that rolling would make mud, wouldn't it?"

Michelle laughed in answer, the two walking toward the kitchen where Liz had been trapped by Christina while the stunning blonde showboated about her love life. "Coffee or something stronger?"

"Coffee for now," Dana said, giving a wink to Liz. The other woman, obviously desperate for a rescue, mouthed, "Thank you," then turned her back on Christina to pour.

Michelle pressed her fingers to her lips, hiding her smile. Christina would always be Christina: the center of attention, the life of the party, the monopolizer of all conversations. Still, the others loved her, so like animals in the wild had learned over time to adapt.

Dana, adapting, went on. "I'll save the hard stuff for later, when talk turns to the lack of time most of us have for dating, and the lack of men most of us have to date. I figure I'll be needing a buzz by then."

Her attention pricked, Christina hurriedly swallowed, holding her drink to the side and fluttering her fingers. Her brightly lacquered nails looked like tiny brake lights flashing. "Time is one thing, sure. But lack of men? Totally a rumor. They are coming out of the woodwork."

"And that right there is the problem." Gathering the crushed bronze silk of the ankle-length skirt she wore with macramé roman sandals, Liz wiggled her way out of the kitchen, moving to the seat with her name card. "I don't want to date insects. Or vermin. They're disgusting, diseased, and too big to squash with your shoe."

"Some parts of them are small enough," Dana put in, taking her spot across from Liz. "Their wallets, for starters."

"Tell me about it." Michelle set a basket of sliced poppy-seed loaf on the table before going back to the fridge for the fruit salad.

"The last guy I met for dinner? He walked out on the tab while I was slipping on my sweater. I don't mind paying my part of the bill, but good grief. How cheap can you get?"

Nibbling on one of the almond crescents intended for dessert, Christina settled into her chair. "You're going about this dating thing all wrong, Michelle. All of you are. Take charge of your destiny. Stop hoping a guy in a club will actually deliver, or relying on friends for fix-ups."

Dana fluffed her napkin and draped it over her lap. "I dunno, Chris. Fix-ups aren't so bad. As long as whoever's setting you up knows both you and the guy. Dating sites give off a really bad tempting-fate vibe."

"True, though they have almost as much compatibility data to work with as friends do," Michelle said, sliding a knife through the quiche she'd pulled from the oven and serving a wedge to each of her guests.

"What they don't have is the personal touch that can make all the difference," Liz countered. "A computer doesn't know that smelling Drakkar on a man's skin makes you want to throw up. Or that you hate having a date suggest something on a menu when he has no clue what you like."

Christina overruled Liz's objections with a snort. "Even friends can get those things wrong."

"I've thought about signing up with a service," Michelle offered, surprised to hear the words spilling out. Thinking of doing so was one thing. Admitting she'd considered it had a whole lot of backfire potential.

"But?" Christina queried. "Not willing to put your money where your mouth is?"

Bang! "It's not about money as much as time. I don't have any. But it's some of what Dana says, too. Tempting fate. A recommendation from a friend goes a long way to soothing nerves and fears. Hooking up with a random stranger, not so much."

"You're overthinking things. Trust your instincts." Christina turned for the pitcher of mimosas behind her on the kitchen bar. "It doesn't take much reading between the lines of a dating-site profile to separate the wheat from the chaff."

Pushing her fringe of strawberry-blonde bangs from her eyes, Liz gave Christina a look of disbelief. "You're saying there are no rats and roaches online? Because from what I hear, that's where their kind thrives."

"Of course there are, but we're not talking about stalkers and pedophiles here," Christina said as she poured her second drink. "Just singles like us looking for company. Taking precautions isn't that hard. Make sure someone knows where you are and work out a code. Keep your phone handy with their number on speed dial. That sort of thing."

"I think I'd rather try eight-minute dating," Michelle said, wondering why Christina hadn't gone into the business of selling luxury cars instead of becoming a literary agent—though, she supposed, both took the same sort of playing hardball that made Christina Christina. "At least that much face-to-face time gives you a sense of their personality."

Dana licked a spot of the poppy-seed loaf's orange glaze from her fingertip, then said, "Not to mention their nose hair and breath."

Giggles erupted, fueled by champagne and appeased appetites and the letting down of hair that only happened in the company of close and trusted friends. Savoring the tang of the cheese in the quiche, Michelle listened as the others discussed the ups and downs of dating, of men, the creeps, the players, the basement dwellers, then moved to argue the pros and cons of settling for good enough versus waiting for true love.

For a moment, Michelle wondered if her friends were as happy as she was, content with their lives the way she was. Or, she thought, smiling as she reached for her coffee and cradled the cup in both hands, if they felt they had to have a man to complete them because that's what the movies said.

She understood the sentiment, that joining, that two becoming one, but for her it went both ways. She wasn't that needy and wouldn't want a man who was.

"Care to share what's going on in that pretty little head of yours, Ms. Snow?" Christina asked, meeting Michelle's gaze over the rim of her flute.

She figured it wasn't a big deal, and confessed, "Jerry Maguire."

"The movie?" Liz asked, halving the last bite of her quiche. "Or were you thinking about Tom Cruise?"

Tom's *Oprah* moment was a perfect example of the crazy, obsessive behavior Michelle wanted to avoid. "I was thinking about the line the movie made famous."

"'Show me the money!'?" Dana asked.

"No. 'You complete me.'" She toyed with the bread on her plate, pinching off a corner of the crust. "I mean, yes, I'd love to be in a relationship, to eventually have the two-point-five kids and, well, not a white picket fence, but whatever the urban version might be. But I'm happy now. I don't feel incomplete at all. Seriously, how bad would it be living the rest of my life as Single Snow?"

She looked from Liz to Christina to Dana, getting a mix of reactions, though none vocal. She wondered what was going through the women's minds, if they were worried about her seeming indifference to dating, or if they were looking inward, stacking their own emotional responses on the opposite side of the scale from the one she used to weigh her outlook on love. Surely she wasn't so different from them.

Was she?

Liz finally spoke. "It wouldn't be bad if you really are happy."

Brows knitted, Michelle gave a brisk nod. "I am—"

"But," the other woman continued before Michelle could explain. "I hate thinking of some really great guy missing out on all the love you have to give."

"Not to mention the gorgeous home you keep." Dana gestured toward the accessories Michelle had carefully chosen to pull the look together, the peaceful taupes and creams and accents of brown on light aqua. "I can't think of anyone else who has your sense of style."

"Or your cooking skills that are incredible," Christina put in, as she took another bite of her quiche.

"Stop already, you guys!" Michelle laughed, a blush heating her neck and creeping toward her face. "Next thing I know you'll be writing ad copy and auctioning me off to the highest bidder."

"Or writing an online profile to find you a perfect match," Christina said, not bothering to hide her pleasure in bringing the conversation back to her current obsession.

"Do you really believe in perfect matches?" Liz asked, licking cheese from the tines of her fork.

Christina considered the question. "Of the happily ever after sort or the happily right now sort?"

"See? That's the thing." Finished with her food, Michelle laid her napkin across her plate and poured her first mimosa. "I am happy right now. I don't need to test-drive a bunch of lemons to get me there. But happily ever after? That's a trip worth taking. The pièce de résistance. The crème de la crème. The—"

"The icing on the cake," Dana said.

Michelle raised her glass in a toast. "Exactly."

"And how many people get that?" Liz asked, frowning. "Is happily ever after even realistic these days?"

For others? Michelle couldn't say. But for her . . . "I can't hope for anything else. And I definitely won't settle for anything less."

Christina huffed. "That would explain a lot."

Uh-oh. "A lot of what?"

"When's the last time you took a guy home to meet your parents?"

Michelle thought back. And back, and back, and back. All the way to college. And . . . him. Really? Had it been that long? Had he turned her off relationships for good, or had she just been too busy to do more than date casually? Maybe she'd stayed busy so she didn't have to put herself out there and risk suffering that much hurt a second time.

Men who cheated sucked. She screwed her face into a grimace as the reality swept through her. "Ten years?"

Sighing, Christina shook her head, pushed out of her chair as if this intervention had been a long time coming. She headed for the cushy brown club chair in the living room and the laptop out in the open on the side table.

Michelle knew what the other woman was up to but didn't give a moment's thought to putting a stop to the madness. Maybe it was the champagne taking advantage of the fact that she was a total lightweight. Maybe it was the relief of giving up control to someone better versed in the games the sexes played. Maybe it was just time.

Because, really? She was so out of practice she was picking up more than her fair share of tabs these days. And it wasn't about not wanting to be a mooch. It was just that the guys were the pits. Telling her she'd be hot if she put on a few pounds? *Yeah. No goodnight kiss for you, Mister Cheap Creep.*

Back in her chair, Christina pushed her plate aside to make room for the laptop. She booted it up, clearing her throat and bringing Michelle back to the moment just as, red nails flashing, she launched a browser window and typed www.match.com into the address bar.

"Here's what we're going to do. It won't take more than ten minutes to get your profile started. You can pay for the service later and add all the stuff you don't want us to see." The website came up, and Christina looked over, her sharply arched brows daring Michelle to argue.

Sigh. It wasn't like Michelle was having such great luck on her own. The bar scene was so not her thing. Coffee shops, bistros ... those locations didn't have the same meat-market vibe as did so many nightclubs and even the gym. But neither had any of the connections she'd made in such places panned out.

Christina went on. "Honestly, Chelle. What do you have to lose?"

"Certainly not her virginity," Liz said, snickering behind her mimosa glass as she sipped.

"You are so not funny," Michelle snapped, though she couldn't stop the grin that followed.

"Hold that pose." Christina abandoned the keyboard and brought up both hands as if framing Michelle's face. "Who's got a camera?"

"Ooh, ooh. I do. In my purse." Dana was up and edging her way around the table before Michelle could stop her.

"You guys. This is crazy." Crazy enough to work? Dare she do it? The idea was exciting, true, but excitement didn't last, and first attractions were way too quick to fade. She hedged, sweeping her bangs to the side with her fingertips. "I'm sure my hair's a mess."

Liz shook her head. "Your hair is perfect. The dress is perfect. The necklace is perfect. You look amazing, and guys are going to wink and nudge you to death."

"Not exactly the outcome I'm hoping for," Michelle muttered, ducking as Dana leaned across the table to hand Christina her sleek Nikon Coolpix, and wondering how the dating talk had gotten so out of hand. She didn't have time for this, and yet she found herself pondering the possibilities.

Was *The One* really out there? Someone not to complete her, but to complement her? To see the good in her and make her better? To allow her to do the same and to build on that trust, creating something together that would be bigger than either of them could be alone?

Or would this mission, should she choose to accept it, turn out to be a big waste of time?

"Smile." Christina clicked the shutter before Michelle was ready.

"I need a bit more notice than that, Chris."

"Just getting your attention." Straightening in her seat, Christina prepared to play photographer. "This one's for real, so sit up straight, look sexy, all that good stuff."

Fortifying herself with a sip of her drink, Michelle canted her head just a bit to the side and gave the camera—and the man of her dreams—the sweetest, most honest and inviting smile she could. Being sexy with the right man was no problem, but if she went through with Christina's plan, she wasn't putting herself out there as an open invitation for those only interested in notching their bedposts.

"Perfect," Christina said after snapping the shot and viewing the result on the LCD screen. She handed the camera to Michelle to see for herself.

Not bad. And it was sincere, resembling the real her, not some airbrushed or Photoshopped version intended to dupe a potential suitor into expecting more than he'd be getting. Casual, relaxed, her smile of contentment reaching her eyes. It would do—if she worked up the courage to post it.

"Listen," Christina said. "I've got a train to catch and a manuscript to read before tomorrow, but none of us are going anywhere until Michelle swears on her future firstborn that she'll try Match.com."

Hoping she wouldn't come to regret it, Michelle raised her right hand. "I swear on my future firstborn that I'll give a month of my life to Match.com."

"There now. Was that so hard?"

"I suppose not." Though of course she didn't let on to any of her friends that the fingers of her other hand had been crossed the whole time. And thankfully, not a one of them commented on the time limit she'd set as they left.

But as soon as Michelle shut the door behind the last of her guests, the excitement faded so quickly, she forgot the thrill that had carried her on its wings all afternoon. Monday morning loomed and, with it, a full agenda that required one-hundred percent of her attention.

She took one last look at the website that seemed to be mocking her, calling her a fraidy cat and a fuddy duddy and a fool. Annoyed, she stuck out her tongue and clicked the X that sent the cruel voice into the ether. Silly? Maybe.

But she, not some website, would be making decisions about her love life. And her promise to Christina aside, it would happen on *her* terms and when *she* had the time.

Online dating—and any men who might like to do more than give her a wink or a nudge—would have to wait.

Two

*Ba-nilla: banana bottom with vanilla buttercream top

HER ATTENTION ON THE PROPERTY TAX analysis she'd just received and her head pounding, Michelle reached blindly for the phone ringing on her desk. "Michelle Snow."

"Well? Any hot dates lined up yet?"

"Hey, Christina." She sat back, rubbing the tension from her nape, knowing she was in for the third degree and accepting she had no one to blame but herself.

It had been a week since their brunch, a week since she'd sworn on her future firstborn to give a month of her life to Match.com. And yet, here she sat, working her fingers to the bone, no closer to having a firstborn than she'd been that Sunday. Things at the office had been bananas, and dating had been the last thing on her mind.

Listening in the background as Christina answered her assistant's question about titles, Michelle thought to head off the impending interrogation, saying, "No dates yet. I haven't even finished my profile."

Christina, returning to the conversation, gasped in Michelle's ear. "Michelle! You prom—"

13

"I promised. I know." Since heading off hadn't worked, she gave cutting off a try. "I haven't had a minute to spare in days. Work is insane right now. The trouble the real estate market's in is hardly a secret."

This time Christina huffed into the phone, but her voice was no longer shrill when she spoke. "You're going to die old and shriveled and alone."

"Thanks for that," Michelle grumbled, rolling her very tired eyes, then letting them close. She couldn't deal with talking about herself. Not now. "And how're things with you? Meet Mr. Right yet?"

"Actually," Christina began, lowering her voice. "I'll be meeting him for the first time tonight. We've been texting all week but this is the first chance we've had to get together. We're having drinks at a place near his office. Look out your window around ten for the fireworks."

"You're two hundred miles away, Chris."

"They'll be bright enough. Trust me."

Michelle chuckled softly to herself. Only Christina would have the confidence to assume a man she'd never met would be around longer than one night. "Just a drink? You're not picking out china patterns?"

"You mock, but you're going to look like a movie star in your gold lamé bridesmaid dress."

As crazy as it sounded, Michelle could so see Christina pulling off something that outrageous. Maybe with bouquets of purple calla lilies, and a jazz band playing Ella Fitzgerald's Our Love Is Here to Stay. Or Etta James's At Last, with Christina and her new husband swaying together on the dance floor as had the Obamas while Beyoncé sang.

Dropping her gaze to her lap, Michelle toyed with the ribbed hem of her sweater, wondering what songs she and her husband would choose to dance to at their reception. Or if she'd ever have a reception, much less a wedding, and need to decide on things like fabric for bridesmaid dresses and flowers for boutonnieres and flavors for the cake's filling.

Enough. Seriously. Brooding was ridiculous, and not the least bit productive. Shaking off the fatigue that was obviously presenting as melancholia, she said, "Only for you, Christina, would I wear gold lamé."

On the other end of the line, Christina snorted. "How about for me, and for the sake of your future firstborn, you go home tonight and finish your Match.com profile? Dana e-mailed you the photo, yes?"

"She did. And I suppose it will do." If she was going to do this, and that was still a big if, then the photo from the Sunday brunch would also be a nod to the girlfriends who'd encouraged her to go for it.

"It'll more than do. It's perfect." Christina let the air between them go silent for a minute, then said, "You know I love you, Chelle, right? This isn't just me being the pushy broad that I know I am. I want good things for you, and that includes the relationship you deserve. You're a peach, and I want you to have it all."

Oh, great. On top of the hellacious day Michelle was having, now she was going to cry. Her voice, when she spoke, was all watery and weak, but she was so lucky to have such good friends that she couldn't help but laugh through the tears. "I love you, too, Christina. If I didn't, there's no way you'd get me into as much as gold lamé underwear."

Christina caught back what sounded like an emotional sob of her own before clearing her throat and getting back to business. "Okay, but lovefest or not, I'm going to keep bugging you about this. It's just a month. A month is nothing. Especially when we're talking about the rest of your life."

"I'll do it. I promise. Because honestly? I'm already pretty

attached to my future firstborn." She found herself sighing wist-
fully. "He's got his father's eyes."

Why was it when Friday night rolled around, Michelle was too
exhausted from the workweek to enjoy the start of the weekend
and the freedom from what had become a daily grind?

This should be her time, the time she shed the job, the stress,
the uncertainty of what would happen when she went back to
the office on Monday. Instead, she was wrung out from leaving
dozens of balls up in the air after putting in fifty-plus hours.
Juggling was for clowns.

Her run in the morning would help, as would a good night's
sleep tonight, but that meant leaving the cushy brown chair
where she lived these days for the bedroom, and the idea of
dredging up the energy to do so tired her even more. She'd given
ten years of her life to real estate marketing. Coming home
chewed up and spit out was not the carrot she'd expected to find
at the end of that very long stick.

She'd told her girls the truth last month at brunch. Two-point-
five kids, with a doorman and the city's amenities at her fingertips was exactly the life she'd dreamed of. The life she'd hoped by
now to be sharing with *The One.*

And if believing in the fantasy of soul mates made her a
Pollyanna, so be it. She liked thinking that somewhere out there
waiting was her own Jerry Maguire. But then, it made a lot of sense
that she'd see things that way based on the marriage she knew best.

She couldn't imagine her mother with anyone but her father.
They fit as if formed from two sides of the same mold. Years
together had made it impossible to think of one without the
other, but that only proved her perfect partnership theory.

Her parents brought out the best in each other. The strength of their union had seen them through good times, but had been even more vital during the bad. And no doubt her brother Michael's future would follow a similar path. He couldn't have found a better match than his fiancée Colleen.

There was that word again. Match. As in Match.com? Michelle sighed, and with no small amount of reluctance, reached for her laptop on the side table. Was Christina right? Would a relationship make everything better?

Would having someone at her side help with the burnout that was sucking her dry? Would sharing her days with a husband enrich her existence? Was having a man in her life what she needed?

Maybe it was, though she hated thinking it would take a man to make everything better. Better was something she should be able to do for herself, by herself. That didn't explain why, right now, the only thing that could make her forget the week she'd just had was not a man but a cupcake.

Something with frosting and filling and sprinkles. With cream cheese and creamy ganache and buttercream. Vanilla, chocolate, strawberry—it didn't matter. In this very moment, nothing else would make her happier than such an extravagant, calorific indulgence.

Except that wasn't true. What would make her the absolute happiest would be making the cupcakes herself; mixing, icing, filling, decorating, and doing so in a quaint little bakeshop of her own. The hours would be even longer than those she worked now and the responsibility solely on her shoulders. In this economy, she was nuts to even go there, but she'd dreamed for ages of running a boutique business, of being her own boss, of involving her entire family in the enterprise.

She could so see herself scooting along on a Vespa to the store where she would create baked goods as dazzling as they were delectable. Her mother would help, of course. Tapping her mom's years of experience as a caterer only made sense. And her dad and brother Brian had just as much in architecture, meaning her shop would be a haven. How could she be anything but a success with so much brain and brawn behind her?

It was the planning holding her back. The time it would take. The start-up costs. Vendors. Personnel. Marketing. Equipment from ovens to mixers to dishwashers to pans. Deciding on a product line and sales strategies. Finding a location that would work with her vision, one suited for the chandelier she knew she wanted as a focal point of the décor.

She was insane to even be considering something so monumental when the entire country was cutting back, not looking to splurge on extras. Why would anyone want to buy gourmet cupcakes when they could whip up a batch of Betty Crocker at home?

Now, if she had a partner . . . not her mom or dad or brothers, not a financial planner or investor, but someone to share the niggling worries that came late at night while drifting off to sleep or bubbled to the surface during morning showers . . . things might not seem so dire or beyond the realm of possibility.

If she had a shoulder to lean on, an ear to listen, an invested opinion to tap, a voice of support in her corner, she might sway further to saying yes and away from the barrage of hammering noes.

Okay, Match.com. I give up. I surrender. You win.

Last month, after promising Christina during their conversation about gold lamé bridesmaid dresses that she'd sign up for the wondrous world of online dating, Michelle had gone home that evening and done just that. Since then, however, she hadn't once used the service she was paying for. A financial planner would thwap her over the head for the waste, so she pulled up the website and logged into her account.

Well, now. Apparently, there were more than a few men out there who found her wink-and-nudge worthy. Or at least thought her profile deserved flirting with. Part of her thought it was sweet; who didn't love attention? But part found it silly, the whole sending winks and nudges thing. The super pokes and fish slaps and sheep thrown on Facebook were bad enough. Maybe she was a fuddy duddy, but she'd much rather skip the games and see for herself who was out there.

To start, she filled in the parameters for her search, building a man pretty much the same way she'd built her dream car at the manufacturer's website. Nothing like reducing romance to a series of drop boxes, but if she was going to date, it wasn't going to be long distance.

And since her end goal was a relationship, she had no interest in players wanting only to hook up for a good time. Also, since she knew she wanted a family, and her children to have a father capable of chasing them around the playground, a big age difference wouldn't work. She capped that search field at forty.

Political views, religious beliefs, hobbies, income, and education—those things she preferred to find out through conversation. A few words on a form weren't enough to explain what drove one to make those choices or to end up where they had. Having seen her father and Brian struggle for—then lose—their place in the family business, she would never judge anyone for getting hit by the curve balls life threw.

She shook off the thought, focused again on the screen. Though she wasn't so shallow that she'd consider a man solely on his looks, there was a lot to be said for chemistry. She wanted fireworks as much as anyone. In fact, she wanted explosive Christina-bright fireworks. Besides, if gentlemen could prefer blondes, well, so could she. There. All done. Taking a deep breath, she clicked the search button and got started.

When a dozen pages of possible profiles in she caught herself
yawning, she glanced at the clock on the taskbar. Good grief!
She'd been sitting here way too long, nothing to eat, nothing to
drink, still wearing the clothes she'd put on after her shower this
morning. This was ridiculous. She was not so desperate to date
that she was going to allow this to become an obsession, but she
clicked to the next page anyway, scanned those profiles and
clicked again, then again.

Honestly, she was more than a little bit surprised. Were there
really this many men looking for love? No wonder Christina had
pushed her so hard. It was a man buffet. A smorgasbord of testos-
terone. A dessert cart stacked with beefcake. Oh, sure. She'd
noticed a couple of lemons, a bad apple or two. And no doubt
some of the photos were years old and hair had been lost, pounds
found. But, wow. A girl could come back for seconds and thirds if
her first serving left a bad taste.

But enough was enough. Someone obviously needed to get off
her butt and eat dinner. And if that same someone was going to
get up early and run, she had to get some sleep. One more page of
profiles and she would. One more, number fifteen. A good place
to stop. After a quick scan, she would toss herself a salad and—

Oh. Oh. Oh. Her stomach tumbled. Oh.

He was blond. He was cute. She looked closer. He was exactly
the right age and less than an hour away. An hour didn't count
as long distance. An hour in the D.C. area was nothing. His eyes
were bright blue, full of mischief. His hair tousled and funky.
And his smile . . . his dimple . . . he seemed to be saying, "I've been
waiting for you."

Wouldn't it be amazing if he had? If he'd been right here all
this time? Okay, but she was not going to get too excited too soon,
no matter the tingle sweeping through her. She wiggled her toes

in her shoes, then kicked them off and curled her legs beneath her to see what he had to say.

She came back to his profile name. *DieselCat*. Hmm. Dare she hope the moniker had a personal significance and that he didn't have a thing for cats? The dimple was killing her, but cats just weren't her thing. Still, compromise wasn't out of the question. As long as he promised to clean the litter box. She moved to the quote next to his profile.

I wonder what the smartest thing ever spoken was that started with the word dude. "Dude, these are isotopes."

Cute. Oh, he was cute. And clever. And she was wide wide awake and not hungry at all. Now to see if what he'd chosen to share about himself sealed the deal. She shook off the buzz of excitement and settled in to read.

My headline about the "dude" thing is a quote from one of my favorite comedians—Demetri Martin. I used that one because unfortunately I still call too many people "dude." Even my mom gets it from me every once in a while. It's probably a bit of growing up with blond hair and emulating every surfer I'd ever seen. The problem is—I was landlocked in central Ohio.

Ok, so a little about me. I'm a transplant from the Midwest going on eight years now. I'm in the technology sector and love my job managing a team of software developers. My job is challenging and rewarding, and I have an incredible work ethic, but also like keeping a balance in my life.

I'm ridiculously funny, smart as a whip and handsome, and can pull a small airplane with my teeth—oh, and I can be modest, too (wink wink). Seriously—I'm the third of three kids and was always the comic relief for the family. I'm pretty athletic and love the outdoors, mountain biking, martial arts, throwing around the lacrosse ball, skiing, and have a huge desire to learn snowboarding.

I love music of all kinds and would love to go see a concert, or do karaoke (I do a pretty mean Whitney Houston) with the right someone. I'm a big fan of animals, especially dogs. No pooch at home right now—but my last one was like a member of the family.

I know it sounds pretty worn, but what I'm looking for is the girl next door with a great/twisted sense of humor who can be as much of a smart aleck as I am. I really like to be challenged and think that wit and smarts are as important as how someone looks. Honesty, openness, and sincerity are also big things with me.

Ok—so I have written more than I thought I would, and I'm not sure I really got across what I wanted to, but hey—what are you gonna do?

Wow. Just wow. He'd hit every one of her buttons. Athletic, intelligent, loved his family, well-employed. She ignored the voices of her girlfriends whispering about liars online and blew out a long, slow breath.

What *was* she going to do? Besides, well, respond because that was a given. Her fingers hovered over the keyboard. She clenched them, flexed them, rested them lightly against the keys.

Telling him that she loved his dimple seemed too flirtatious, so nodding as inspiration struck, she typed out the next best thing.

Three

*The "G" Man: gingerbread bottom with a
lemon cream cheese buttercream top

BENGAY, DAMP TOWELS, SPORTS TAPE, LEATHER, and hard-earned sweat. The smells of the gym and Krav Maga. Todd Bracken had taken up the study of the martial-arts form as part of what he referred to—with a healthy dose of wry—as his own personal renaissance.

He wasn't sure when it had happened, but after hundreds of miles run in high school as part of his lacrosse training, he'd let himself go. Not badly, but enough that he felt it like bands of sluggishness binding him. The why was easy. Work. Hours and hours spent developing software solutions for a government client's cutting-edge tech.

Not that he was a slob of a couch potato or anything like that, but he'd never met a pizza he didn't like, and it had started to slow him down. Krav Maga had been a big part of his getting back into shape, and advancing to the second level had been a hell of a physical challenge, one he was probably more proud of than he'd been of anything in a while.

But none of that explained why, on a Friday night, he was sitting in the gym's locker room having showered after working
every muscle he owned, breathing in the smells of dirty socks and
dirtier jocks instead of the perfume on a woman's skin.

"Yo, Bracken. Wanna grab a beer or a burger or something?"

Todd scrubbed his towel over his face while he made up his
mind. He'd worked late, he'd worked out even later, and he had
plans to work more once he got home. He could go for a beer and
a burger; it was Friday night, after all, and he'd burned enough
energy the last couple of hours that he could afford to refuel.

But for some reason, he just wanted to go home. He looked at
Blake who'd slung his gym bag over his shoulder and was checking that he hadn't left anything in his locker before checking out
the lay of his hair. Blake had it bad for his hair.

Todd shook his head. "Rain check, dude? I've got . . . stuff
going on."

Blake arched a wicked brow. "By stuff, you mean a hot date you
don't want me to know about?"

With his DVR, maybe. He was way behind on *LOST* and *The
Office*. And admitting he planned to curl up with the remote
would no doubt save him a lot of grief. But Todd was more
straight man than fall guy. And Blake had a hard time leaving his
competitive streak inside the gym.

Blake also liked knowing he'd warmed himself in the beds of
more women than the rest of the guys in the class. Not that Todd
had been doing much in the way of warming lately, but knowing
Blake would be scrambling over the weekend to maintain his lead
gave Todd a reason to live.

Add to that the fact that he wasn't the one who'd scorched a
path through his intestines on a bowl of tom kha gai soup last
week at lunch and Todd was loving his upper hand. "Hotter than
spicy Thai the next morning."

Blake closed his eyes, shuddered, then slammed his locker door. "Do not bring that up again. Me and my hammer strike will be all over your ass if you do."

Todd wasn't worried. His classmate might flatten him in the weightroom, but Todd's lean frame and reflexes would win on the mat every time. To mess with Blake's head, he countered with the Krav Maga motto. "'So that one may walk in peace.' Might wanna bone up on the discipline, dude."

"Yeah. Right after I bone your sister."

Todd dropped his towel and shrugged into a clean T-shirt. "I'll tell her you're on your way. Give her time to wax her back."

This time Blake tossed out a half dozen ear-singeing words. "Bracken, you are one sick freak. I think I like you."

"Not sure if I should be worried or flattered." Todd winked. "I've never had a boyfriend before."

"And on that, I'm outta here."

"I'll tell Sis to expect your call," Todd tossed back, earning a flip of the bird in response. He snorted, shook his head. Blake was so freaking easy; Todd got better action sparring with him on the mat.

Then again, Blake was the one who'd be scoring tonight while Todd went home. Alone. Again. To the house he'd spent too much money on, and now with the market in the toilet, would never recoup even if he managed to sell.

He bounced his locker door shut, hefted up his gym bag, wondering if working instead of playing this weekend would prove him to be a dull boy. Because suddenly? He was feeling the throbbing ache of his age to the marrow of his bones.

He needed more than a renaissance. He needed an extreme makeover. Him and his house both.

Picking up a pizza on the way home did little to alleviate the sensation that—renaissance or not—Todd hadn't made all the changes he wanted. Not that there was anything wrong with pizza, but he was letting things settle, giving in to routine.

He needed to get back to shaking up his life, doing what he most enjoyed—like running—to counter the activities he'd just as soon avoid, like spending the weekend mired in repairs to his money pit instead of spending his days off on the go.

And so he settled on the sofa, the TV on CNN in the background, his laptop on the coffee table, and surfed the web while he ate. He looked for any charity runs—10Ks, 5Ks, any Ks would do—he could find in the area. Running was when he did his best thinking, made decisions and plans. Running wiped him out, left no room for the day-to-day stressors that otherwise sapped him.

He bookmarked registration forms for three events and added the deadlines and dates to his calendar to later sync to his phone. It was a start, and looking forward to the challenges was better than the boredom that loomed on his horizon.

He was a half second away from shutting down his laptop when his e-mail notifier dinged. He launched his e-mail client and saw he had incoming from Match.com. Interesting, but no longer exciting. He hadn't had a whole lot of luck hooking up online, and the games were getting old.

But he had nothing on the weekend schedule he couldn't easily talk himself out of, so why not close out Friday night with a bang? Maybe close out Saturday night with a date.

You have a great profile, and an even better smile.

Okay then. Simple. To the point. He liked it. He was used to cleverly constructed double entendres in place of honest communication. Most of those he didn't respond to. That wasn't why he was here. But this one . . . he didn't know why but it spoke to him, as if the sender were inviting him into a conversation, one where they could take their time.

He clicked through to her profile. A single white female, thirty-one, living in Bethesda—out of his account's geographic search area—and calling herself Snowstar. So far, so good. And cute pic. Really cute pic. He reached for the last slice of pizza and read on.

I'm a small-town girl trying to make it in the big city. I worked hard to get where I am financially, emotionally, and personally and would like to meet someone with the same track record. I have a big, warm heart, an open mind and spirit, an upbeat personality, and try to circle myself around people of the same nature. I take pride in myself, my appearance, my virtues and morals. I come from a wonderful family, falling in the middle of two great brothers. I work extremely hard at all my relationships in life as they all require love, attention, dedication, trust, and time.

I'm looking for the final piece of the puzzle who completes me. Someone who shares my passions, interests, ethics, and morals but has his own individuality. We all have our standards and mine are definitely not unreasonable, but I know what I want and have never settled for anything less. Life is too short and at the end of the day, I just want happiness and luv from my friends, my family, and The One and in return I will give it all right back plus some. :)

Hmm. The last line of her profile unsettled him a bit.

Life is too short and at the end of the day, I just want happiness and luv from my friends, my family, and The One and in return I will give it all right back plus some. :)

The One? Was she referring to a higher power or a soul mate? Though definitely not an atheist, he wasn't overly devout, so wasn't sure going into a relationship with a woman who was would be smart. Still, he was getting ahead of himself. He wasn't going to judge a book by its cover, or a really cute little number by two words.

And so he wrote back, not holding out hope that he was about to change his life, but being enough of an optimist to walk through when doors opened.

Saturday morning dawned clear and cool. Michelle skipped coffee and took a bottle of water to her balcony, spending a few minutes watching the sun rise before locking up and heading out to run. She loved this quiet time as night gave way to day, the world waking on its own schedule—though admittedly her love was tempered this morning by the three hours of sleep she'd had instead of the six hours she'd needed.

Halfway to the front door, she stopped, squeezing her keys in her hand, and aggravated with herself for allowing the delay. Had he answered? Had he read the note she'd sent him? See, this was why dating drove her nuts. She had plans to run before getting on with her Saturday, yet here she was, wondering if the mysterious *DieselCat* had written back.

It wouldn't take but a minute to find out; she could check on her phone and get the wondering out of the way. Plus, knowing would free her mind for her run, and in the end, that was the deciding factor. Cutting short her workout because of a gnawing curiosity was not going to happen. She refused to give that much power to Match.com—or to a man she didn't know. Decision made, she locked up and headed to the elevator, tapping the e-mail icon on her phone while waiting for it to arrive.

Your profile's even better, and your smile's got mine beat by a mile. I'm Todd, btw. Nice to meet you.

He'd responded! He liked her smile! Giddy, she jumped up and down where she stood. And then, before she could stop herself, she typed a quick reply.

Hi, Todd. I'm Michelle Snow. I've gotta run, but I'll be back later this morning. Talk more then?

That done, she plugged in her earbuds and snugged her phone into its armband as she rode the elevator to the first floor. Waving at the doorman as she scurried to the exit, she broke into a run, then broke into a smile that felt as wide as the Washington Monument was tall.

Todd. His name was Todd. And he—Todd—liked her smile.

After a loop that took her up Wisconsin Avenue, past the U.S. Naval Hospital, and back home along Old Georgetown Road, Michelle was nicely winded, but energized and ready to get home. She should probably add more miles to her weekdays to help with the stress as it happened, but at least she had the weekends to detox. She'd thought about *DieselCat*—about Todd—while she'd run, but knowing he was interested was a lot easier on the nerves than the wondering would've been.

Of course, now she was fretting about the reply she'd sent. Would he think she was putting him off? That she didn't have time for him already? That his answer to her original note had fallen flat? She didn't want him to think that!

Outside of her building, she took a minute to catch her breath. She used the same minute to pull up her e-mail, and when she saw that yes—Yes!—he'd replied, she ran inside, hopping and skipping to the elevator, crushing her phone to her chest. She felt like a schoolgirl, tingling with excitement, and was ready to explode by the time she turned her condo's deadbolt and leaned back on her door to read.

You're out and about awfully early, Michelle Snow. Do you have a paper route?

Oh, this one was funny. Funny and cute and within driving

distance. Phone in hand, she climbed onto a barstool with her water bottle. She needed to shower and change before meeting her parents, but she had a couple of minutes to spare. Besides, her wicked love of competition meant she couldn't resist beating him at his own game.

Her fingers hovered as her mind considered one comeback, then another. Too coy, and she might turn him off. Too much of a wiseacre, and she might scare him away. Finding a middle ground was not the easiest thing she'd ever done, but she had to admit she hadn't had this much fun in ages.

Here goes nothing, she mused, hoping her sense of humor came through and that she didn't sound dumb.

I've been a workaholic most of my life, but no, there's not a paper route on my C.V. I was a towel girl once, and got up just about as early. Hope that doesn't disappoint you?

She carried the phone with her to the bathroom, shed her clothes, and turned on the shower. Before she'd done more than drop her top into the hamper, her e-mail buzz sounded, and naked, she let the water run while she read.

Are you kidding? I've always wanted a girl to take care of my towels. And I wouldn't say no if she offered to do the rest of my laundry, too.

She laughed. Out loud. And was still giggling like a teenager when she hopped into the tub. Covered with soap suds and shampoo, she swayed back and forth, slinging bubbles this way and that, singing The Beach Boys' *Surfer Girl* at the top of her lungs. She was way out of tune and didn't even care.

She had a feeling this surfer dude from landlocked Ohio might just be the one to make her dreams come true.

Four

*Frenchie: french toast bottom with maple buttercream top

IT MIGHT'VE SEEMED STRANGE to her girlfriends if they'd known, but Michelle's idea of a perfect Saturday afternoon was to spend it with her parents, and that was exactly what was on the agenda today.

Long before the distraction of Todd—What was his last name? She hadn't even asked!—she and her mother had signed up for a technique class on baking cupcakes at the Williams-Sonoma store in Tysons Corner Mall. Her dad, not one for the mixing and measuring of the process but a lover of the end result, would then join them for lunch at Coastal Flats.

Standing in the mall in front of the store's main window, Jack Snow was the first to see her arrive. He pulled a hand from the pocket of his gray trousers and raised it in greeting, nudging her mom with his elbow. Her black and white Coach tote hooked over one arm, Ann took a minute to pull her gaze from the deep rusts, reds, and yellows of the autumnal display before waving Michelle over.

"Look at this." She pointed at the tiered arrangement of cornucopias that had once been seriously squat and oblong pumpkins.

"I would never have thought to do something so clever. And then to stuff the big pumpkins with the smaller gourds and the crab apples? Very very clever."

"It's Williams-Sonoma, Mom. Clever is the name of the game, or in this case, the name of the store." Michelle slipped her arm through her mother's, breathing in the familiar scent of Estée Lauder's Beautiful before leaning over to kiss her dad on the cheek. He, as always, smelled of Old Spice. "Do we have time to look around before the demonstration? Dad? Are you going to hang out or go do some man shopping?"

"The Apple Store's down the way," he said, inclining his head in that direction. "I can make an hour of it there while you two learn how to make me even fatter."

Michelle laughed, pinched his side. "You, sir, are anything but fat."

"And for that, daughter, you won't have to worry about finding coal in your Christmas stocking." He glanced toward his wife who seemed to be ignoring them both. "Now, be a good girl and convince your mother it's safe to let me go."

"As long as your credit card stays in your pocket," his wife told him, patting distractedly at his shoulder, "you can stay there as long as you'd like."

He shook his head, giving a wink to Michelle. "And you make sure hers stays in her purse."

Michelle had to take her mother's side on this one. "I doubt she and I combined could do the same monetary damage as you could."

"Your mother was a caterer for years. You have no idea the monetary damage she has done in her quest to have just the right pan for every occasion," he countered, though his eyes twinkled as he settled his gaze on the woman he loved. "Not to mention this need of hers to own every rare spice ever milled, and any utensil that could pass for an instrument of torture. I think she collects those just to keep me out of her kitchen."

As her mother gave a long-suffering shake of her head, Michelle turned, poked her father in the shoulder. "Believe it or not, I've seen her use most of them, but I promise. No utensils or spices or pumpkin-shaped pans—"

"Unless I pay cash," her mother interrupted to put in. "And let's not forget. Your father has never met an 'i' product he couldn't live without. If anyone's responsible for breaking the family bank . . ."

There was nothing in the world Michelle loved more than watching her mother and father tease each other. Their accusations and threats were made in jest and were the stuff of a great relationship. If she were to get truly sentimental, she'd have to admit watching her mother plant a quick kiss on her father's cheek and her father respond with a warm smile was the sweetest thing ever.

But she wasn't going to admit anything of the kind to anyone but herself. And she certainly wasn't going to admit that seeing her parents together sent her bubble of hope rising. More than she wanted the bakery she dreamed of, she wanted what they had, a partnership that would last a lifetime.

"Ready?" her mother asked, bringing Michelle back to the present as she made her way to the store's entrance.

Michelle followed. "I'm ready to eat the finished product."

"You're as bad as your father."

"A happy tummy means a happy Michelle."

"I take it back. You're worse than your father."

Breathing in the wafting aroma of whatever yeasty, garlicky goodness was cooking inside, Michelle said, "If by worse you mean I share his love of good food, then yes. I am definitely worse than my father."

Their steps softened by the warm wood floors, they bypassed a cheerful employee clad in a green apron, listening to him ask another customer, "Did you know if you roll a lemon on the counter before slicing it releases the oils?"

"I did, yes," Michelle whispered devilishly. "But I'll bet you've never tried it yourself."

"Michelle Elizabeth! Behave yourself."

Though she nodded that she would, Michelle knew her mother was on the verge of breaking into laughter over her antics. And as they moved through the store, she began to fear she was going to have as much trouble as her mother keeping her credit card tucked away. Lacking as much as a spare inch to store the things she most coveted was all that kept her from whipping out the plastic several times.

The stainless steel coffee grinder required too much counter space, so she bought her beans at the market and ground them there. She really didn't need to coordinate oven mitts and hand towels by season, so stuck with the linens she had.

The vignettes of bowls, spatulas, and retro muffin mixes were cute, but she preferred cooking from scratch, and she had almost as many utensils as her mother. And no matter her lust for the Le Creuset cookware, those items weren't in her budget any more than were the big ticket ones she'd need to buy for a bakery.

She looked over as her mother fondled a lasagna turner. "Would you think I was crazy if I said that I wanted to open a bakery?"

Peering from above the dark rims of her glasses, Michelle's mother gave her a questioning look. "Would I think you were crazy if you said it, or if you did it?"

"Either or, I guess." She reached up to push her hair from her face. "I'm just ready to go to work and breathe in hot sugar and vanilla instead of all the desperation and anger stinking up the office."

"There's a reason I've spent most of my life in a kitchen," her mother said, gesturing with the turner before dropping it on top of the others in the barrel.

Michelle picked up a tiny silicone pinch bowl and squeezed. "Because at the end of the day you've got something to show for your blood, sweat, and tears?"

"I've shed a few tears, mostly due to onions, but yes. Hard work poured into a béchamel sauce was always more rewarding than that poured into paperwork. Not that I didn't have a lot of book-keeping to do, but most I handed off to my accountant."

"So you wouldn't think I'm crazy?" Michelle asked as they neared the rear of the store where the registered crowd had gath-ered for the baking class.

Another pointed, over-her-glasses-frames look. "I'd think you were crazy if you didn't follow your dream."

"I don't know that I'd call it a dream—"

"I would." Her mother stepped into a side aisle and pulled her along. "I've watched you in the kitchen, Michelle. I don't know if I passed down some Julia Child gene, or if cooking is just something that gives you pleasure, but I've seen your face when you're test tasting dishes you've created. You love being in the kitchen as much as I do, and I'll wager you love it more than you do marketing."

These days, a paper route—and the thought had her mind drift-ing to Todd—sounded better than marketing, and she wondered for the first time since meeting her folks if he'd answered her last e-mail. Not that she was going to stop now and look . . .

"I don't know," she said, not even sure what she meant. That she didn't know about Todd? That she didn't know about loving cooking more than marketing? That she didn't know if she'd be crazy to start a business?

"What's stopping you?"

She looked from the cloud of her mother's silvery blonde hair to a sale table showing off last season's cookie cutters with this one's holiday baking mixes. The old and the new together. Would her ten years of marketing give her the needed leverage to get ahead in the competitive bakery game?

Maybe so, but she knew the biggest roadblock stopping her was fear of giving up what security she did have for none at all. "The fact that I have a very good job that already takes up fifty hours a week? Then there's the cost, the economy, the uncertainty."

Her mother held up a finger to get her attention. "'No one ever went broke underestimating the taste of the American public.'"

"Thanks, Mom," she said, laughing softly. "But somehow I don't think the author of that quote was referring to cupcakes."

They spent the next hour listening to the instructor explain how to measure liquids and solids, how to order the addition of ingredients and mix for the best texture, how to adjust for the impact of humidity and altitude on baking times and temperatures.

They watched as she piped icing into flawlessly tiered mounds, swirled it in fluttery waves with neat edges, squeezed out tiny dots that circled a surface of smooth ganache. All of that was then followed by decorative dustings of coconut flakes and crystallized sugar and chocolate sprinkles. Finally, it was time to eat.

Michelle sighed with pleasure. Sinking her teeth into the finished product was like taking a bite of a dream. A dreamy, heavenly concoction of flavors, of soft cake and rich icing and mousse in the middle, but also of her dream, her bakery.

Her future.

Why, when surrounded by the things she loved, the people she loved, could she see it all so clearly?

She wasn't one to take this outing as a sign, but with her mother's encouragement coming on top of the morning's e-mail flirtation with Todd, she couldn't deny she was in a better mood than she'd been in a while.

Maybe it was time to work up a preliminary business plan, see if she could manage such a venture, or if her first step would take her directly into the deep end and way over her head. Would Todd be around to breathe life into her if that happened? Better question: why was she getting ahead of herself? They hadn't even met!

Just outside the Williams-Sonoma entrance after the class, Michelle turned to her mother and, before they started for the Apple Store to retrieve her father, blurted out the question she'd been batting around for weeks. "Have you ever wondered what your life might've been like if you'd married someone besides Dad? Or if you'd never married at all?"

Her mother frowned as if the change of subject from cupcakes to marriage had her concerned about Michelle's state of mind. "Why would I have married anyone besides your dad? I love your dad."

"I know that. I just mean . . ." She glanced over her mother's shoulder at the store's window and cornucopia pumpkins, looking for the words that had suddenly vanished. "If you'd met someone else first. Married him instead."

"I did meet someone else first. I met several someone elses first. Your father happened to be the one who tickled my fancy," her mother said, looking down the mall as if waiting for her Prince Charming to appear. "And who I wanted to tickle back."

"So, he completed you," Michelle said.

That got her mother's attention. "Completed me? Why are you quoting movies, Michelle?"

It was such a long story, and not one she had wanted to get into—or maybe she had. Maybe her mother could quell the misgivings that had been nagging Michelle for weeks. "I had the girls over for brunch last month. We got to talking about men and dating and relationships and *Jerry Maguire*."

Walking, her mother led Michelle to a bench out of the way of the mall traffic. "And they convinced you that you needed someone to complete you?"

"Not at all." Michelle shook her head, clutched her purse in her lap as she sat. "In fact, I told them I didn't. That I'm quite happy, totally content."

Her mother took her time responding, as if she wanted Michelle to look for the truth in what she was saying, then finally asked, "But now you're doubting it?"

Doubt? Was that the same as wondering? Or was there something else she was doubting? Maybe it wasn't about being happy and content, but being on her own that was getting to her. And that bugged her most of all. She didn't want the desire for a partner to get in the way of living.

She crossed her ankles, stared at the blush of pink polish on her toes where they peeked out of her sandals. "Did you ever think you might spend your life alone? That you'd never find someone you trusted enough to marry?"

"Trusted? Not loved?"

"Loved then," Michelle said, brushing off the slip and ignoring the sting of her mother's question. Was her approach to relationships all wrong? "You know what I mean."

Her mother gave her an arch look. "Is this about you still being single? Because if it is . . ." She stopped, took hold of Michelle's closest hand and held it, rubbing her thumb over her knuckles. "I know how bad things were for you in college. I know that put you off relationships—"

Michelle shook her head to interrupt. "I'm not so sure it did."

"I am," her mother said, patting Michelle's hand before letting her go and getting to her feet as her father appeared in the Apple Store's entrance and stopped to search them out. "Maybe not consciously, but there's no way for any woman to go through a betrayal like that and not be cautious."

Swallowing a lump of choking emotion that had come out of nowhere, she asked, "You think I've been cautious for ten years?"

"I think you've been working your butt off for ten years, keeping too busy to have a relationship, but yes." Her mother stepped in front of her, speaking softly, hiding their conversation from her father. "I think you've held everyone you've met in front of that mirror from the past, looking for something to tell you they won't cheat."

She didn't know what to say. That betrayal was a part of yesterday, and she'd long since moved on with her life. At least she thought she had . . . but was her mother right? Did she see things Michelle couldn't see in herself?

"When you find the right man, you won't need the mirror anymore," she went on to say, leaving Michelle to realize that neither would she ever need a therapist with Ann Snow for a mother.

Earlier that morning, Todd had laid out the tools he would need to replace the back door from frame to flashing. The wood was warped, and no amount of weather stripping was going to make a good seal. Brisk fall weather was on the way, and as much as he enjoyed running in the cold, he wasn't much for sleeping in it. The door had to go.

Next to the tools he'd lined up on the living-room hearth, he'd placed his iPhone, and not for the iHandy Carpenter app either. He was still working on a response to the last note Michelle had sent. And if she wrote again before he got back to her, well, he wanted the phone close.

Towels. He'd teased her about towels. Like he was looking for a maid or something. He'd braced his shoulder on the door then, wrapped his hand around the knob, and used all of his weight to shove it open—and to punish himself with the pain that shot down his arm.

He'd deserved it. As soon as he'd hit send on that email, he'd wished for a button to retrieve it from the ether. He'd sweated through his T-shirt waiting for her to write back and couldn't blame all of it on the effort required to pry the facing from around the door's frame.

Most of the sweat was due to thinking he'd screwed up a good thing by doing nothing but being himself. There was no way to be sure a personality came across in an online profile, even when the words were cobbled together with the best of intent. Hmm. He should've remembered the care he'd taken then. It would've made his morning—and the wait for her reply—a lot easier to get through.

Her response had come just in time. His door wouldn't have been able to take much more abuse. And he hadn't stopped smiling since reading her words.

They make laundresses for that. They do it right and don't expect anything but cash in return. Trust me. It's worth the investment. Plus there's no messy mixing of business with pleasure, or colors with whites. But if a laundress is what you want . . .

What he'd wanted then—and still wanted now—was to meet this woman. And not because he wanted her to wash his clothes. Her flirting was smart. Thoughtful. Not coy or ribald. He'd enjoyed both in the past, but he didn't live there anymore. So while he'd knocked dried paint from the door's hinges with a scraper, he'd weighed in his mind what to say.

He didn't want to scare her off more than he had already, but he was who he was, and his sense of humor had been honed during a very rough time in his very young life. It had been the one thing he'd been able to give his mother after she and his father divorced, and being the youngest of three siblings, he was already known as a clown.

As the years passed, he'd grown to use the trait some found annoying as a defense; better than fists, he figured, and better than running away. But he knew, too, that not everyone got his jokes or the sarcasm with which most were delivered. It made getting to know a woman through e-mail a crappy proposition.

One thing was certain. He was not going to give Michelle Snow a reason to think he was anyone but Todd Bracken. And as big a kick as he got out of the way he saw the world around him, he prized honesty above the rest of his outstanding and highly desirable traits.

So, he mused, with a healthy dose of self-deprecation, while he was being modest, he might as well tell her exactly what he had on his mind. Leaving the door on its own for the moment, he tossed the paint scraper into the toolbox and picked up his phone, dropping to sit on the edge of the fireplace hearth as he typed.

E-mails are fine for business. Let's make this personal. Meet me for a drink one night this week? You pick the place and I'll come to you. Just let me know when and where.

Five

*Jackie-Oh!: chocolate bottom with almond buttercream top

MON AMI GABI WAS A CLASSIC FRENCH BISTRO specializing in crepes, quiches, French onion soup, and any number of similar items. Michelle was so nervous she doubted she'd be able to handle more than a glass of Riesling—assuming she ever reached the restaurant.

Though she'd told Todd she'd be coming straight from the office, she'd rushed home first and changed clothes. A woman's prerogative, right? To look her mind-blowing best on a first date?

It hadn't been hard to decide what to wear. A French bistro, drinks, and a man with a dimple to die for called for a simple little black dress. She had the perfect one and saved it for special occasions.

Meeting Todd counted as special in so many ways she'd lost track. The pressure had brought on a major case of performance anxiety. Nerves had never been her friends, but tonight they'd ganged up to make her the butt of their jokes.

Because she was missing one of the earrings she'd wanted to wear, she'd had to default to her second favorites. She'd discovered a scuff on the heel of her left shoe, but had been halfway

43

across her building's lobby by then, and running late already. The wind, as she walked, mussed her bangs and whipped her ponytail like a mane at her neck. She would need to slip into the ladies room and make repairs when she got to the restaurant and hoped she could manage unseen.

Small disasters, true, but as a whole, enough to tempt her into turning around for home. Instead, she reached for her phone. Though her mother had no idea she was out on a date, she tried her first, needing someone to calm her down. Or better yet, talk her out of going through with the evening that had seemed like a much better idea when she'd given Todd the when and where he'd asked for.

When the call went to voice mail, she hung up and tried the next person on her list—someone who did know what she was up to and wouldn't let her back out. Or would demand her soul if she did.

"Oh, Christina, what am I doing?" Michelle rubbed away the stress she knew must be lining her forehead. Such an unattractive first impression to present. "I'm not cut out for this online dating thing."

Christina *tsk'd* loudly in her ear. "Get yourself together and have fun, Michelle. You deserve more in your life than ten plus hour days in the office."

"Maybe so, but this is not my idea of a good time."

"Where are you?"

She dropped her hand from her face and looked up. "Down the street from the restaurant."

"You haven't even made it inside and you're complaining about not having fun? Egads, woman. Call me after you meet him. Sneak off to the ladies room if you must. If he's a dud, I'll pay your way to the city for the weekend."

"You're coming here, remember? If we didn't have tickets to the symphony tomorrow night, I'd take you up on it." And she was considering doing just that when her phone beeped in her ear. Hopefully her mother getting back to her. "I've got another call. I've got to go."

"Okay, but tomorrow I'm going to want details."

Not a promise Michelle was willing to make. If tonight was a disaster, she did not want everyone in their shared circle of friends to know. "Later, Chris," she said, clicking off to take the incoming call. "Hello?"

"It's Todd."

"Hi," she said, and just like that, the world stopped spinning and stilled.

It was the first time she'd heard his voice and all she could do was stand there, the wind whipping her bangs, the crowds on the sidewalk parting like the Red Sea to flow around her. They'd exchanged numbers in case either had a problem. Neither wanted the other to think they were being stood up. There was a bit of the Midwest in his tone, and he sounded as easygoing as his e-mails.

A shiver ran through her, and wondering what had gone wrong, she repeated herself. "Hi. Everything okay?"

"I'm parking now," he said, and she could hear his engine humming in the background. "Running about five minutes late."

That made two of them. She was still walking. But it looked like she'd be able to reach the ladies room before he got inside. Or she would if she hurried instead of standing here like a lamp post.

She took off, her heels clicking like dance taps on the concrete, not sure what else to say. He'd called her just to tell her he was running five minutes late. Five minutes. Who was nice enough to do that? Obviously not her, as she was going to be just as tardy and hadn't bothered to let him know.

A big fat fail of a date. That's what she was. "I'll see you in a minute, then. I'm wearing a black dress. And a ponytail."

"Great. Can't wait. Oh, and I'll be the guy in the white shirt and the Hula-hoop," he said and hung up.

By the time she flew through the bistro's front doors, her nerves had their claws in deep. A Hula-hoop? Where did he come up with this stuff? Thank goodness he'd disconnected so quickly. She'd been too tense to even think to laugh; how in the world was she going to pull off appearing to be cool and collected when she was wound rubber-band tight?

She checked her hair, her lipstick, the line of her dress, her eyes for smudged mascara, her breath. When there was nothing left to check, she inhaled deeply and told herself to get out there and rip away the bandage. The quicker she got this first meeting over with, the quicker her heart would stop pounding, her stomach tumbling, her head whirling in Hula-hoop circles.

More than five minutes had passed by the time she left the ladies' room, but the instant she stepped into the dining area, she saw him. He was there, at an intimate table for two, watching for her to arrive. Tumbling stomach or not, this was it. There was no backing out, so wearing her very best smile, she headed his way.

He stood as she walked toward him, a fluid rolling up from his chair, not jerky, not awkward, but confident and sure. He was tall. Not too, just perfect for her, and he was lean and wore casual well. Classy jeans and loafers. A button-down oxford in a soft ivory tucked in. It took an overly long moment for her to pull her gaze from his hips to his face.

He was waiting when she finally did. "Hi. I'm Todd."

Oh. Oh. Oh, my. He was cute, not the scary monster she'd feared he'd turn out to be, but cute. As in *real* cute. As in cuter than his picture cute, his hair a sexy mess, his eyes flashing, his dimple a crescent in his cheek when he smiled, and his smile was simply gorgeous.

"I'm Michelle," she said, and stepped close for a hug. His arms came around her, and she closed her eyes. She didn't want to let go. He smelled great. He felt great, his hands in the small of her back possessive, pressing, making her think about having them there against her skin—a thought she shelved for a more appropriate time.

And then finally—but with a reluctance she knew she wasn't the only one to feel—she stepped back. Todd, his smile bedazzled, moved to pull out her chair.

"Thank you," she said, setting her clutch on the table and holding on as if needing an anchor. She was going to float away; she just knew it. People in dreams floated, and this had to be a dream. He was too yummy for it to be otherwise. "I hope you didn't have any trouble finding the restaurant."

"GPS is a man's best friend," he said as he sat, signaling at the same time for their server. "Do you want a drink? Coffee? Milk? Tea? Rum and Coke?"

Milk? Had he really asked her if she wanted milk? Silly, yes, but the ice breaker seemed to work. She took the relaxing breath her lungs desperately needed, then decided relaxing a bit more wouldn't hurt. "A glass of Riesling?"

He relayed her order to their server as the young man stopped, then sat back, one leg squared over the opposite knee. Running a finger around the rim of his highball glass, he studied her from beneath hooded brows. His eyes were the blue of a California sky, his beach-boy smile warm and sunny—all which she hoped forecast a perfect night ahead.

"So," he said as he continued to consider her. "Here we are. Snowstar and DieselCat, together at last."

Holding her clutch helped since her own drink had yet to arrive, and her trembling hands were going to give away the tsunami of her nerves. Her stomach fell to her feet, a surfing rush of up and down, to and fro. How could he look so cool when she felt totally wiped out?

Scrambling for her balance, she lifted her chin, turned up the heat on her feminine charms. "I hope you're not disappointed."

"Are you kidding?" He let go of his glass and sat forward, his forearms crossed and braced on the table as he leaned as far as he could into her space. "I'm enchanted. And right about now very happy I decided not to bring my laundry." When she laughed, he grinned as if the sound made his day. "I'm really having trouble imagining a gorgeous woman like you as a towel girl."

She looked down, warmth creeping into her cheeks. Enchanted. What a wonderful word. "It was a long time ago."

"And there's a story behind it?"

"There is." And telling it would at least loosen her voice. "Since I promised myself I'd never get bogged down in debt, I worked two jobs for a while. The paycheck from the gym went straight into savings for the down payment on my condo."

He bobbed his head, appreciative. "So you've lived in the D.C. area awhile?"

"Most of my life, yes." She let go of her clutch, crossed her legs, and rested her hands in her lap. "I grew up in Pennsylvania, but my father's job brought us here when I was thirteen. I've been here ever since."

"What does he do?"

"He's in architecture." And rather than going into the history of the family business, she changed the subject since no doubt he would ask. "And my mother had a catering company for years.

She's retired now, but you wouldn't know it. It's like every breakfast, lunch, and dinner is a special occasion. Oh, and our birthdays. Her celebrations make them so memorable.

"When I was ten or eleven," Michelle went on to say, not sure if she was rambling but too caught up in the memory not to share, "she threw me an English tea party. I loved Princess Di, and Mom knew it, so she sent out fancy invitations, and served hot tea and cocoa, and tea sandwiches and scones, to ten little girls, mind you, in her best china. I had the hat, the scarf, the jewelry and shoes, like I was queen for the day. Which, I guess, I was. It was great."

"Sounds like a lot of fun," he said, and his eyes started twinkling as he added, "And all good to know. I've been thinking I need a cook as well as a laundress. Plus, I've got a birthday coming up soon."

His teasing set her at ease, and she gave him a sly smile. "Getting ahead of yourself, aren't you?"

He took a drink, returned his glass to the table, shifting to lean his chin in one palm. "You said she's retired. Might as well toss my bid into the pot."

"Trust me. Between me, my dad, my two brothers, and my future sister-in-law, Mom has her hands full. And this time of year? With all the holidays coming up? Her kitchen is insane. You can't imagine the Thanksgiving dinner she serves, or the table she sets. Martha Stewart could take lessons. Seriously."

And then she stopped because this time she was sure she was rambling. It was just hard not to go on and on when talking about her family, and since his profile left her with the impression that he was equally close to his . . .

She rubbed a fingertip back and forth on the tablecloth, gathering the courage to meet his gaze. "Sorry. I didn't mean to take over the conversation."

He shook his head. "Nothing to apologize for. I enjoyed every word. But now I'm waiting for an invitation."

"An invitation?" she asked, frowning.

"To Thanksgiving," he said, as if it were obvious.

The funny part? He had no way of knowing her mother always set extra places at the table for unexpected—but welcomed—guests, and if things worked out, well, he might just be getting what he'd asked for.

Instead of telling him all of that, however, she allowed herself a private smile, and settled for saying, "We'll see."

He nodded, said nothing. Neither did he look away. Around them, diners chatted and a rolling wine cart rattled and servers danced with the doors of the kitchen, trays held high as they stepped lightly and spun.

Michelle let her gaze skitter over the art on the walls, the wine list, and specials in gold script on crackled mirrors. The low hanging light fixtures, the heavy dark wood, the mosaic-tiled floor—all of it was designed to set an intimately Parisian mood.

Her mood had flipped so many times tonight already, she doubted at this point a prescribed stabilizer would do her any good. Lacking one, she reached for the wine the server had left on the table moments ago and sipped.

Todd drank, too, then asked, "Did you stay in the area for school?"

Her profile had mentioned her degree, so it wasn't like he was fishing to see if she had one. Returning her glass to the table, the wine sweet on her tongue, she said, "George Mason University. I majored in marketing with an emphasis on advertising."

"And that's what you do now?"

She named the firm she worked for and saw the recognition she'd expected. It would be hard to live and work in D.C. and not know of it. "I've been there for ten years and was made marketing director in March."

"Congratulations." He paused, nodding as if in thought, then asked, "And I'm guessing everyone there does their own laundry?"

"As far as I know, yes," she said, enjoying the ongoing joke, but putting down her foot. She was done talking about herself. "Your turn. I know you're from Ohio and that being landlocked didn't stop you from wanting to surf."

"I wanted it more than anything," he said, passion bright in his eyes. "I would've traded my lacrosse stick for a surfboard in a heartbeat."

"Lacrosse?" He'd mentioned playing in his profile. She wondered if he still did. He was leanly muscled, not bulked up as if he spent hours lifting weights. "Is that why you're in such good shape?"

He brought his fists together in front of his chest and flexed playfully, à la Hans and Franz. "Thank you for noticing, but no," he said, sitting back. "I haven't played in years. I got into Krav Maga a while back—"

"Sorry, but Krav Maga?" she asked distractedly. She'd felt his hands when he hugged her, and she'd watched them as he'd held his glass. But until he'd flexed, made those fists, she hadn't realized how large they were, how . . . capable, and her mind was still marveling when he spoke.

"It's a hand-to-hand combat system. Employs a lot of the same moves as boxing or wrestling, but with more of a street-fighting vibe. You use your opponent's strength to put him at a disadvantage." He brought up both hands defensively, pretended to spar then throw a punch. "It's practiced by Mossad, SWAT teams, special ops forces."

Wow. Intense and a little bit scary. "Remind me to stay out of your way."

"I'd rather you not. But if it makes you feel any better, all I do on the streets is run."

"Really?" Oh, this was great! "I run."

"No way! You do?"

"I do," she said, loving the animation in his eyes and the thrill vibrating down her spine in response. How cool that they shared this! "That's why I was up so early when you e-mailed on Saturday. I was meeting my mother for a baking class at the mall that afternoon, but knew I'd never make it through the day without getting in a few miles first."

"How many?"

"About four."

He lifted a brow. "Explains the legs."

"My legs?"

He leaned to the side to check them out. "They're amazing."

"Thank you," she said, reaching for her wine again, needing the diversion to give her heart time to calm before their chemistry did her in. If this went where she thought it might, she was going to be in so much trouble. "So, DieselCat. Todd. Do you have a last name?"

"Bracken. It's Bracken." He gave a self-deprecating snort and shook his head. "I can't believe I haven't told you."

"You haven't told me much of anything," she said, pressing. She wanted to know everything: details, secrets, the minutiae of his life. "Besides the fact that you hate doing laundry. And that you can take care of yourself on the street."

He smiled at that, but then went on. "Well, the Ohio part you know. My folks divorced when I was nine, so that was tough on the three of us kids. I learned pretty quickly to put bad stuff behind me, and was as independent as a latch-key kid can get, reading, hanging out with friends, usual stuff.

"I did the lacrosse thing in high school, then left home for college, and got out of Michigan State after five years with a degree in, wait for it, interdisciplinary studies in social science with a focus on pre-law. Way generic, and it landed me in collections, which was not a good fit."

"What did your parents do?"

"Doctors. Both of them. And both retired now. My mom was a psychiatrist for twenty years, and my dad—" He stopped, frowned, seemed to shake off whatever he'd been thinking. "My dad's a surgeon."

Instead of pressuring him for more, she asked, "Did you ever make it to law school?"

"Nope. After more crap jobs, I went back to Wayne State in Detroit for a graduate degree in computer science."

"A better fit?"

"Oh, yeah. I head up a team that works out software solutions for a government technology client."

She picked up her glass, swirled the wine in the bowl. "Impressive."

"Ah, but not as impressive as my karaoke skills," he said, waggling both brows.

"That's right." She smiled, humoring him. "Whitney Houston, wasn't it?"

"I can bust out with 'The Greatest Love of All' if you need proof."

She wanted to request he sing "Saving All My Love For You," but managed to bite her tongue before making a complete fool of herself. Tonight wasn't about love.

It was, however, about like. It was definitely, *definitely* about like. So much like she thought she would die from the fluttering in her belly, the warmth raising the tiny hairs on her skin. "I'd rather they not kick us out of here yet."

"Does that mean you're having a good time?" he asked, more uncertainty in the question than she would've expected him to be feeling.

She took great pleasure in setting him at ease. "Yes. A very good time."

Six

*Happy!: vanilla bottom with chocolate fudge top

THIS LAST WEEK OF WAITING to meet Snowstar had been one of the longest Todd remembered. He'd had plenty of work to keep him busy, and he'd hit the gym or the streets every night after. The plan had been to exhaust himself to sleep. The reality was that he'd ended up lying awake thinking about her a lot more hours than he'd liked.

They'd continued to e-mail, sporadic notes to make sure the other hadn't forgotten about their Thursday night date, but neither had shared anything personal. It was if they'd agreed to save the good stuff for their first face to face. As lousy as his jokes came across in e-mail, that was fine by him.

Though that bit in her profile about looking for *The One* had him wondering if he should expect a girl in a nun's habit, his hopes for the evening were high . . . so he wasn't exactly sure why he'd been so uncharacteristically nervous when he'd called her while parking his car.

He had no reason to think she'd stand him up, but he didn't want to sit alone waiting should she be a no-show. He'd been relieved beyond reason to hear she was on her way, but had still ordered a gin and tonic as soon as he'd found a table in the corner with a view of the door.

He'd seen Michelle's picture. He'd expected hot. He hadn't expected smoking, and he'd been glad he'd had that drink to hold onto. Her black dress was killer, her legs outstanding, her eyes bright and honest, and he'd learned through the evening that her mind was the same. The bounce of her ponytail as she'd walked made him want to pull out the clip holding it and bury his face in the golden brown strands. It still did.

He watched her again now as she returned from a trip to the restroom, enjoying every bit of the package a second time, knowing he wouldn't say no to a third. Or to watching her let down and shake out her hair. He was intoxicated, though alcohol had nothing to do with the buzz zinging through him.

And as much as he hated to squash the simmering tension, another drink might be in order . . . though on second thought, he was pretty sure making his first a single was the only thing keeping him in his chair and out of hers.

Once she was seated, he nodded toward her glass that was only half empty. "Do you want more wine?"

Reaching for the rest of the Riesling, she shook her head. "I've got too much work on tomorrow's agenda to risk anything close to a hangover."

Then he'd stick to just the one, too. "Not the type of job you can leave at the office, I guess."

Her brows creased. "For the most part it is. But it's been so crazy lately, and so eggshell tense, that I tend to overthink my schedule. I don't want to get into a morning meeting and not have the information I'm expected to have. Half the time I need a checklist for my checklist."

And how familiar that sounded. Two of a kind maybe? OCD workaholics? "Maybe a vacation's in order?"

This time her eyes brightened, and the crease gave way to tiny little smile lines at the corners. "I'm taking one in November with a friend of mine, Eileen. She's my favorite travel buddy. We've been to Paris, Costa Rica, the Dominican Republic. This time we're going to London and Dublin for a week. I am so ready, you can't even imagine."

Running, and now traveling, not to mention the career-focused thing. He wondered how many other loves—and bad habits— they shared. Then he wondered how long it would take to find out. "I'm actually heading to Munich later this month with some buddies of mine."

"Oktoberfest?" she asked, and he nodded.

He was ready for a break from the daily grind, too. "We're going to drink enough beer to float Europe like a battleship."

Her laugh was soft, appreciative, as if she approved of his choice of destinations and of his plans to have fun. "I haven't seen Germany. Or Switzerland or Austria. I would love to visit Bavaria someday."

"With Eileen?" he asked, thinking how much he'd love to make the trip with her. And when, eyes sparkling, she replied, "Or . . . someone," it was all he could do not to toss her over his shoulder and head for the airport.

Yeah. He either needed more alcohol or less. "I guess with ten years and a marketing director title under your belt, you could afford the time away."

"I could, but I think the trip with Eileen will be my last for a while," she said, the crease back as she considered the level of wine in her glass.

Interesting. Especially the frown. "Oh?"

She acknowledged his query with a nod, but kept her gaze averted, watching as a server rolled by with a wine cart, the wheels clicking over the floor's tiles. "I've been thinking a lot lately about opening a business."

He sipped his drink. "Something to do on the side, or instead of what you're doing now?"

Gutsy move to give up a marketing director's position in this economy. Even more so to exchange a long-term gig for self-employment. Most interesting, though, was the uncertainty he sensed in her tone, her body language.

"Oh, it would definitely have to be instead of. It would be a full-time investment of time, energy, focus, and probably every cent I have to my name."

He didn't want to pry, but a business venture was no place for the doom and gloom he heard in her voice. "That sounds like hesitation."

"Hesitation, reluctance. A healthy dose of fear and a big fat dollop of 'am I crazy?' hair." She brushed back her bangs, took a deep breath, and blew it out as if blowing away the chance of a lifetime because the odds were stacked high and leaning against her. "I'd have to devote as many sleeping hours as waking ones to getting it off the ground. It exhausts me almost as much as it scares me to think about it."

"But you are thinking about it."

"I am." She looked away again, sighed. "It seems to be all I think about these days."

Wondering, he returned his glass to the table. Her own ad firm? Cardio classes for wannabe runners? Kids' birthday parties? She had him curious. "What is it you want to do?"

Color tinted her cheeks. "It's going to sound crazy."

Crazier than a bunch of ten-year-olds dressed up like Princess Di? "Try me."

She looked at him for a long moment, as if weighing whether she wanted to trust him with something that meant so much. He was a stranger. What did his opinion matter? And yet the moment she made her decision to share felt like a weight lifted from his shoulders, not hers.

"I want to open a bakery," she told him.

"A bakery." A simple response. Not a judgment. She hadn't asked for that.

"Except not just a bakery. A . . . cupcake bakery."

So that's where she was going. "Like Sprinkles? In L.A.?"

Her head came up. Her eyes brightened. "You've heard of it?"

He watched the news, read the business section, flipped through *People* magazine at the gym. "I thought I heard some valley girl in your voice."

"Sprinkles started in L.A., yes, but they've since branched out across the country. Plus, there's Babycakes in New York, and dozens of similar specialty shops." She paused, swirled her wine, added, "Though nothing in D.C."

"Yet," he said, catching on.

"I would love to be the first—" She stopped as if she'd said too much, then found her footing and the thread of the conversation she'd dropped. "So, no, it has nothing to do with being from the valley, which would be a stretch anyway since I'm an East Coast girl."

He toyed with his glass, the ice cubes melting into the gin and tonic, letting what she'd told him sink in, then lining it up with the rest of the things about her he'd already learned.

Simply, she wore her heart on her sleeve. That wasn't to say she had no depth or didn't hold her private side close. He'd sensed some of that, too, but this conclusion didn't take a huge leap of logic.

"It's about having English tea parties as a kid," he finally said, and her smile nearly melted him. What emotion she was feeling, he couldn't say, but he knew his paying attention had snagged hers. It wouldn't take her long to learn that among other things, he did that one well.

"It is, yes. In a way." She hooked a finger through her necklace, slid it back and forth along the chain. "It's about loving to cook, too, and to bake, and doing something my whole family can be involved in. But it's also about wanting to run a boutique that's small and cozy and inviting. It would be a place for people to feel welcome. To know they would always find a comfort treat when they were in the mood."

"Like going to Starbucks every day for a latte and a croissant."

"Is that what you do?"

He shook his head, thinking about Vikram's addiction. "I have a coworker who does. A croissant or scone once a day, but coffee at least three times."

"I have all sorts of ideas for products, and I want to have a coffee bar, too," she said, returning her glass to the table. "I've been baking test batches off and on for a while, fine-tuning the recipes and the look."

"The look?"

"The look is the best part." Her expression grew animated, her body bursting with energy. She talked with her hands, as if the motion was the only thing keeping her from jumping up to pace. "Each menu item will get its own. I mean, the cupcakes themselves will be similar, but the toppings will be customized, and the baking papers will be coordinated with the flavors. Like ivory for the vanilla and pink for the strawberry."

"Brown for the chocolate."

"Probably not brown. Maybe cream for contrast, and ginger colored for the carrot cake."

"Carrot cupcakes?"

"Why not? Oh, and I've got an absolutely scrumptious recipe for one where the bottom is sort of a cake doughnut and the icing is mocha. Your morning coffee and breakfast all in one."

He took her in, the flush staining her cheeks, the smile that didn't stop, her eyes that gave away the fast spinning wheels of her mind. "You love this stuff, don't you?"

"I do. And I hadn't realized how much thought I'd really given it until putting it into words . . ." She sighed, sat back. "And I'm probably boring you to tears."

He leaned toward her. "Not bored at all. Fascinated, really. You'll be a great cupcakeress. How can you not, all that passion, so many ideas, all those details, and you haven't even started to plan?"

"Scary, isn't it?"

"Why scary?"

"That I'm so obsessed."

"Isn't that what dreams are about?"

She considered him a long moment, her head cocked to the side. "What are yours?"

"My dreams?" When was the last time he'd had one? "I guess right now the only one I have is to get out from under the house I bought for way too much money. I'm having to pour buckets more into it. I mean, it's not a bad place, but I'd like to be closer in. I'm in the city all the time. Might as well live here."

"You'll love it. I promise. Granted, I live in a shoebox, but I'm close to everything. I walk everywhere."

"No car?"

She gave a quick shake of her head. "No, I have a car. I drive to work, but I walk everywhere that I can."

"The legs." He arched a brow. "I remember."

This time when she looked up at him from beneath her lashes, she wasn't blushing at all. "You, Todd Bracken, are an incorrigible flirt."

"Hmm," he hummed, trying to catch his breath. "I thought I was just being a guy."

"Same thing," she said, then dropped her gaze and smiled as if holding onto a secret.

As the wheels of the wine cart clattered past, he downed a swallow of the gin and tonic, studying her while drinking and while he lowered his glass. "Does it bother you? The flirting? I mean, you're not a nun or anything, right?"

"A nun?" she asked, laughing. "Nothing like that. I hope I didn't give you that impression. I sure didn't mean to."

"What impression did you mean to give me?"

"A good one?" She shrugged, held her wineglass by the stem and twisted it. "It's just so strange to sit and be able to talk to you as if I've known you forever. I've told you things I haven't told my best girlfriends."

"About the cupcakes." Because he couldn't imagine her best girlfriends not knowing the rest.

She nodded, changing the subject. "Your turn. Tell me something no one else knows."

"My life is an open book," he said, though the minute the words were out of his mouth, he knew exactly the story to tell her. "Most of my life, anyway."

"Ooh, sounds juicy," she said, leaning forward.

He caught a whiff of perfume or shampoo, maybe soap, and breathed deeply. "Trust me. My life is anything but juicy."

"But the deep dark secret is?"

Not as juicy as it was dumb. And embarrassing. "It happened at work one night. I was late leaving, and rode down in the elevator with a guy taking the flat screen TV from his office in for repairs. The thing was huge, and he was a pretty small guy, so I flexed all my Krav Maga muscles and helped him get it to his car."

"And it wasn't his," she said, snatching away his punch line before he could deliver it.

Shaking his head, he grinned sheepishly. How gullible could he be? "Man, am I a moron or what? He was stealing it, and I had to look through some photos at the sheriff's office and couldn't have picked out the guy had my life depended on it. Such a loser."

"And you've never told anyone else that happened?"

"I'd rather tell it to a complete stranger." And that was the truth.

"Wow," she said, and after a moment, her eyes went wide. "I'd forgotten that we're strangers."

"Doesn't feel like it, does it?" He reached across the table for her hand, stroking his thumb over her knuckles, swearing he saw a spark. "I think sometime during the last few hours we moved up a step."

"Good grief. Has it been hours?" She pulled her hand from his and glanced at her watch. Then glanced around the dining room to find the place nearly empty, the serving staff hovering, chatting quietly with each other as they waited to clear the last of the occupied tables. "As much as I hate to say it, we'd probably better leave."

She got to her feet. Todd did the same, reaching for his wallet and tossing down enough bills to cover their tab. She watched him, waiting, and he wondered if they could continue this night somewhere else.

He wasn't ready to let her go. "Let me walk you to your car."

"I didn't drive. I walked."

Huh. He hadn't known she was so close. "Then I'll walk you home."

"You don't have to. I walk in this area all the time. I'll be perfectly safe."

It wasn't about her being safe. Well, it was, but it was about placing his hand in the small of her back, which he did, and opening the bistro's door for her, which he also did. It was about walking at her side, being seen with her, being the man she'd chosen to be seen with.

But mostly it was about being who he was. "I do have to," he told her once they were on the sidewalk, the evening air still holding the warmth of the day. "My mother would take me out behind the barn and switch me if she found out I didn't walk a date to her door."

"I didn't know you had a barn."

"As drafty as a couple of my windows are, sometimes it feels like I'm living in one."

"Is it full of cats?"

"No. I'd fill it with dogs, if anything."

"I was wondering. Because of your profile name, and all."

Oh. That. "Think cat, like hip, groovy. A real cool cat."

"Is that how you see yourself?"

"Let's just say . . . well, let's just say no," he said and reached for her hand when she laughed.

They walked in silence for the next several blocks, neither one wanting to break the spell cast by the physical contact. All they were doing was holding hands, and Todd felt as if his skin was alive. He didn't want the feeling to end, and it was way too soon when Michelle slowed.

"Here we are."

She stopped just this side of the portico leading into her building. He stopped beside her, leaving room, his fingers still laced with hers. He hated the idea of letting her go, of saying goodnight. He turned her to face him, their wrists brushing, her skin soft and warm.

Heat sizzled down his spine, settled at the base, burning. "Tonight was a blast. You give great conversation."

She looked down, smiled, looked up. "You just like that I'm a cheap date."

He would've paid for a dozen drinks if she'd wanted them, but the night wouldn't have been as much fun if she had. Or if he had. Staying sober left him with a whole lot to remember and to think about. He'd be recalling bits and pieces for days.

But the memories weren't going to hold him long. And he was pretty sure she felt the same. He saw her interest in the flicker of light in her eyes, in the way she touched the tip of her tongue to her lips. She was nervous. He got that. But he wasn't worried.

They'd made it through the nerve-wracking first act of meeting. They'd made it through the second with butter-smooth conversation. He was ready to get started on the third, and he'd really like it to begin tonight.

"I like a whole lot of things, Ms. Snow. I like that you run, that you travel." He liked that the reference in her ad to *The One* meant a partner, and not a religious experience. "I like that you're close to your family, that your mother makes a mean pumpkin pie."

"And that I don't mind doing laundry?"

"That, too." He swung their joined hands, pulled her closer. She came, she didn't stumble, she took a deep breath. "I want to see you again, Michelle."

"I'd like that."

"Soon. Not weeks from now."

She nodded, her eyes extra bright, her smile drawn tight by anticipation, her hand trembling.

He squeezed it, leaned near, breathing in the soft florals of her perfume, the same scent he'd notice earlier. He had to get close to do so, as if she'd worn it just for him, and he thought he liked that most of all. "You won't think I'm too pushy if I call tomorrow?"

"As long as you won't think I am if I call later tonight."

"Please. Push." Push hard, he wanted to add, but his voice was stuck, and he didn't want to talk anymore anyway. He wanted to kiss her, to taste and feel her, and so he leaned in . . .

. . . just as she leaned away to give a jostling crowd of loudly laughing friends more room on the sidewalk to pass. And then he lost her. She was gone, tangled in the group, waving as she rushed to her door.

He waved back as the doorman ushered her in, then stuffed his hands in his pockets and turned, kicking out and scuffing the sole of his shoe over the concrete.

Ah, well. Even if she had taken off like a butterfly who'd barely escaped having her freedom clipped by a net, she hadn't told him not to call.

He did have that going for him, though it didn't really offer much in the way of comfort as he walked alone to his car.

Seven

*Bleubelle: blueberry bottom with streusel crumble top

STUPID. STUPID, STUPID, STUPID. Wigging out was *not* the way to impress a man who'd spent an entire evening impressing her all over the place. What in the world was wrong with her? It wasn't like she hadn't wanted to kiss him. She'd wanted to kiss him from the moment she'd stepped into his hug and felt his hands press her close.

Michelle kicked off her shoes, tossed her clutch on the side table, then curled up like a kicked puppy in her cushy brown chair. The worst part? She was the one who'd kicked herself! What must he be thinking of her? Running off as if she was the nun he'd thought she might be?

Before she threw up all over the place, because that's where her stomach was headed, she had to set things right with Todd. She had to let him know he had nothing, *nothing*, to worry about, that she wanted to see him again and soon, as soon as possible, just like he'd said.

She didn't want to e-mail him—doing so was, as he'd told her, about business—but neither did she want to call. Considering the state of her nerves, she'd no doubt stumble over her words and make things worse.

Texting seemed the best option. She could touch base, assess the damage, then figure out what in the world to do from there. She dug her phone from her purse and typed.

Thank you, DieselCat. Although I didn't get a Whitney Houston performance or a kung fu chop, your company was très fantastique! Safe travels home. ;)

One quick read through and she sent the message before she could wig out even more. Then, phone cradled in her hands, she leaned back and closed her eyes.

She was tired—it had been a long week and it wasn't yet over—but she was not the least bit sleepy. The one drink she'd ordered had relaxed her but not wiped her out. Because of that, she couldn't even blame the alcohol for making her stupid. Nope. That she'd accomplished on her own. And for no reason that made any sense.

Instead of worrying, she needed to go to bed. She wanted to get to the office early tomorrow and clear her desk before leaving mid-afternoon. She had plans to meet her girlfriends for drinks and they had tickets for the symphony. Yet here she sat, counting the seconds since her message had winged its way through the airwaves to Todd.

Maybe he'd turned off his phone, never wanting to hear from her again in this lifetime. Maybe he'd run all the way to his car, afraid to look back and see her chasing after him, a crazy woman flagging him down. Maybe—

The vibration of her phone sent her heart into her throat. She took a deep breath, telling herself bad news wouldn't be the end of the world, before hitting the button to read.

Sorry I didn't have a chance to show off my karaoke skills. Next time for sure.

Oh, thank goodness, thank goodness! The tension keeping her on edge washed away, leaving her wet-noodle limp. She'd been given a reprieve and swore that *next time for sure* she would not run off and leave him standing on the sidewalk alone. She wrote back to let him know.

You owe me one mad performance on the second date? Deal?

She sent the text, thinking about what she'd said. If she were to be honest, she was the one who owed him. Her wigging out wasn't about him. He had to know that. To know it was about her wanting so badly not to screw things up that she'd done just that. She typed quickly.

You make me . . . nervous.

Was she stupid to admit that? Was she giving him more ammunition to use against her with each text? And what was wrong with her? She was acting like this was her first encounter with a man, when the reality was this was anything but. The buzz of her phone kept her from having to dig and find out why she was such a wreck.

No being nervous, babe. I'm just a guy looking to get out of doing his laundry.

Babe. She read the note again and sighed. Who knew dirty clothes could become a long-running joke? And why in the world was the idea of washing his so . . . comforting? She disliked doing her own with a passion, but the size of her condo meant she couldn't let so much as her delicates pile up.

It was as if she were mentally nesting, caring for him, for his possessions, embracing the traditional female role when he was a grown man, capable of caring for his laundry and himself. But on this, her girlfriends were right. She had oodles of love to give and that meant making sure those she loved lacked for nothing— even clean clothes.

And anyway, her nurturing instinct was only one part of who she was. Any man who wanted her was going to get it all. The cook, the laundress, the career woman—whether in her position as marketing director or as proprietress of her own boutique bakery—and the lover.

She pulled in a deep breath, blew it out slowly. The thought of being Todd's lover . . .

Her phone vibrated again.

You still there?

Should she confirm that she was? That she couldn't stop thinking about him? That doing so was keeping her up?

I am.

Was he still thinking about her? Obviously he was or he wouldn't have texted, right?

Good. I like knowing that you're out there.

Her heart fluttered. Her stomach took flight. It was like he was in her mind, reading what she was thinking about him, using the very words she would've chosen.

She loved knowing he was out there, wondered if some cosmic event had occurred to bring them together when they were both ready. Smiling softly, she formed her response, one that came from the bottom of her heart.

I've been here all this time.

"Every detail. I want to hear everything. Don't leave out so much as a speck."

"Hey to you, too, Christina," Michelle said, climbing onto the bar chair at the small table around which Christina, Liz, and Dana were gathered.

Obviously Michelle's panicked call to Christina last night had been the topic of conversation while the group waited for her to

THE ICING ON THE CAKE   71

arrive. She wasn't surprised, though she wished she'd thought to ask the other woman to keep the details to herself. She wasn't ready to talk about Todd.

The four were heading to Strathmore Hall to listen to the Baltimore Symphony. All had checked out of work early, wanting a head start on the weekend—though what Michelle really wanted was to skip the concert altogether and head straight to Todd's.

Allowing for traffic, she could be in Springfield in less than an hour. But she and her friends had set up this girls night out weeks ago, and bailing now for a guy would create a lot of questions she wasn't ready to answer. She had no problem spilling the details of bad dates, but this one had been so good she wanted to keep it close to savor.

She could, however, give them the simple stuff, the stuff that still had her heart doing cartwheels, and her cheeks aching from her constant smile. She took a deep breath and rushed out with, "He was amazing, and I owe Christina a hundred apologies for badmouthing Match.com."

"Christina accepts every one," said the woman in question. "But amazing is too broad of a brushstroke. We want the nitty gritty. Paint us a picture with a toothpick. Tiny little detailed lines of what went on."

Michelle looked from Christina to Liz to Dana. All three wore the same expression, though Christina's curiosity seemed rather prurient, Dana's hopeful, and Liz's doubting. This was not a position Michelle loved being in, and she took a sip of her spring water while weighing her words.

She wasn't of a mind to divulge the minutiae her girlfriends wanted. She didn't fear jinxing her connection with Todd, but she was still relishing their time, revisiting their playful moments, reliving the sizzle of their flirtation. Those things were all hers, private and special and too intimate to turn into a conversation had over drinks.

She settled for what felt safe. "His name is Todd. He's got big blue eyes and great, summery blond hair, all tousled and sexy. A very Martin & Osa style. Casual cool. He's smart, and works in the tech sector. We had drinks, only one drink, actually, because we were too busy talking. After the restaurant closed, he walked me home."

"You closed down the restaurant?" Liz asked.

"He walked you home?" Dana asked.

"Did he kiss you goodnight?" Liz wanted to know.

"One drink and hours of conversation? That's hardly the juice I was hoping for." Obviously disappointed, Christina shook her head and reached for her martini.

Michelle looked from the face of one friend to the next. She would love to tell them more, she really would, but now was not the time. "Sorry, guys, but that's all the juice you're going to get."

At that, Christina's brow lifted. "So I was right. There is more."

"Not really," Michelle assured her.

"But you're seeing him again, yes?" Liz asked, then looked down, frowning as she rifled through her pocketbook for cash to cover her drink.

If not for the guilt that would've consumed her for bailing on her girlfriends, Michelle would be seeing him tonight instead of sitting through an evening of Gustav Mahler and Johann Sebastian Bach.

She gave a quick nod. "We didn't make specific plans, but I hope so. I really liked him. I liked him a lot. A whole lot."

"I'm so excited for you," Dana said, squeezing Michelle's wrist, her grin infectious.

"Just think. Before you know it, you'll be naming your first-born Christina or Christopher. A little reminder that if not for me, you'd still be a corporate slave, incomplete and unfulfilled and sleeping alone." Christina emptied her glass and stood along with the others. "I need to make a stop in the ladies' room. Meet you out front?"

"I'm coming with you," Liz said, while Dana, marching as always to her own drummer, headed for the exit.

That left Michelle alone, debating whether she could feign a sudden migraine and weasel out of the evening's plans. Doing so would make her feel like a weasel, but rather than a grimace, the thought brought a smile. Todd would appreciate the humor of a weaseling weasel, and thinking of him had her reaching for her phone.

On my way to symphony. Would luv to see you tonight. I'll try and skip out early. If we can meet, I can come to you or somewhere close as I know you have to be up early???? ;)

She sent the text, then left payment for her part of the tab on the table. She'd barely tucked her wallet back into her purse when her phone buzzed, and she grabbed it before Liz or Christina made it back.

How soon can you get here?

Not soon enough was the only answer that came to mind. And every step she took through the bar and toward the parking lot moved her closer to begging off the evening and heading to Virginia, where Todd lived. In the end, however, she couldn't do it. Even knowing her friends would forgive her for ditching them, guilt for such rudeness wouldn't let her go.

Once in her seat at Strathmore Hall, she told herself to relax, to enjoy the company and the show. Todd wasn't going anywhere, and a little bit of hard to get wasn't a bad thing. Besides, this was her music, what she'd grown up listening to instead of boy bands or garage grunge. And it had been too long since she'd spent an evening enjoying it.

The Snow home had been filled with show tunes, classical favorites, and operatic arias, many sung by her grandfather, Joseph Gargiulo, in a voice reminiscent of Luciano Pavarotti. Even in her twenties, when friends raved about the latest album from Three Doors Down, Michelle had been more familiar with the Three Tenors.

Tonight's presentation of Gustav Mahler's arrangement of music from Bach's orchestral suites was one she knew her mother would love. She should've loved it, too, and she did, but if not for the program, she wouldn't have been able to identify *Air on a G String*, much less Mahler's grand Seventh Symphony that followed.

She could, however, identify the reason for her distraction, and it took every good manner she had not to pull out her phone and text Todd during the program or to see if he'd texted her. By intermission, though, she'd had enough, and while her girlfriends stood in line for the ladies room, she made her excuses.

"Hey, guys. I'm going to cut out early." She reached up, rubbed at her temple. "My head is killing me."

"Oh, sweetie, I'm sorry," Dana said, slipping the skinny strap of her purse higher on her shoulder. "Do you need me to drive you home?"

Since she wasn't going home . . . "I'll be fine. It's just been an insane week, and I think tonight I need some quiet time more than I need to hear Bach."

Christina's arch look conveyed her skepticism better than words, but that didn't keep her from saying, "Or maybe you need another night with your Todd."

That was exactly what Michelle needed, but she wasn't about to confirm Christina's guess and admit it—especially with the way the other woman stockpiled ammunition. Michelle looked Christina up and down, took in the clean lines of her scooped-neck sheath in a gorgeous ivory and yellow floral. "Did I tell you how much I love that dress?"

"Uh-uh-uh." Christina shook a copper-tipped schoolteacher finger like a metronome. "I'm not falling for the compliment or the claim of a headache, but I'm not about to stop you from leaving. If not for me, you'd have no reason to."

Before Michelle could ask Christina for the expiration date on her gloating, Liz took hold of her shoulders and turned her toward the exit. "Go with God, my child. It's the weekend. Enjoy it. I know I'd rather be spending Friday night with a man than the bunch of you singletons."

"Speaking of singletons," Dana began slowly, clearing what sounded like an I-told-you-so from her throat. "Christina. What happened to your dream man and all those fireworks you told us to watch for?"

Thankfully, that was all of that particular conversation Michelle had to—or wanted to—hear. She was already swimming upstream and lost in the crowd, fighting for the exit and her freedom.

Eight

*REDiculous: red velvet bottom with vanilla
cream cheese buttercream top

KNOWING THAT MICHELLE WAS ON HER WAY made this
Friday night the longest Todd could remember. A week ago he'd
spent the evening exhausting himself at the gym then coming
home to a pizza. He'd had no weekend plans but attending his
Krav Maga class on Saturday morning and seeing how much
more cash he could sink into his money pit of a house.

Tonight, as good as a pizza sounded, there was no way he'd be
able to eat a pie if he ordered it. The workweek had been as
insanely busy as always, but he hadn't even considered working
off the stress at the gym. And tackling the repairs to his house
could wait until he had nothing better to do.

A different Friday night. A whole different story.

A week ago, he hadn't met Michelle Snow.

It was hard to believe he hadn't known her forever. He'd certainly never clicked similarly—or so immediately—with another
woman. Even the relationship he'd ended a couple of years ago
hadn't been so comfortable straight out of the gate. It had
become easier, but had required a lot of work to keep it running

smoothly, and he'd always felt like he'd been the only one putting in the effort.

With Michelle, there was no effort needed. Zero. Nada. Zilch. Sure, it had been one night, one drink, one hug. There'd been a lot of conversation, a lot of laughter. He couldn't remember the last time he'd held hands with a woman while walking her home. As first dates went, it ranked at the top of its class. A kiss would've made it better, but she'd had her reasons for taking off like she had.

And waiting never killed a guy—or so he tried to convince himself while he died a little more with each minute that passed. It didn't matter that each of those minutes was bringing her closer. Until she was in his driveway, in his house, in his arms, she'd be too far away.

He had just walked from the bedroom to the kitchen when car lights flashed across his front window. He opened the door and saw Michelle pull her German-engineered six-speed into the drive. Wow. Things were getting better and better. He wouldn't have thought it possible. Nor would he have put her behind the wheel of that tight little machine.

He stepped onto the porch and watched as she swung her gorgeous legs from the hot Audi A4. The sight was worth every minute of the hours he'd waited to see her again. And as she approached, her heels clicking on the pavement, he found his appreciation for the woman multiplying.

"Hi," he said once she drew near.

She cocked her head to the side, giving him a shy sort of smile. "Hi, yourself."

"You have any trouble finding me?"

"GPS is a girl's best friend," she said, stepping onto his stoop and into his arms, not shy at all.

Relieved, he hugged her, closed his eyes and held her, kept her body as close to his for as long as he could without his pounding heart scaring her away. It was too soon to expect more than this, and he didn't want her to think it was only her body he wanted. Pulling back, he looked down, grinned.

"You want the ten-cent tour?"

Her mouth quirked, her eyes in his porch light full of mischief. "You might want to charge more than ten cents if the place is the money pit you say it is."

"That's not a bad idea." His hand in the small of her back, he guided her into his home. "Charge a few bucks and give a walk-through lesson on what not to look for when buying a home. Then again, that would probably kill any chance I might have of selling it."

"I don't know," she said, taking in the main room he'd deco-rated in modern cave with some early Spartan thrown in for good measure. "It's not a bad place. Maybe a little short on personality—"

"Maybe?" His place had the personality of mud. It had been a place to crash when he wasn't traveling for work, an investment he'd hoped to flip before the market went to the dogs. All he wanted now was to get out from under it before the renovations leveled his bank account.

Michelle circled his sofa, ran her fingers over the back of the cushions before leaving the living room for the back of the house. She continued to peek into doorways, though never turned on the lights, and halfway down the hall, called out, "Nothing some paint and pillows and family photos can't fix."

"I'll keep that in mind," he told her, though paint was about as far as he was willing to go. And even then he was sticking to neu-tral colors to up his chances of unloading the place. He waited for her to finish checking out his lack of taste before saying more.

Waited, because she'd walked into his bedroom and he wasn't sure if she would be able to hear him. Waited, because it gave him a quiet moment to pull himself together. Waited, because following her into the room with his bed couldn't be any kind of good idea when he was wound so tight.

"You want to get a quick drink?" he asked once she'd returned. He hoped she'd say no. Now that he had her here, he didn't want her to leave. "We can go to Mike's. It's just around the corner."

She nodded. "Sure. I'm parked behind you, so we can take my car if you want?"

"Sounds like a plan." A plan he didn't want anything to do with, but one too late to take back. And since he'd been the one to make the suggestion . . .

He locked up and they headed outside. Once at her car, he climbed into the passenger seat and buckled up as she backed out of the drive. "Did your friends know what you were up to, ditching them?"

A smile teased the corner of her mouth as she shifted into gear and put the car in motion. "I'm sure they suspected, but I didn't give them any details."

He liked watching her hand as she shifted, her leg as she lifted it to clutch. Her handling of the car was sure, confident, and he liked that, too. "Hmm. I thought that's what girlfriends did."

"And just what do you know about a girl and her friends?" she said, giving him a quick teasing glance.

He shrugged, sat back, enjoying the company and the ride. "Everything I ever wanted to know about a girl and her friends I learned from *Sex and the City*. Not that I watched it."

At that, Michelle laughed. "Trust me. Our lives aren't half so exciting."

"No revolving bedroom doors? One man barely out before the next one's in?"

"Who has the time? Or, more's the question," she continued, downshifting through the turn he pointed out. "When did those girls work? Weekend brunches, sure, but they went clubbing or went shopping more than they did anything else."

"Not much for clubbing?"

"Billy Idol may have enjoyed dancing with himself, but I don't, and since I'm such a lightweight . . ." She gave a wry shake of her head. "Clubbing while sober seems a bit of an oxymoron."

Can't argue with that, he mused, glad they had that in common, too. "What about shopping?"

"Ah, now shopping's a different story," she said, slowing for the corner stop sign. "I could beat those girls at their own game, and for pennies on their dollars. I love bargains even more than shopping. Especially finding one of a kind pieces in out of the way places, boutiques, antique shops. Really. I could shop for a living."

"If you weren't going to be a cupcakeress, you mean."

"That's still to be decided. For now, it's being a marketing director that's keeping me from shopping for my life."

"It can't be too bad a gig considering . . . He waved a hand around the car's luxury interior."

"You like?" she asked, a note of pleasure in her voice.

"I like. I like even better watching you drive it."

She accelerated evenly, then shifted from first to second in an equally smooth motion. "You think a woman can't drive a stick?"

Oh, there was no question that she could, and she looked damn sexy doing so. So much power controlled by such a small package. He adjusted his position, enjoying too much the direction his mind was going. "It's more that you'd choose to drive a stick. Clutching's got to be hell on your heels."

"I know a sexy car when I see one." She shifted again, giving all those German horses their head. "It's an indulgence, but I work hard and don't splurge on much else."

"Except travel."

"Eileen and I booked a package deal. No first class anything involved."

He'd buy that. The price tag on his own upcoming trip had been a steal. "Clothes, then. Jewelry. Your antiques shops and boutiques. Bargains or not, there's got to be splurging involved in looking like that."

"Like what?" she asked, the streetlights and the light from the moon dancing off her frown.

Like a fashion advert. Like he wanted to see what she wore next to her skin. Like he wanted to see her wearing nothing. He swallowed hard, pointed out the entrance into Mike's. "Put together, I guess. Nothing out of place."

Her frown lightened, curled into a smile as she slowed the car, bumping into the lot and cruising the rows of parked cars. She maneuvered into an empty space and turned off the engine. Only then did she turn to him and respond.

"Thank you." It was simple. It was all that she said, accepting gracefully the compliment he'd delivered with no grace at all. It wasn't his business if she splurged or pinched pennies, so why had he even gone there—unless it was about self-preservation and finding a fault to put him off this fiery attraction before he got burned?

He'd seen her twice, and both times had been seriously wowed, but he didn't think his reaction had as much to do with her looks as it did with her. The smile, the eyes, the shy laughter, her intense focus on him. She paid attention. And, yeah, he liked that; who wouldn't?

Still, those were the things that could get a guy in trouble if he wasn't careful, if he let the danger zone of his lower body do his thinking instead of using the head on his shoulders.

He pushed the thought away, walking her inside where they found a quiet corner at the bar to order a drink. They sat close, facing each other as best they could, Michelle's crossed leg swinging in and out of the open vee of his spread thighs, her calf brushing his calf, her ankle skimming his like a match head to a striking pad.

Suddenly, danger zone or not, Mike's was the last place in the world Todd wanted to be. "Listen, Michelle—"

But it was all he got out before she shook her head, placed her hand on his thigh. "I'm so, so sorry about running off last night."

He hadn't given it more than a second thought. Well, maybe a third. "I told you not to worry about it—"

"I know you did. But texting an apology isn't the same as talking. And I needed to say it. I need you to know . . . " She'd been looking into his eyes all this time, giving him all her attention, potent and intense, but now dropped her gaze.

He tamped down the pulsing tide of apprehension "Need me to know what?"

"I'm not that girl," she said, lifting her chin, her expression sincere, troubled, as if she feared what he might be thinking of her. He liked that it mattered to her. Liked it a lot. She went on. "I'm not a prude. I don't run from a kiss. I don't . . . run."

"You ran last night." He didn't want her to grab onto that one moment and make it bigger than it had been. He'd let it go, and she needed to. Yeah, a kiss would've been great. But he was a patient man. And it didn't hurt to hear that she wasn't a nun. "But it was dark, and I couldn't get the really good look at your legs that I wanted."

Her smile was back, her leg swinging again, her hand on his thigh pressing, her fingertips rubbing tiny circles on the denim of his jeans. "We're going to have to go running together, you know.

I love to do the park trails at night when I can't sleep. I just don't want to go alone."

Yeah, he thought, her touch growing bolder, the circles wider, his skin warmer. Definitely not a nun. "I just looked up some charity runs last weekend. I haven't registered yet."

"Ooh, yes, let me know when they are. I ran the St. Patty's Day race earlier this year. It was my first."

"Mine was the Capital Hill Classic. I managed ten minute miles after almost no training."

"Not bad."

"No, but I've gotten a lot better. I like the crowds." He reached for his drink, swirled the ice in the scotch. "Makes it easy to set a good pace."

"I've wanted for years to have someone to run with," she said, watching him lift his glass and swallow. "Someone to push me while I push them."

"Years? So you've been at this awhile?"

"I started in college, I guess? Then just kept it up as I got into advertising. That world is wicked intense." She gave a small shudder. He felt the vibration from her fingertips. "Running made for good stress relief. And therapy."

"And killer legs."

She squeezed his thigh, squeezed again when he flexed. "Hmm. You know, I think you're right."

There was only one thing he knew. "Why don't we run right now?"

"Right now?" she asked, letting him go.

"Right now. Back to my place. It's too noisy here. Too . . . public."

Her eyes flashed a fiery agreement, and she didn't give as much as a nod to his drink when she asked, "You don't want to finish your scotch?"

"I didn't want it in the first place." And she'd hardly touched her chardonnay.

Still, she frowned. Confused? Concerned? "But you brought me here anyway?"

"I thought you might be more comfortable here, with the crowd. Instead of alone, at home, you know, with just me," he said, wondering why all of a sudden he was tripping over his tongue.

She shook her head, shook away the frown. "I came here to be with you."

He tensed, watched her brush her hair from her neck, her fingers toying with her earring where it dangled, and tossed back the last of his drink before reaching for his wallet. "Good. Let's get out of here."

They rode back to Todd's house in silence, and this time Todd drove, Michelle willingly surrendering her keys. While caught up in each other and conversation in Mike's, they'd been oblivious to the noise from outside, where the bulging gray clouds that had threatened all evening had burst into a downpour.

Since Todd was the one familiar with the neighborhood, Michelle had asked him to take the wheel, admitting she wasn't thrilled with the idea of making her way to his house through the storm. And that was fine with him. There was something primitive about being in charge and protective.

With the only sound as he drove that of the rain on the car's roof and the rich hum of the engine with each change of gears, the cockpit became a cocoon of comfortable silence, even if it was somewhat tense. Comfortable in that neither felt compelled to talk. Tense in that the lack of conversation gave both time for thought, creating a bit of a strain.

Todd was thinking he was a jerk for rushing her out of the restaurant. Nice job, letting on how selfish he was. But damn if he didn't want to get her alone, no Friday night crowds disturbing them, no solicitous bartender hovering, no blaring music making it hard to hear.

What he didn't know was if Michelle was regretting her decision to leave with him when she knew they'd be returning to his house unchaperoned. She'd seemed more than ready to go, and her silence could be nothing more than allowing him to concentrate on navigating the streets and the storm.

As he did so, he cast quick glances toward her, her legs, her hands in her lap, her pulse in the hollow of her throat. The way she caught at the edge of her bottom lip with her teeth, the only clue to her state of mind.

His state of mind was simple. He wanted to hear everything she had to say. He didn't want to shout above the noise or censor himself due to eavesdroppers. Or see anyone he might know and have to explain Michelle. He wanted her all to himself. That's all there was to it. And with that, he pulled into his driveway and parked her car behind his.

He turned off the engine and looked over at her. Raindrops picked up as she'd dashed from Mike's clung to strands of her hair like tiny white lights, and her eyes were huge and liquid and blue. He was going to drown in her before the night was over, give up his air, and pull in everything she was.

Her expression haunted him, left him aching to know what scared her. Was it him? Was it the anticipation? Was she waiting to be disappointed? Or like him, was she wondering if things had moved beyond fast to rocket-powered before either one of them was ready for blastoff?

He leaned closer. She leaned toward him. The air in the car stood still, grew heavy, as if waiting for the time that had stopped to start ticking again. Todd swore his chest was about to explode, and so he closed the final few inches between them and pressed his lips to hers.

She opened beneath him like a flower, welcoming him, offering herself up, a sacrifice of sweet nectar, and then she was pushing into him, turning in her seat to drape herself over him, and all of it with her mouth kissing his.

She tasted like the glass of chardonnay she'd sipped, like grapes and heady earth and hot sun, like he couldn't get enough. He slanted his head farther to the right, trying to find the best way to fit. There wasn't room to get to her the way he wanted, but he did what he could.

His hands roamed her back, gripped her shoulders, held onto her arms and cupped her nape. Her hair was down tonight, and he threaded his fingers into the thick strands that smelled of fresh herbs and mint and cool rain, breathing deep of the scents and of her.

Her hands were just as busy learning him, and when she moaned deep in her throat, he chuckled, not expecting her to pull away at the sound, feeling the loss like a shot to the heart when she did.

"You're laughing at me?" she asked breathlessly.

"I'm not laughing. I'm enjoying." Too much to put into words without fear of scaring her off. The things going on with his body were base and raw and best kept to himself until he was certain she felt the same way.

And then, because he had to, he laughed again, kissed her again, pouring all of what he was feeling into the press of his mouth to hers. She was the sweetest thing ever, the good, good woman he wanted in his life, and he had a hard time letting her go. The rain beat down on the car's roof, a timpani rhythm creating a safe harbor in the storm.

But then the clouds broke, and the percussion around them calmed to a snare drum patter. It was now or never, he decided, pulling back and looking at the longing in her eyes. "Do you want to come in?"

Nine

*P.B.J.: vanilla bottom with jelly filling &
peanut butter buttercream top

HOLDING TODD'S HAND, Michelle scurried to keep up as they ran for the closest entrance. Once he worked his keys from his pocket, unlocked the door, and ushered her inside, she found herself standing in his kitchen. She turned to thank him for driving, but never got the chance.

He backed her into the counter and bracketed her thighs between his. With one hand in the small of her back and the other in her hair, he lowered his head, wasting no time in picking up where they'd left off in the car.

It was exactly what she wanted him to do, and this time it was so much better. She could feel him, all of him, his legs around hers, his chest pressed to hers, the hard length of him bold against her belly.

A perfect fit, his body to her body, her mouth to his mouth. Her stomach tingled, then sizzled, fireworks popping the harder he pushed. His tongue swept over hers, needy, greedy, and she gave him back the same. Oh, this was good. Oh, he was good, tender when that's what she wanted, demanding when she let him know to ramp things to rough.

The symmetry of their fit, the synchronicity of their movements, the simpatico of their passion. The trail of singed skin his fingers left behind as he slid them under the hem of her blouse. It amazed her. All of it. She wanted to stop just for the pleasure of longing and aching and starting again. But she didn't. She couldn't stand the thought of parting.

Todd, though, as if reading her mind, put some distance between them. "Am I hurting you?"

In every good way she could possibly want him to, yes. But what she said was, "No. Not at all. Not nearly enough."

He was right. Things were on the edge of getting out of control. She loved the sensation of tiny sparks lighting along her skin, but sparks meant flames meant fire, and it was much too soon.

She slipped out of his arms, but didn't pull away, allowing him to keep hold of the hand she'd let linger too long on his chest. "Maybe we should turn on the lights? Sit at your table and talk?"

He groaned, releasing her, the mood bubble finally bursting. "I've got a dozen projects going on and the kitchen is the least of it. I let you see the mess, and I'm afraid you'll run screaming into the night."

Her fingers cold without him, she glanced around, but it was too dark for details. "What's wrong with your kitchen?"

Rubbing a hand over his forehead, he sighed, then stepped away to flip the light switch, squinting at the sudden glare. "Besides the chipped tiles in the corner by the door, and the stains in the sink, and the paint being a whiter shade of pale than the yellow it's supposed to be?"

Once her eyes adjusted, she looked around. "Those are cosmetic fixes. Easy to make."

He gave her a look, leaning against the refrigerator as he considered her. "Easy if it's not your shoulders and back making them."

"What happened to Mr. Krav Maga muscle man?" Respecting the space between them, she reached out and squeezed his biceps. "Nice ones, by the way. Muscles, I mean."

"So you noticed," he said, but didn't move.

She pulled back her hand, hating the tension that was rising like a wall between them. "I did."

He seemed to think about that, several seconds passing before he asked her, "Then why are you all the way over there when I'm over here?"

Being honest was the only thing she could do. "Because neither one of us is here just for that."

"By that, you mean sex?"

She nodded. They were consenting adults, and this was the sort of thing that deserved a discussion. She didn't want to find herself involved with someone who turned out to be hot to trot but uninterested in all the things involved in getting a race started.

Todd took another minute but finally relaxed, grinning, his dimple deepening as he blurted out, "But you do like sex, don't you?"

"Yes," she said, laughing, so glad they'd gotten that out of the way, but beyond embarrassed now as a flush crept up her neck. "I like sex."

Pushing further, he arched a brow. "And you're not into using it as a weapon or a bargaining tool?"

"No. Not at all. Never." She'd known women who'd made a bad name for the rest of their gender by doing just that.

"And you're not opposed to a . . . compatibility check?" he asked, his legs crossed at his ankles, his arms crossed over his chest. "Down the road, I mean. If things should head in that direction."

The man was a nut, and his defensive posture tickled her. "If by compatibility check you mean premarital sex, why don't you just say it?"

"Because I'd rather hear you say it."

She shook her head. "Is there anything you can't turn into a joke?"

"I got an early start at it," he said with a shrug. "My mom did not take the divorce well, and cutting up at the dinner table was the least I could do to put a smile on her face."

"Did it work?"

"Most of the time. She was a great mom. It was hard to see her hurting."

Michelle thought she felt her heart breaking. "And you were a great son to see that and to try and ease the pain."

"It was tough on all of us. I don't know. Maybe being the youngest allowed me to get away with more shenanigans."

"Were you the shenanigans type?"

"Absolutely. I still am."

"Thanks for the warning. I'll be sure not to let my guard down."

"I kinda like it when you do. Makes me all warm and fuzzy inside."

Inside made her think of being wrapped up together in the close quarters of her car. He'd been so warm. So very warm. She couldn't suppress a shiver or say no when he pushed off the fridge and reached for her again.

His mouth opened over hers, and she melted, wishing the kiss didn't have to end, the night didn't have to end. She pressed hard against him, her lips, her tongue, nipping with her teeth when he leaned away, wrapping her hands in his shirt collar and pulling him back.

It was when she could no longer tell her heartbeat from his, the sounds she was making from those rumbling up his throat, her labored breaths from the short strangled ones he struggled to suck in ... that was when she knew things were headed in a direction she wasn't ready to go.

She took his hand, led him to the living room and to the corner of his couch. They were still close, still in contact as she sat tucked to his side, but they weren't pressed front to front, their bodies urgent and seeking.

And so instead of touching, they talked, hours and hours of sharing everything about their lives. He mentioned Scott Tucker and another of his buddies from Ohio who'd be traveling with him to Germany, and a third, who they'd all played lacrosse with in high school.

They'd been state champs three out of his four years there, such a highly competitive team a Midwest anomaly, he told her. She expounded on her friendship with Eileen, her travel partner she'd mentioned previously, and about Christina who'd been the one to urge her to try Match.com.

Todd explained how his last relationship had ended in a big ball of flames, and related his ups and downs of online dating since then. Michelle confessed that she'd spent those same ten years dating casually after a crushing breakup and admitted that his profile was the only one she'd responded to since signing up for the service.

"Really?" He shifted to look into her face, his expression way too pleased. "I'm your first match?"

"I wasn't super thrilled with putting something so personal into a third party's hands."

"Yeah, but isn't that what we do every time we go out on a blind date?"

She frowned up at him, thinking his ten years with one woman had kept him from going through the same dating hassles she'd had during the same time span. "Have you had a lot of luck with those?"

"Not so much, no."

Facing forward again, she brought his arm tighter around her shoulder and laced her fingers through his. "Sometimes I wonder if my friends know me at all."

"Maybe they want to see you with someone so they spin the roulette wheel and hope for the best."

"That might work for some, but I've always known I wouldn't settle just to keep from being alone." She cuddled closer, liking so much being near him. He was warm, solid, a good place to land. "I mean, it's not like I'm lonely. I've got great friends and an amazing family, and between the things I have going on with all of them, not to mention work, I stay plenty busy."

"People who stay busy can still be lonely," he told her, and she wondered if he was speaking from personal experience or if he was wanting her to look for a deeper truth behind what she'd said.

"I know, and I guess from time to time I am. But I want the sort of relationship my parents have. I want to raise children in a home filled with love, not one that's about nothing more than companionship. Don't get me wrong. I know couples who've made such relationships work, but what they have is not what I want to have. I'd rather be the doting single aunt or perpetual third wheel."

And she really needed to shut up. Babbling about what she wanted from a relationship when on a second date was no way to guarantee a third. Granted, neither tonight nor last night were typical of any dates she'd ever been on, and she had a really good feeling about her connection to Todd, but too much too soon was a perfect romance killer.

"You want children then?"

Uh-oh. "I do, yes. Very much."

"Good," he said, rubbing his thumb over her knuckles. "I'm kinda fond of rugrats myself."

His confession came as a relief, though it also had her deciding it was time to go. Things were moving so fast she wasn't thinking, and she feared making an unforgivable blunder. This was one reprieve, his forgiving her for running off last night another. Tempting a third was not something she wanted to do. She glanced at her watch and didn't have to feign shock when she saw the time.

"Oh my God. It's so late." It was four a.m. How had she not realized it was four a.m.? How could they have talked all night and still have so much to say? "I've really got to go. I've got a work thing all day tomorrow, uh, today."

"Today's Saturday."

"It's our company picnic." And she'd really been looking forward to the food, fun, and games until Todd. "You know how that goes. Attendance isn't mandatory, but you get grilled to death on Monday if you don't show up."

He pushed up off the sofa. "I'll drive you home then."

"And get back how?" she asked, smoothing the wrinkles from her blouse, the tangles from her hair, knowing she wasn't wearing a bit of lipstick anymore. She had to look a mess.

"They have these things called cabs. You might've heard of them?"

He was so sweet. So, so sweet. His smile sleepy and sexy, his frown concerned. "I'm fine. It's not that far, I'm not going to fall asleep at the wheel, and the one drink I had wore off hours ago. A lot of hours ago."

"Then call me when you get home," he told her once they reached the front door. "I want to know you're safe."

"I'll be fine," she said, pulling her keys from her purse, waiting for him to let her out. When he made no move to do so, she added, "But I'll call you. I promise."

He gave her a look that said she'd better, and walked her to her car. She slid into her seat, expecting him to close her door so she could go. Instead, he stood there, one hand on the frame, one on the roof, looking down as if afraid he'd never see her again.

It tickled her, that forlorn expression, and also had her on the verge of climbing out of her car to stay. She chose a safe middle ground, reaching for the front of his shirt and tugging him down for a kiss. A strangled sound escaped his mouth just before he pressed his lips to hers.

His kiss told her that he was going to miss her. Hers told him not as much as she would miss him. When he slid his tongue along hers, she heard him whisper how much he wanted her even though he never spoke the words. She wanted him, too, and hoped he could understand the language she used to tell him.

But she had to go, she *had* to go, and she dropped a final peck to the corner of his mouth, knowing without looking back that he watched her until he couldn't see her anymore, and only then did he return alone to his house to wait for her to call.

At the time he'd signed up, a Saturday morning Krav Maga class had seemed like a good idea to Todd. On this particular morning, it did not. It had been close to dawn when Michelle had left, and even closer when he'd called because she hadn't.

He'd waited as long as he could, long past the time she should've been home. He'd caught her buying groceries—who did that at five a.m.?—and she'd promised once she was behind the locked door in her condo, she'd text him. She had, and he'd read her note so many times he knew it by heart.

You are amazing. ;) I'm so lucky to have gone out with someone so special two nights in a row. Thank you! Made it home! Sweet dreams!

He hadn't wanted to go to sleep until he was sure she was off the streets and safe. Then he hadn't wanted to go to sleep because he couldn't get her out of his mind. He wasn't sure he liked giving that much power to a woman he'd just met. As a rule, he wasn't the leap-without-looking type.

But he was sure that he liked her. He liked her a lot. Enough so that making an exception and taking such a leap seemed worth the risk of a bad landing. He was light on his feet. He'd survive. No matter what happened.

Grabbing his gym bag from his car, he slammed the door, jerking at the noise as if hung over. Bad enough that he was squinting behind his dark sunglasses to keep out the glare of the sun. At least he wasn't puking.

Probably be smart to skip the workout and head home for the sleep he'd missed last night. Except he knew his mind—unlike his body—was too wound up for any decent shut-eye. He could only hope it was wound up enough to keep him on his toes during class.

Shaking off the daze and keeping his feet rooted to the pavement, he pocketed his keys—just as his cell phone vibrated against his thigh. Not a call, but a text. And since there was only one person he could imagine texting him this early on a Saturday morning, he found his daze falling away like scales from his eyes.

I had to pinch myself when I woke up this morning. I'm glad it wasn't a dream. It really was a very sweet night with you. Enjoy this beautiful day!

The night had been many things, though sweet wouldn't have been his first choice of words to describe it. Steamy, sizzling, not nearly wild enough, hot as the business end of a bottle rocket. Still, he liked that she thought it sweet. She certainly was . . . as well as being hot, engaging, the best time he'd had in ages, enough to make a grown man lie down in surrender.

Good thing he was headed for a morning of pain.

He was beginning to sound like someone who needed his priorities knocked back in place. Working, working out, working on himself, working to fix his money pit of a house so he could get out from under that albatross. One, two, three, four. The list wasn't hard to remember.

He couldn't let a woman distract him. But since he already had, he typed back.

Sweet. Like a doughnut. Like a cupcake. Like you.

He sent, then hoped an hour of kicks and punches would toughen up this soft and gooey side of himself he wasn't familiar with and that he blamed on too little sleep and an overdose of Michelle Snow.

"Yo, Bracken. You look like cold zombie leftovers. Tough Friday night?"

Pocketing his phone, Todd turned toward Blake. The other man was flapping his way through the parking lot in board shorts and flip-flops, his eyes hidden behind sunglasses darker than Todd's and most tinted windows. "How do you know what I look like? Those things are illegal to wear while driving in twenty-three states."

Stopping at the front of Todd's car, Blake dropped the shades down his nose and gave him a once-over before pushing them back into place. "You still look like crap. Which means you're going to be crap on the mat."

"Better than being crap on a stick." Which was pretty much how he felt. "Though at least a stick would keep me upright."

Blake slapped him on the back, jarring him out of his coma and into walking. "Did you hit the bottle too hard, or just the ladies?"

A gin and tonic Thursday night. A scotch on Friday. Todd wouldn't consider that hard, though it was more than he usually drank. And he wasn't about to mention Michelle to Blake who played sex like Drew Brees played football. "The only hard you need to worry about is my foot to your ribs and your face to the floor."

Blake laughed as they headed into the gym. But two hours later, winded, unwound, and more than a little bit wired, Todd was the one wearing a smile. Blake, on the other hand, was wearing sports tape on two of his toes as he limped through the lot to his car.

Sliding behind the wheel of his own and starting it, Todd dug his phone from his duffle and saw that he had another text from Michelle. Feeling a whole lot more like himself, he sat back to read.

Hope you're enjoying this gorgeous day! Food for thought. If you don't have plans in the morning, would you like to meet for brunch at the diner across from Tysons around 11?

That was a no brainer, he mused, typing a quick response while the car idled.

It can't get here fast enough.

Michelle must've had her phone in her hand because she got right back with him.

Bet you type that to all the girls.

She was sweet. Man was she sweet. And quick. And smart. And he would much rather have met her for brunch now. Knowing she was at her company picnic somewhere in Maryland kept him from making the suggestion. It was the same reason that he texted her back instead of calling.

Only the ones who know I can't wait till noon for lunch.

Speaking of lunch, it was time. He'd had just enough breakfast to get him through the morning without making him sick, but now the well was empty. He started his car, buckled up, sat idling while reading Michelle's next text.

Pout. And here I thought you were anxious to see me.

He found himself smiling like a fool. One more, then he had to go. He had miles of home renovations to get through before he could get to her tomorrow.

I am. And I'll be looking at you over a plate of hotcakes the whole time.

Ten

*Joe-n-Dough: coffee cake doughnut bottom
with mocha fudge buttercream top

I'M BREAKING ALL RULES. *I really cannot stop thinking about
you. Is it Sunday, 11 a.m. yet?*

It was, and Todd reread Michelle's text from the corner booth
in the Silver Diner where he sat waiting, a cup of coffee in front
of him, a privacy wall behind.

He'd asked the hostess for the most out-of-the-way table she
had. He wanted to get his hands—and his mouth—on Michelle,
and he didn't want the disapproving looks from a hungry audience dampening the mood.

Even though he'd gone home from the gym and spent a whole
lot of yesterday with a hammer in his hand, he still hadn't slept
much last night. This wasn't like him, this being distracted, unfo-
cused, this having a woman on his mind to the point of obsession.

He wasn't obsessed. Except he was. And this brunch was going
to be about making sure he wasn't being stupid with it as much
as it was about making out.

He pocketed his phone, palmed his mug, brought up the coffee to sip. It was hot, strong, caffeinated, and gave his system a

much-needed jolt. But it was nothing compared to the jolt he got when he glanced over the rim to see Michelle walking toward him. As if hit with a live wire, his heart leapt, his blood heated, his skin burned.

Yeah. It was going to be hard to keep his cool when she was so freaking hot.

He slid from the bench and stood to greet her. Her smile, when she saw him, turned more heads than his. And how could it not? She looked like a million bucks, her hair a cloud of golden brown, her skin glowing. She wore what looked like a tank top that was a dress, loosely belted, very chic, and showing off her killer legs. Not that he knew for chic, but she did, and she wore it well.

"Hi," she said when she reached him, wrapping her arms around his neck for a hug that wouldn't quit, then letting him go and sliding into his side of the booth.

He slid right in beside her, cornering her, crowding her. She turned into him, her arm along the back of the booth, her crossed leg tucked between his.

And then he finally said, "Hi."

Still smiling, she ruffled the hair at his nape. "I never knew twenty-four hours could seem so long."

He glanced at his watch. "It's been more like thirty-one."

"Well no wonder," she said, coming close to kiss him, her lips soft, pressing, urgent and warm.

He leaned against her arm where it was still draped behind him, leaving his head there when she pulled hers away after a very long, very sexy kiss. "I remember you."

"Are you sure?" she asked, using her thumb to clear a smear of her lipstick from the side of his mouth. "Because if you need another taste—"

"I do," he told her, cupping the back of her head this time, kissing her until neither one of them could breathe, then sitting back, breathless, spent. "I'm going to need my strength if we're going to keep this up. And probably more coffee."

"I could use a cup, too," she said, pulling her arm from behind him to reach for a menu, snuggling up against him again as she read. "Did you sleep well?"

"The better question would be did I sleep at all," he said, then took a long swallow of coffee. "Between class and the rest of the day ripping up and putting down floor tiles, I should've dropped off like a baby. Not so much."

"Well, after all that fun in the sun at the picnic, I slept, but then found myself wide awake at four so decided to get up and run."

"No wonder you look so great. Fresh air and exercise."

"And makeup." She held up a finger, her bracelet jangling as it shimmied down her arm. "Don't forget the makeup. It hides a multitude of sins and sleepless nights."

"Hmm. Maybe that's what I need," he said, causing her to chuckle and elbow him in the ribs. He went on. "A friend saw me yesterday morning and told me I looked like crap. And we were both wearing sunglasses."

"How was class?"

"Brutal. Though Blake had a worse time of it than me. Broke a couple of toes," he said, as their server arrived.

Michelle ordered coffee, Todd a refill. And while she decided on blueberry pancakes with blueberry syrup, he opted for a spinach and feta cheese omelet, figuring the iron and protein would at least give him the energy to care about the dark half-moons under his eyes.

"He broke them on his own, or with your help?" Michelle asked, once they were alone.

"I am *not* a violent man."

She rolled her eyes. "Right. You just punch and kick and chop and pummel and—"

"Only on the mat," he told her, adding sweetener to his hot coffee. "But, no. Blake's responsible for his own misfortune. He wore flip-flops to class and tripped on a bench in the locker room."

She laughed, her expression bursting with it, her mouth smiling, her eyes narrowed, the lines at the corners like tiny little grins. "I shouldn't laugh, because ouch, but that's really kinda funny."

It was, and he liked that she shared his sense of the absurd. "It's even funnier if you know Blake, Mr. Cock of the Walk."

"One of those, huh?"

"And more. Kinda why I haven't mentioned you to him," he said, then took a sip of the steaming brew.

"Why's that?" she asked, lifting her own cup to her lips.

"Because he's never met a secret of mine he didn't like."

She considered him, her eyes busy as she thought, her frown drawing her brows into a vee. After a long moment, she returned her cup to the table and looked down as she asked, "Are we keeping this a secret?"

"Depends on what this you're referring to." For now, he wanted her all to himself. What he didn't want was for her to think his selfishness was shame. Showing her off would be a pleasure, but one that could wait. "Mon Ami Gabi? Mike's? Today's breakfast? You running away before I could kiss you? Me kissing you?"

She stuck out her tongue. "All of it, then. You and me. The Match.com thing."

"Have you told anyone? Besides the girlfriends you abandoned at the symphony?"

She seemed to hedge, giving their server time to set their orders in front of them. "They're the only ones who know I signed up, and that I met you. Actually, they're the ones who made me do it."

He found himself grinning at that. "How'd that happen?"

"Last month I had them over for brunch. That's when Christina . . . I told you about her Friday night," she said, refreshing his memory. When he nodded, she went on. "That's the day she made me swear to give the service a shot. It turned into this big deal, taking my picture and everything. So at the symphony, they were curious about you. I think it was pretty obvious I wanted to leave long before I did."

"Ah, then you told them about running away from my kiss and needing to make up for lost time?"

"No, I did not," she said, her cheeks flushing. "I didn't tell them much about you at all except that I'd enjoyed our evening."

"So I *am* your secret."

She toyed with her food, dragging a square of pancake through syrup before asking, "Does that bother you?"

Since he wasn't doing much talking himself, he couldn't say that it did. He sliced into his omelet, the smells of hot spinach and feta making his mouth water. "Tell me more about this brunch."

"What do you want to know? It was just a girls' day in." She shrugged, ate a bite of her breakfast.

He waggled both brows and ate another bite of his. "My favorite kind."

"Oh, so that's it. You're looking for prurient details."

"The only kind worth hearing about."

"Well, the only details you'll get from me will bore you to tears. Or put you on the defensive."

"Because you talked about men."

"Of course," she said, reaching for her coffee.

"Hmm," was all he said, and the buzz of the restaurant rose to fill the void. He smelled bacon and sausage, heard boisterous voices and laughter, wondered why the thought of Michelle discussing other men made him itch.

"Please." She drank her coffee, spoke into the silence he'd let settle between them. "As if you and your friends don't talk about women."

Uh . . . no. Best not to go there. "Not in any way you want to hear about."

"Exactly," she said, and he knew from her tone he'd been owned. Change of subject time. "Did you cook? For your brunch?"

"I did, yes. A quiche, a poppy-seed loaf, a fruit salad. Almond crescents for dessert."

"Girl food."

Her eyes on her plate, she shook her head. "Are you trying to convince me you're sexist? Because it's not working."

"Sexist? Me? Hardly," he said, and found himself grinning. "More like I'm trying to convince you to cook for me."

"First your laundry, and now this." She looked him over, sized him up. "Let me guess. You're a steak and potatoes man."

"I like both. I like burgers, a good cheese pizza. I'll eat pretty much anything. I like sushi—"

Her eyes went wide as she interrupted. "I love sushi. And pizza. But sushi especially." She paused, stared into his eyes for a long moment as if looking for a truth or a sign, something to help her make whatever decision she was weighing. "Would you like to come over tomorrow night after work? I'll pick up some rolls, maybe a salad?"

Still holding her gaze, he reached for his coffee, the delay tactic all about keeping his cool when his body was heating, her words like sticks of kindling. "You're inviting me to your place?"

"I am."

"I showed you mine so now you're showing me yours?"

She waited, said nothing.

"Could we make it Tuesday?" he asked, hating to turn her down but stuck. "I've got a late meeting tomorrow."

"Tuesday works." She gave him the number. "You know the building. Is seven okay?"

"Seven is fine." He cut a bite from his omelet. Three dates in four days and they were making plans for another. The speed, the ease . . . it had him shaking his head.

Michelle noticed. "Is something wrong with your food?"

"No, it's great, but I think something's wrong with the world."

"The world?" She laughed, swirled another bite of blueberry pancake through blueberry syrup. "Something more than wars, and people losing their jobs and homes, and the drain on natural resources—"

"That's what I'm talking about," he said, gesturing with his fork. "How in the world is a woman like you still single and out there on Match.com?"

"A woman like me?"

He thought about all the things she'd told him. "Someone so caring, so involved. So smart, so driven. So devoted to her family, a good friend."

"You make me sound like a saint."

"Saint Michelle. Patron Saint of Perfection."

"I'm not a saint. I'm not a nun. I'm hardly perfect." She gave a soft laugh as she blushed. "I'm just an old-fashioned Catholic girl. Besides, I could ask the same of you. You've been out there a lot longer than I have. Why haven't you been snatched up?"

"Many have called. Few have been chosen." That had her rolling her eyes, and this time he was the one to laugh. "I exaggerate. But I would never have found you if I'd been the one searching. You were outside my area."

"Then I guess it's a good thing I was more open-minded."

"Open-minded? Hey, you're talking to the most open-minded guy I know."

"You weren't open-minded enough to look for me twenty miles away."

"Guilty as charged. But then I like having my women close."

"Your women?"

"I'm trying to cut down."

"Oh, right. The many who have called." She nudged her hip flush to his. "Is this close enough."

"For a public display of affection, yeah," he said, his voice strangled by the need to have her nearer. "But I wouldn't say no to another night of the private kind."

Her mouth quirked, a sexy tease of a smile. "We'll see what happens on Tuesday."

Damn. That was two days from now. "No hanging out for the rest of the day?"

She shook her head. "I've already got hanging out plans, sorry."

"Are there other men involved?"

"Two, actually," she said, laughing.

"Uh-oh. Should I be worried?"

"My parents and I, and Michael and Colleen are hitting the outlet malls."

"I see what you mean about shopping."

"It's a vice, I admit it. Don't say you weren't warned," she said, pointing a finger at him, the bracelet he'd noticed earlier sliding down her arm and jingling as she did.

He nodded toward the jewelry. "You pick up that bracelet in one of your boutiques?"

"No. This belonged to my grandmother Gargiulo. My grandfather gave it to her early in their marriage."

"And the charms all mean something?"

"They do, yes." She placed her fork on the edge of her plate, pulled the bracelet around and fondled a tiny horse. "This is for their hometown. Goshen, New York. Goshen Historic Track is the world's oldest harness track."

"Cool. Didn't know that." He pointed at the next charm. "The heart and the key. Not a lot of subtext there."

"She held the key to his heart."

"How long were they married?"

"Forty-seven years. He was one-hundred percent Italian, and she one-hundred percent Irish, so he gave her—"

"The four leaf clover," he said, finishing the sentence he'd cut off.

"Yep," she said, moving to the next. "The masquerade mask commemorates a trip they took to New Orleans in their twenties. They traveled once a month when my mother was young."

"And the musical scale?"

A smile softened her face. "That's one of my favorites. Before marrying my grandmother, my grandfather Garguilo sang opera."

"No way."

"Yes way," she said, nodding. "He performed on the Major Bowes Amateur Hour and on Broadway with Eddie Albert."

Okay, now this was fun. "So I'm dating into a showbiz family?"

"I suppose you are." Her eyes twinkled as she fingered the next charm. "Bermuda was always one of their favorite vacation spots."

"And the phone?"

"My grandmother was, and still is, a social butterfly, and my grandfather loved to tease her about all the time she spent on the phone."

"You inherit that trait? Talking a lot?"

She gave him a teasing glare. "I can hold up my end of a conversation. Does that bother you?"

He shrugged it off. "Just wondering about your social butterfly wingspan."

"I've got Eileen, and my tight group of girlfriends from college, then a more extensive circle I flutter through." She forked up a bite of pancakes, gestured with it as she said, "Most are coming to my Halloween party. You could meet them there."

He watched as she chewed, as she reached for her coffee and drank, never breaking eye contact as she waited for him to respond. Was he ready to go there, inviting her friends—or his friends, even—into what they shared? Would he be ready in another month?

A lot of things could happen between now and then. He kinda liked living in the moment, and he was really liking this one a lot. He settled for saying, "We'll see."

Michelle frowned. "What? You don't want to risk having me make fun of your costume?"

That he'd need a costume hadn't even crossed his mind. "I guess you've got yours all picked out?"

"Eileen and I are hosting together, so we're going back and forth between a couple of themes."

"Will there be cupcakes?" he asked, scooping up the last of his omelet.

"Of course. And candy, since it's Halloween. And Jell-O shots. And tapas. We're working on the menu now. Oh, and we always end up hitting the local bars to see what craziness they have going on."

"Real party animals, huh?"

"Does that scare you?"

"I like to think of it more as a challenge. How to dress to impress the woman who loves a good costume party."

"Well, you've got a month and a half to come up with something, so I expect to be blown away."

"Have I failed to do that so far?"

She shook her head, her smile huge and bright and smelling like blueberry syrup. "You, Todd Bracken, have blown me so far away, I'm not sure my feet will ever touch ground."

"They will. I'll be here to make sure."

Eleven

*Whoopie Pie: chocolate bottom with whoopie
cream filling & chocolate ganache top

*IN ROUTE TO MEETING and thought I would say good morning!
Hope you had a great night. Please email me later and let me know
what rolls you like besides eel. Wine, beer, h2o or pop?*

Standing in line and waiting to place her order for spicy tuna
rolls and seaweed salad, Michelle read through for the fifth time
the text she'd sent Todd almost ten hours ago—ten hours that
had passed at a snail's pace. A snail's pace made worse by her
wondering if she'd ever get home on this, the one night she really
needed to. Todd was coming over for the very first time. And
everything was going wrong.

The traffic had been terrible, and it seemed everyone had
stopped at Raku for sushi takeout tonight. At this rate, Todd was
going to get to her building before she did. She wanted to be there
when he arrived, calm, cool and collected—not rushing through
the door like a madwoman.

She'd done everything she could to make tonight perfect.
Skipped her morning run to clean every inch of the condo.
Prayed all day for the gorgeous weather to hold. Mother Nature

had done her part, setting the stage for a romantic dinner on the balcony, but at this rate they'd be eating by moonlight—not exactly the cozy tête-à-tête Michelle had planned.

Todd was the first man she'd invited into her home. At least the first man who wasn't a family member or a friend, or even a friend of a friend. Though the size of her place forced them to keep the guest list small, it was where she and Eileen hosted their annual Halloween party, and where she held the occasional dinner or other holiday fete.

But tonight was a private party for which her condo was perfectly suited. No rolling wine carts rattling, no laughing dinner crowds. She and her single guest could talk about anything and everything without being overheard, and they could touch, kiss, even be silent and alone with their thoughts if they wanted. Or they could if she ever got home!

She made it from the garage to her door and was inside gathering plates, napkins, bottled water, and ramekins for the soy sauce and mustard when the doorman rang to let her know Todd was on his way. She hurried to the restroom to check her face and hair, hurried back to the door when he knocked. She pulled it open and had trouble waiting to shut it behind him before jumping into his arms.

He brought them around her, brought his mouth down on hers as if he, too, had spent the last two days desperately hungry. She kept her eyes open, and he did the same, and she fell into him, drowned in him, lost herself in the sensation of being with him until his stomach growled.

She pulled free, sputtering with laughter, but all Todd did was give her a shrug and a grin.

"What can I say? I'm starving."

For more than sushi? she wanted to ask, but gestured toward the balcony doors instead. "Go on out. I've got everything just about ready."

"Need some help?" he asked, following her to the kitchen instead.

Tickled that he had, she set the food on a serving tray and handed it to him, put the dishes and drinks on another and led the way. The light was enough to eat by, but it was near to dusk and darkness not far off. At least the buildings held the day's warmth. They should be able to enjoy a couple of hours before the cool night air drove them inside.

They settled across from one another at her balcony's small wrought-iron table, the sound of the traffic below, of the pedestrians on the sidewalk, the Metro rumbling on its tracks, that of another world. This was their world, intimate, enclosed, the exhausting pace of the day forgotten.

Michelle had been looking forward to it for so long, emotion overwhelmed her, and all she could do was smile when Todd stretched his arms overhead and sighed. "Sushi on the balcony. Life doesn't get any better than this."

She just looked at him. So relaxed, laid back. So at ease. If anything ever bothered him, he didn't let it show. She hadn't once seen him out of sorts. "I don't know. Sushi on the deck of a thatched hut in the islands sounds pretty good."

"Rough day?" he asked, a brow arched.

To be honest? "It wasn't the day so much as it was waiting for this evening to get here."

"I took off an hour early," he admitted, and leaned an elbow on the table, watching her. "I didn't want to get caught in traffic."

"I should've done the same thing," she told him, gathering a serving of salad onto both of their plates, glad to know she wasn't the only one who'd been anxious. "I did get caught, and then Raku was a madhouse."

He picked up a tuna roll with chopsticks. "How was your Sunday with your family?"

"It was great. Colleen and my mother and I did more window shopping than we spent money, which made Dad and Michael happy. But they're good sports, and Brian joined us for dinner, so it was a great time."

"I'll bet your parents love having all of you so close."

"They do," she said, hoping her joy didn't bother him, what with his family so far away. "How often do you go back to Ohio to see your folks?"

"Not as often as I'd like to, or should. Holidays, mostly, but I've been here eight years and this is home now so . . ." He let the sentence trail, looked away, and reached for his water bottle, leaving Michelle to wonder if the distance between him and his family was as much emotional as it was physical.

She didn't want to pry but it was hard not to, especially as close as she was to her mom and her dad, Brian, and Michael. "You have two siblings, right?"

"An older brother with two kids of his own, and an older sister with three. Two half brothers, too, both younger, from my father. My mother never remarried. Between her career and raising the three of us, I guess a relationship was the last thing on her mind. Or at least on her schedule."

"I can't imagine the strength it would take to raise three children alone."

"She did her best. She did a good job. With everyone but me," he told her, his dimple flashing though his smile never reached all the way to his eyes.

"You're a hopeless case, you say."

"Most women think so."

"I, sir, am not most women," she said, gesturing with her chopsticks.

Todd shook his head. "Which begs the question of what you're doing with me."

Not as much as she would like to be doing. But she kept that thought to herself. "Are you close to your half brothers? And your stepmom?"

He shook his head, but she didn't think he was saying no. It was more like something was on his mind. She'd noticed it earlier, an emotion in his eyes that she couldn't define and didn't want to pry into.

"I was in my teens when my half brothers came along, and too into sports and music and girls to be much of a big brother. Plus, I wasn't crazy about the whole divorce and remarriage thing. How it happened wasn't pretty, but my stepmom was nice enough, and my father was happy. Is happy. I guess."

Yeah, something was definitely wrong. "They're still together then."

He nodded, toyed with his salad. "They are. For now."

Uh-oh. She swallowed, hesitated. "Todd? I know it's not any of my business—"

"My dad has cancer," he said, cutting her off as if he'd been needing to unload and only waiting for an opportunity to release the words that were choking him.

"Oh, Todd." Michelle's throat swelled, and she struggled to find her voice. "I'm so, so sorry. What can I do? Please, anything, just tell me."

"You're doing it by being here. By caring." He sat forward, laced his hands between his spread knees. When he spoke, he looked not at her but at the ground. "He's managing it with chemo, but it's a bad one. Bone cancer. It's tough, especially because he's always been this larger-than-life kinda guy."

"You said he was a surgeon?"

He nodded. "A pretty prominent one, so I grew up thinking he was a real big shot. That nothing could take him down. Cancer's the great equalizer. It's also a son of a bitch."

"Have you seen him recently?"

"I go back for the weekend a couple of times a month. Or try to." He looked up then, smiled softly. "He'd love you. He's a real ladies' man. Not that that's always been a good thing, but yeah. You he would love."

"Then I'd love to meet him, too."

"Maybe next time I go . . ." He let the sentence trail, and she didn't know if he thought his father might not be around for a next time, or if the two of them might not be together. She didn't know what to offer him when this moment was the only thing of which she could be sure.

It had been five days since they'd met in person at Mon Ami Gabi. Five days spent talking and texting, touching and teasing. Five days imagining the rest of her life with Todd. Five days during which she'd told herself it was too soon to be in love.

That didn't mean her emotions weren't involved. She cared for him. She didn't want him to hurt. And looking at him now, the sadness he was trying so hard to conceal, the baggage he was working to shoulder alone . . .

She didn't want him to regret an invitation that he may have made while feeling vulnerable. She could be a shoulder, a friend, a confidante. She could also be—and wanted to be—so much more.

And there wasn't a doubt she was taking the most important step in her life when she stood and said, "Let's go inside."

"I'm sorry. I wasn't even thinking." He got to his feet and started gathering the detritus of their meal. "You've got to be cold."

"A bit," she said, watching him, waiting for him to turn for her intent. "But it's getting late."

"Right. You've got work tomorrow and I'm sitting here unloading on you. You're probably wishing you could toss me off the balcony right about now."

"Todd—"

"I know, I know." He ran a hand over his hair. "Morning will be here way too soon. I'll get going."

Oh, this was so not going well. She twisted her hands at her waist, gestured with one to get his attention. "You've got to be up early, too."

He gave a little laugh, still futzing with the food and the dishes, still not meeting her gaze. "Can you tell that I'm having trouble saying good-bye?"

"Then don't say it."

His head came up. "What?"

Finally. "If you spend the night here, you don't have to say good-bye."

He stared for a long, quiet moment, then gave a quick shake of his head as if he wasn't sure he'd heard her right and needed to be sure.

"By spend the night—"

"Yes." Her hands were back at her waist, her fingers threading in and out of each other like a nervous needle and thread. "I mean what you think I mean."

His throat worked, his jaw, too. His pulse jumped at his temple. "Are you sure? Because if you're not, I can just sleep on the couch and pretend . . ."

Circling the table, she came to him, pressed the fingers of one hand to his lips to silence him, then reached for both of his hands. She brought them up to cover her breasts, raising up on her tiptoes to brush her lips over his.

"I've never been so sure of anything," she told him, her voice shaking as she whispered against his cheek.

If she said anything more, she knew she would cry. The emotion that filled her was as powerful as the need to draw breath, but she didn't want Todd to misunderstand her tears. And so she lowered her head, took him by the hand, and led him down the hall to her bedroom.

Having him here was a step forward into her future. She wanted him to know that, but her tongue was tied, her fingers shaking, her stomach drawn into a tight rubber-band ball. All she could do was lead him to the bed.

Once there, she stopped, her gaze on his chest as she worked the buttons of his shirt through their holes. She'd touched him when they kissed, caressed his skin; she knew how warm he was, how resilient. How firm his muscles. But touching him like this was different. This was about learning what aroused him, what he liked. What she could do to make him feel better than any woman ever had.

She tugged the tails of his shirt from his pants, pushed the fabric from his shoulders down his arms. He shrugged the rest of the way out of it, dropped it to the floor, then returned the favor, reaching for the hem of the sweater she'd worn to work and pulling it over her head.

They stood that way for a very long moment, staring into one another's eyes, their hearts beating, the room still as if it, too, was holding its breath. Michelle was afraid to move, of breaking the spell, but finally, trembling, skated her palms up Todd's bare chest and hooked her hands at his nape.

He brought his mouth down on hers, his hands finding the clasp on her bra and releasing it. She lifted her arms to allow him to skim it away, then pressed as close to him as she could while their mouths mated.

It was pure magic, the feel of being skin to skin, no shirt in her way as she rubbed against him, no sweater or bra keeping him from her. He was hungry, demanding, his tongue sliding between her lips to find hers. She moaned, the sound a vibration deep in her throat, and he growled in return.

Then just like that it wasn't enough. She kicked off her shoes. He toed off his. He found the back zipper of her skirt and lowered it. She shimmied her hips and the garment fell. She worked down the zipper of his jeans, her fingers careful as she brushed his erection. He shoved the denim to his feet.

Her heart was pounding, her blood rushing and heating her as he pushed her onto the bed, as he covered her, his body warm and heavy. He tangled his legs with hers, pressed her down, and she rubbed her soles over the muscles in his calves. Running muscles. Solid. Strong.

With a heavy groan, he shifted to the side, reaching down, his palm sliding the length of her thigh, to her knee. She pulled it to her chest, and he continued his exploration, learning the curve of her calf, her ankle, his hand closing around her foot to squeeze.

She shivered, shuddered, shut her eyes.

"Cold?" he asked softly.

She shook her head on the bedspread, the fabric cool beneath her. "No. Just . . . waiting. This feels so good."

He moved his lips to the column of her throat. "And this?"

"Yes. Oh, yes."

He trailed kisses over her collarbone, leaving her skin damp. "And this?"

She nodded, clawed her fingers into the bedclothes on either side of her hips.

He moved lower then, finding her breast, his tongue circling the tip, his teeth nipping . . . all the while his hand moving up her leg, to the inside of her knee, her inner thigh. He stopped when he reached the elastic band of her panties, teasing her there, sliding his fingers along the barrier she wished he would breech.

"Do you know how good you feel?" he asked her, his mouth on her shoulder, moving to her neck, to her ear. His breath was hot, his lips warm, the tips of his fingers burning where they played.

She gave a light laugh, a desperate, needy sound. "I know exactly how good I feel. You're making me feel that way."

"Glad to hear it. Would hate to be the only one here finding it hard to breathe."

"Trust me. If I had to think to breathe, I'd be unconscious."

"Don't think. Just be," he said, rolling up to his knees between hers and shucking his boxer briefs away.

He was gorgeous, full and thick, and she lifted her hips when he urged her to, wiggling out of her panties as he pulled them down. And then he lowered his weight, covered her, letting her feel him, his arousal caught between them and hot where it pressed into her belly.

He kissed her, a soft exploration with his mouth while moving above her, seeking her, finding her, and slipping deep inside. She caught back a breath and he stilled.

"You okay?"

She nodded.

"Am I hurting you?"

She shook her head. Torturing her, yes, but she'd been wanting this since the night they met. Since the night they'd kissed in his kitchen. Since the morning she'd eaten pancakes with no taste at all. Wanting him forever.

"Are you sure?" he asked and she searched for her voice, telling him, "You're doing everything just right. You're just not doing enough of it."

He chuckled, a low rumble in his throat, and he started to

move, rocking against her slowly, filling her, his eyes like blue flames in the low light of the room. She wanted to look away, to close her eyes, to give herself up to sensation. Except she wanted him to know just as much pleasure.

She brushed the backs of her fingers over his cheek, down his neck to his shoulder, turned her head to kiss his arm where it rested on her pillow. Hooking her heels over his ankles, she braced herself there to push up as he pushed down.

They moved as one, a perfect synchronicity of rhythm, their bodies joined, dancing, mating, rising, and falling. She moaned, whimpered. He buried his face in the pillow at her neck and groaned, surging forward into completion.

She came with him, shattering, falling into so many pieces she knew she'd never find them all—especially the ones that became a part of him and would belong to this moment forever. She'd enjoyed sex before, but this went beyond. It was body and soul, mind and emotion.

And she sighed deeply, consumed with pleasure, a puddle of sensation beneath him.

He raised up on one elbow, smiled down at her. "You okay?"

"I'm perfect."

"You are perfect."

"Well, not that perfect. I have a couple of scars."

"Show me."

She laughed, wiggled beneath him, loving the feel of him still inside her. "I don't think so."

"You mean I'm going to have to turn on all the lights and find them for myself?"

"I think it would be a lot more fun if you discovered them by accident."

"Hmm. That could take a lot of time. And a lot of exploration."

"I'm not going anywhere."

He brushed her hair from her face. "You're an amazing woman, Michelle Snow. I think it's going to take a long time to learn all your secrets."

"You're welcome to stick around for as long as it takes."

"Good. Because I wasn't planning on going anywhere."

"Then you'll stay the night?"

"You couldn't get me out of this bed if you tried."

Twelve

*Edelweiss: almond bottom with
almond buttercream top

FRIDAY NIGHT AFTER WORK, Michelle and Todd ran together
for the first time. They took one of her favorite paths, down the
Capital Crescent Trail into Georgetown. The weather was gorgeous, the evening as perfect as autumn could be in D.C.

She'd made him promise that he'd run at his regular pace and
not hold himself back for her. She wanted to see how they fit as a
team, and found they made for perfect running partners. Still,
Todd checked often to see that he wasn't leaving her too far
behind, to which she'd responded that he'd better watch out or
he'd be choking on her dust.

The evening was the best. Though they spent a solid hour on
the trail, she barely noticed the burn. Instead, she enjoyed the
added high of having Todd beside her as they passed the Arizona
Avenue Trestle, the Dalecarlia Tunnel, and the River Road Bridge.
Once back at her condo, they showered and changed, and made
the quick drive to Ledo's for pizza.

"Mmm-mmm-mmm," Todd mumbled, biting into a slice and
coming away with long strings of mozzarella he wound with his

tongue. He chewed and swallowed, reached for his pop. "Right now, I can't imagine even a cupcake tasting this good."

Her stomach empty, Michelle couldn't argue. "Maybe I could come up with a pizza cupcake."

"Hey, why not. I've seen bacon-flavored chewing gum."

"Eww," she said, scrunching up her nose. "That's just gross."

"And a pizza cupcake wouldn't be?"

She tossed a square of crust across the table. It hit him center chest. "I was kidding about the cupcake. Though I could see an Italian-style bread. Chunks of cheese and tomatoes. Lots of good garlic and oregano."

"For sandwiches, or just noshing?"

"Either or. I mean, I'm not opening a sandwich shop," she said, winding a string of cheese from her pizza with her fingertip. "But I've already thought about adding my poppy-seed loaf to the menu. And my sour cream coffee cake. I've also got amazing recipes for vanilla and almond frosted sugar cookies that I know would be a hit."

"So you're more than a cupcakeress."

She grinned. "I have talents you've never imagined."

"Can you tie a knot in a cherry stem with your tongue?"

"Stick around long enough and maybe you'll find out," she said, and just like that, the mood at the table shifted. Her smile faded. Todd's expression grew pensive, and he looked off over her head as he brought his iced pop up to drink.

Drat her big mouth. He was leaving tomorrow for his trip to Germany. She'd been doing her best to put his absence out of her mind and enjoy their time together. Teasing about him sticking around had been just that, nothing but a flirtatious joke.

She wanted him to want to know all her secrets. She didn't want him to go. But more than that, she didn't want him to have any second thoughts about leaving.

A deep breath filled with the aromas of tomatoes and garlic and Parmesan cheese, and she said, "I'm sorry. I should've worded that differently."

"No." He set down his cup, looked at her. "No eggshells between us. You were playing. I like that. I don't like you second guessing or holding back."

"I don't like seeing that look on your face."

"What look?"

"The one that took away your dimple." He smiled at that, though she could tell his heart wasn't fully in it. "That's better."

His dimple deepened, his hair falling onto his brow. "I'll be back in a week, you know."

"I know," she told him, knowing too that the good front she was putting on wouldn't last. He wasn't leaving for another day and already she missed him like mad.

"And it's not like two months from now I won't be pining for you while you trot through the U.K."

"I don't trot," she narrowed her eyes and shot back, hoping that he would nonetheless pine.

"Looked like trotting from my side of the trail." He winked as he reached for the last slice of pizza.

"Oh, you're so going to pay for that," she said, grabbing it from his hand.

"Did you know it's four thousand miles from Bethesda to Germany?" Michelle asked, curled into Todd's side on her sofa. The television was on, the DVR playing the previous week's episode of *Private Practice.*

Todd was pretty sure Michelle wasn't any more involved in the show than he was. It was Saturday afternoon, and he was leaving later that night. Flying four thousand miles. Four thousand miles away from her. "I know. I also know it's about thirty-five hundred to London."

"I'm pretty small." She tucked herself into a tiny little ball, her knees to her chest, her arms around them, and snuggled as close as she could. "You could probably fit me into your suitcase."

"True," he said, wrapping his arm around her. "But that would hardly be fair since I won't fit into yours."

"I could ship you in a steamer trunk."

"Hmm. Might be a tight squeeze."

"You could run off the leg cramps when we got there, though it might cost less just to buy you a ticket with the fees airlines are charging these days."

He laughed, urging her into his lap. "Think of both of our trips as tests. You might forget about me the minute my plane leaves the ground. And some big strapping Irish lad might sweep you off your feet and make you his lassie."

Lacing her hands at his nape, she looked at him, her face drawn into a dark frown. "Excuse me, but why in both cases am I the one forgetting about you?"

He told her the absolute truth. "Because there's no way I'm ever going to forget about you."

She brought one hand down to rub the tip of her index finger over his mouth. "I think I'll have to hurt you now. As if I could ever forget about you."

"As long as by hurting you mean kissing," he said, catching her finger between his lips.

She pulled it free, pulled his head down and kissed him until he couldn't think about Germany or London, about the weeks they'd be apart, about changing his mind and staying. He couldn't think at all, and that was just fine.

"I'm going to miss you so much," she said several long minutes later. "What am I going to do while you're gone?"

She said it as if she'd had no life until finding him on Match.com, and he knew that wasn't the case. She'd be fine. She'd been fine before meeting him, but they both probably needed the reminder. "You'll work. You'll see your friends and your family. You'll eat and sleep and run. The same things you've always done."

She blew out a disgusted puff of breath. "I'm going to assume I haven't been as boring as that makes me sound."

"I think it's called busy, not boring." But he'd been right. A nudge was all she'd needed. Or maybe he was the one who needed to remember that a year ago he wouldn't have thought twice about taking this trip.

And he was thinking twice. He could have just as much fun here with Michelle as he could in Europe with the guys—which was why he had to go. They both had lives. They couldn't forget that.

Then there was Michelle's dream of opening her own business. He couldn't get in the way of that. "What you should do, if you have time, is work up a menu for your bakery."

"What?" she asked, pushing out of his lap to sit on the sofa beside him, facing him, her legs crossed.

He cocked a hip into the corner, propped an arm along the back to better see her, reached for and toyed with the ends of her hair. "Why not? You can decide how you want to describe your cupcakes. Give them catchy names, make them sound out-of-this-world delicious."

"They *are* out of this world delicious."

"Then why haven't you baked me a dozen or two?"

As if he'd flipped a switch, a light went on in her eyes. "I'll do it now."

It was his turn to ask, "What?"

She leaped off the sofa and nearly hopped, skipped, and jumped her way to the kitchen. He got up a lot more slowly, and by the time he reached her, she'd pulled a spiral notebook of handwritten recipes from a shelf of cookbooks.

He was leaving tomorrow. Watching Michelle bake wasn't exactly how he'd hoped they'd be spending their last evening together. "You don't have to do this. Not now."

"I want to," she said, searching the shelves of her pantry. Flour, sugar, salt, baking powder, brown sugar, cinnamon, graham cracker crumbs . . . she lined them up on the countertop, opened the fridge for eggs and butter and milk.

He understood the reason for most of the ingredients, but "Graham crackers?"

"And that's not even the best part," she said, her face brighter than he'd seen it all day as she pulled out a block of baking chocolate and a really big knife.

Graham cracker crumbs. Chocolate. "S'mores? I thought we were having cupcakes."

"We are," she said. "We're having s'mores cupcakes."

Ingenious. "This I've gotta see."

"Pull up a barstool," she said, grabbing two aprons from a hook on the pantry door and tossing him one. "Or better yet, pull up a spoon."

She started him off measuring dry ingredients into colored silicone bowls, while she chopped the chocolate into pieces and scraped them into a stainless steel one. The cream she poured into a pot she set on the stove to warm.

"Making your own Hershey bars, are you?" he asked, and she gave him a look and a grin as he reached for the box of graham cracker crumbs. "And I guess I'm over here making my own graham crackers?"

"More or less."

"Aren't you forgetting something? The marshmallows?"

"Haven't you ever heard of saving the best for last?"

He was pretty sure that's what he'd done, saving the best woman he'd ever met, knowing she was the last one he'd ever want to be with. "I'm familiar with the concept."

"Then get to measuring. I'll do the ganache."

"Ganache?"

"The Hershey bar part. It's a glaze of chocolate and cream, but both it and the cupcakes need to be cool enough before pouring it on. Otherwise, it won't set."

"Sounds like a balancing act."

"Most baking, most cooking really, is. Getting every bit of a meal to the table at the same time, nothing burned, nothing under-done." She set about chopping the block into chunks. "Though life's not much different, is it?"

"Everything I ever needed to know about life I learned while baking s'mores cupcakes?"

"Not just baking them. Baking them with me."

He was beginning to wonder if another time, one when she wasn't on an emotional edge, might've been better. "So the magic ingredient's the cook's blood, sweat, and tears? Because that knife blade's more than a little bit scary."

"I promise. No blood." She continued to rock the knife back and forth, slowing, the chunks now the size of chips. "But I can't swear I've never cried into a batter before."

Yeah, he'd been afraid of this. "A little extra salt never hurt anyone."

The knife stilled. She turned and looked up at him then, her eyes red and swimming. "I can't believe I just found you, and now you're going away."

"Oh, baby. Don't cry," he said, dusting the flour from his hands and pulling off his apron. "It's a short trip. A week. I'll be back before you know it."

He opened his arms and she dropped the knife and stepped into them, wrapping hers around his waist. He stroked one hand down her hair, held her tight with the other, staring over her head at the balcony door and the lights of Bethesda Row.

The feel of her body against his nearly unmanned him. They'd run together. They'd tickled and romped. They'd made love. He knew her body well. But holding her with emotion nearly suffocating them both was too much. His breath hitched when he tried to pull it in, and his chest ached.

Was he ready for this? The responsibility of another's emotions when he wasn't even sure of his own? That was a question he didn't have an answer for, but he knew he was not going to walk away and leave her like this.

"C'mere," he said, and headed for the sofa, this time pulling her to straddle his lap instead of tucking her close to his side. He wanted to see her face, to feel her weight against him. He reached up, brushed back strands of hair falling to catch on her lashes. "Seven days. That's all it is. You can do anything for seven days."

"Says you who will be relaxing, traveling, drinking, and flirting with fräuleins."

"I'll also be spending nine hours on an airplane and almost that many in airports."

"You do not have my sympathy," she said, though she did smile.

He smiled back, stroked a finger over the shell of her ear, down her jaw and throat, toying with the neckline of her blouse. "Do you know how fast a week goes by?"

Eyes closed, she lifted her chin to give him better access. "Depends on whether you're doing something fun, or not doing anything fun at all."

"So do something fun." He closed his hands over her shoulders and began to massage. "Test drive some of those recipes you're not sure of yet."

"Maybe," was all she said as she let her head roll side to side. Then she added, "Or maybe I'll catch up on the sleep I've been missing since you've been sharing my bed."

"This would be a good time to do that, because there's going to be very little sleeping when I get back. I can guarantee you that." His hands were kneading her biceps now, his thumbs brushing her breasts.

She shivered, opened one eye. "Oh?"

Nodding, he shifted beneath her, easing the strain on his erection. "A week without you?"

"You can do anything for seven days," she told him and wiggled in his lap.

Hmm. Nothing like the bite of one's own words. "As long as it's not eight."

"You had me this morning."

"I'll be crossing the international dateline. Twice."

She reached for the hem of her top, pulled the garment off over her head. Then she reached for the hem of his. "Making up the rules as you go along, are you?"

He sat forward so she could strip off his shirt, then he pulled her against him, his arms around her, his face buried in the thickness of her hair. He breathed deeply, remembering, imprinting. "I'm not much for rules."

"Such as?"

"Dessert before dinner," he said near her ear. "I totally plan to eat half the cupcakes before sushi."

"We haven't even put the cupcakes in yet."

He reached for the clasp of her bra. "Should we go do that?"

"I'd rather we do this," she said, reaching between them for the fastenings of his jeans.

They made quick work of buttons and zippers, shoes and underclothes. They ignored the unfinished cupcakes and the drapes left open over the patio doors. They fell onto the sofa and neither complained when they bumped elbows and knees in their effort to fit. And they did fit, perfectly, their bodies familiar and comfortable and at ease.

He rocked against her, a rhythmic thrust that she met with a measured press of her hips, her legs around his waist, her arms around his neck. He pushed up on his elbows where they rested on either side of her head and looked down, watching the play of sensation on her face.

She was beautiful beneath him, she held nothing back, she hid none of what she was feeling. Her dejection was gone, and what he saw in her eyes finished the job of doing him in. This was real, this thing between them. It was going somewhere, and getting there fast. He hadn't expected it. He hadn't been ready. But surging into her, letting himself go as she did the same, he knew there was no turning back.

Once they'd both calmed and recovered and set about finding the clothes they'd tossed off like they'd been on fire, they made their way back to the kitchen. Todd opted for a barstool. His legs weren't up to supporting as much as a marshmallow. Michelle was doing a much better job walking.

He reached over the bar for the ingredients he'd abandoned without whisking. "You know we're going to have to do this again when you leave for the U.K., don't you? So I'll have some batter to cry into?"

She looked over, her face flushed, her eyes sleepy and warm. "What flavor?"

"What do you have that's chocolate?"

"About a dozen varieties."

"Name one."

"They don't have names yet, but there's chocolate mint, chocolate with Oreos, chocolate and vanilla, chocolate and chocolate."

"No chocolate and peanut butter?"

"I do have one, yes. Give me time and I imagine I can come up with more."

He wondered where she got her ideas. Cookbooks, magazines, cooking shows, restaurant menus, the grocery store candy aisle? "Do you ever check out what other bakeries are doing?"

"I do, but not to rip off what they've done. It's more about inspiration," she said, pouring the batter into baking cups lining a muffin pan.

"Like turning a graham cracker, melted marshmallow, and chocolate sandwich fireside treat into a cupcake."

"Just like that. Or like seeing that Oprah loves a key lime Bundt cake and wondering if I can work the same flavors into something to fit in my shop."

"And? Any luck?"

"Not yet," she said, getting back to the ganache. "Lime has been giving me a lot more trouble than lemon."

"So you have a lemon cupcake."

"It's so good. So good. "I'll bake you a batch when you get back," she said, the sadness returning to her eyes.

He refused to let it, breathing deeply of the aromas wafting from her oven. "I'm ready to walk through your doors and buy up the whole place. Man that smells good."

"Wait till you get a taste," she said, setting about preparing the marshmallow topping.

Todd watched her work, asking questions about the process, amazed at how easily she assembled the cupcakes with the ganache and the toasted marshmallow cap. Where he would've been all thumbs, her fingers were quick and dexterous as she wielded the tools of her trade.

Finally, she set the cupcake on a dessert plate and it was the most decadent-looking thing he'd ever seen. And when he bit in, getting marshmallow on the tip of his nose and more chocolate on his face than in his mouth, he swore he'd found a woman capable of creating heaven on earth.

READER RESPONSE CARD

We care about your opinions! Please take a moment to fill out our Reader Survey online at **http://survey.hcibooks.com**. To show our appreciation, we'll give you an **instant discount coupon** for future book purchases, as well as a special gift available only online.

If you prefer, you may mail this survey card back to us and receive a discount coupon by mail. All answers are confidential.

(PLEASE PRINT IN ALL CAPS)

First Name _____ Last Name _____

Address _____

City _____ State _____ Zip _____ Email _____

1. Gender
❏ Female   ❏ Male

2. Age
❏ Under 20
❏ 21-30   ❏ 31-40
❏ 41-50   ❏ 51-60
❏ Over 60

3. Marital Status
❏ Married   ❏ Single

4. How you did get this book?
❏ Received as gift
❏ Bought for myself
❏ Borrowed from a friend
❏ Borrowed from my library

5. If bought for yourself, how did you find out about it?
❏ Recommendation
❏ Store Display
❏ Read about it on a Website
❏ Email message or e-newsletter
❏ Book review or author interview

6. How many books do you read a year, excluding educational material?
❏ 4 or less   ❏ 5-8
❏ 9-12   ❏ 12 or more

7. Do you have children under the age of 18 at home?
❏ Yes   ❏ No

8. What type of romance do you enjoy most?
❏ Contemporary
❏ Historical
❏ Paranormal
❏ Erotic
❏ All types

9. What are your sensuality preferences?
❏ Wild and erotic
❏ Steamy but moderate
❏ Sweet and sensual
❏ Doesn't matter as long as it fits the story

10. Where do you usually buy books?
❏ Online (amazon.com, etc.)
❏ Bookstore chain (Borders, B&N...)
❏ Independent/local bookstore
❏ Big Box store (Target, Wal-Mart...)
❏ Drug Store or Supermarket

11. How often do you read romance novels?
❏ Every now and then
❏ Several times a year
❏ Constantly

TVA

FOLD HERE

12. What influences you most when purchasing a book?
(Rank each from 1 to 5 with 1 being the top)

Author	1	2	3	4	5
Price	1	2	3	4	5
Title	1	2	3	4	5
Reviews	1	2	3	4	5
Cover Design	1	2	3	4	5
Series/Publisher	1	2	3	4	5
Recommendation	1	2	3	4	5

13. Annual household income
- ☐ Under $25,000
- ☐ $25,000-$40,000
- ☐ $41,000-$50,000
- ☐ $51,000-$75,000
- ☐ Over $75,000

14. How long have you been reading romance novels?
- ☐ 1-2 years   ☐ 3-5 years
- ☐ More than 5 years

15. What other topics do you enjoy reading?

Non-Fiction
- ☐ Family/parenting
- ☐ Relationships
- ☐ Addictions/Recovery
- ☐ Health/nutrition
- ☐ Cooking
- ☐ Religious
- ☐ Spirituality
- ☐ Inspiration/affirmations
- ☐ Self-improvement
- ☐ Sports
- ☐ Pets
- ☐ Memoirs
- ☐ True Crime

Fiction
- ☐ Mystery
- ☐ Chick-lit
- ☐ Historical
- ☐ Paranormal

Comments

Thirteen

*Strawberry Girl: strawberry bottom
with strawberry buttercream top

"MOM?"

"In here, Shelly," came the answer from the same kitchen out of which wafted the smell of hot butter and onions, causing Michelle's stomach to rumble. *And where else would her mother be?* she mused, smiling as she headed that way.

She adored that about her mother. Not that Ann Snow was predictable, but that she loved turning the simplest of ingredients into the most masterful of dishes as much as Michelle did—and had parlayed that love into a business of her own as a caterer specializing in desserts.

Today, however, they were starting with a cauliflower and onion tart, one rich with both mascarpone and Gruyère cheese, and made even richer with whipping cream—not a dish for the faint or weak of heart, but definitely one Michelle was looking forward to sinking her teeth into.

Every week, she and her mother got together to test recipes, to shop for cookware, to attend baking demos, to pick out the best produce the local markets had to offer. Today, she was pretty sure

the time with her mom was going to be the only thing capable of
taking her mind off Todd.

She and Todd had just met. She wasn't ready to be so caught
up in a man, to miss him as much as she did. Or worse, to feel
their separation as a tearing apart of the togetherness, the independence she'd always prided herself on.

Was it supposed to be this hard to balance individuality and
coupledom? Or was she still having issues with trust?

Then again, she thought, tucking her purse into the corner of
the counter before joining her mother at the kitchen's big block
island, she and Eileen would be going to the U.K. in a couple of
months—a trip she'd been looking forward to for ages—and
she'd be plying the same torture to Todd. At least she hoped he
would miss her just as much.

"Did you pick up the truffle salt?"

"Oh, yes." Duh. She was here to cook, not to moon or moan.
She dug the small bag out of her purse. "I hope this stuff keeps
because I can't imagine either of us will ever use enough to justify the cost. And please promise me it tastes better than it smells.
Eww."

"It does, and yes, it's pricey, but not as much as the truffle oil
the recipe calls for. I think the salt will work better." Ann took the
jar from Michelle's hand, studied the label. "I really do hate fussy
ingredients, though."

Her mother wasn't the only one. "Like the cardamom I bought
and have only used once? In the butter chicken I cooked for the
dinner party I threw with Eileen?"

"You haven't made it again?" her mother asked, setting the salt
aside to break apart the head of cauliflower.

Michelle watched the tiny florets pile up, popped one into her
mouth, and shook her head. "That was it."

"Hmm." Her mother reached for a knife, began making thin slices of the florets. "Then we'll have to find another dish to justify the purchase."

"Always looking for more things to cook, aren't you?"

Ann only smiled. "Keeping busy at work?"

"Too busy." Michelle reached for the recipe her mother was using and scanned the ingredients and the directions. "You can't imagine how ready I am for a vacation."

"You're still going to London, aren't you?"

"In November, yes, but I'll be back for Thanksgiving," she hurried to add when her mother frowned at her over her glasses' rims. "I told Eileen when we made plans that there was no way I was missing your turkey dinner."

"Will she be bringing anyone? And what's his name, if so?" For the place cards, of course. "I'll ask her and let you know in plenty of time."

"And what about you?"

Michelle returned the recipe card to its spot on the island, doing her best not to make her hesitation to answer seem obvious. She hadn't brought anyone in years, so her mother's question threw her.

What did she suspect, and why? "What about me?"

"Will you be bringing anyone?"

So much for not being obvious. "Why do you ask?"

Her mother laid down her knife, gave Michelle her full attention. "The flush you've had on your cheeks since you got here? The sparkle in your eyes? The fact that I've known you thirty-one years and can read you like a book?"

Was it really that apparent? Was she wearing her infatuation with Todd like her heart on her sleeve? "I'll let you know on that, too."

"Then you have met someone," Ann said, transferring the cauliflower from the chopping block to a roasting pan and setting it aside.

She'd met him, gone out with him, made love with him, fallen head over heels in a matter of days. But how much of that was she ready to share with her mother? "His name's Todd. I've been seeing him for a couple of weeks."

Her mother frowned. "And you haven't brought him home?"

"I'm working up to it."

Silent, Michelle's mother retrieved a covered bowl from the refrigerator, and a pastry sheet, rolling pin, and tart pan from the kitchen's bakers rack. She began prepping the dough for the shell before she spoke. "I thought we talked about you letting go of what happened in college."

They had. But talk was easy. Letting go . . . not so much. Michelle cleared away the cauliflower remnants to give her mother room to work. "It's a big step."

"Then you should've brought him today and taken a small step first."

"Today would've been impossible. He's in Germany. He left last night." And though she would never have believed it, Michelle had slept straight through the next ten hours after coming home from her trip to the airport.

"On business?"

"With friends."

"You've got a love of travel in common then. That's good."

"Actually, we've got a ton of things in common. We both love travel and sports cars. And sushi. And running. It's amazing, really. And," Michelle found herself admitting, "it's a little bit scary. More than a little bit. A lot."

"Why's that?"

"Because things are moving so fast. We've barely had time to get to know each other—"

"Yet it feels as if you've known each other forever?"

"Yes. Exactly." Michelle picked at the edge of the dough circle her mother had rolled flat. "But we haven't. How can I trust something I know can't be real?"

Her lips pursed, Michelle's mother turned to the sink and washed her hands, drying them on one of the towels Michelle knew was a favorite. She also knew a delay tactic when she saw one, and though her mother wasn't one for lectures, Michelle couldn't help but find herself on edge.

Finally, her mother came close, took Michelle's face in her hands, her expression loving and warm. "Scary is okay. Scary means you're serious and not wanting to mess things up."

Emotion tightened Michelle's chest. "But how do I get past being scared? I don't want to always be waiting for the other shoe to drop."

"Instincts," her mother said, giving a pat to her cheek. "Common sense. You've had enough bad dates to know the difference between a man looking for a woman and a man looking for you."

And how true was that? Michelle mused as her mother went back to her tart. "I just hate to think college ruined me for relationships."

"You wouldn't be questioning your cautiousness if it had."

"Hey, I've worked a long time to build these walls. I'm not sure if I'm ready for them to come down."

"What's the worst that will happen if they do?" her mother asked, carefully folding the dough in half before draping it over the pan.

"I'll get hurt again?"

"You might, but don't you think these ten years have equipped you to handle life's lemons?"

"I suppose so." Though she really wasn't sure she had the stomach for too much lemonade.

"There's a lot to be said for a leap of faith, Shelly."

She knew her mother was right. "Does that mean you'll be my net?"

"Haven't I always been?"

A net with the perfect weave, the perfect give, exactly what it took to break a fall, then bounce her to stand on her own two feet. There was a reason time with her mother always left her feeling better. "Maybe this vacation with Eileen will turn out to be a good thing. It'll give me some time and distance to see what I'm really feeling."

"As long as that time doesn't make you late for Thanksgiving dinner."

"When have I ever been late for Thanksgiving dinner?"

"Have you decided what you're going to bring?"

"I was thinking of a dessert." One dessert, actually, with pumpkin and spice, a vanilla cream cheese buttercream icing, and the barest sprinkling of cinnamon for color on top. "Cupcakes maybe."

At that, her mother smiled. "Does that mean you've been giving more thought to your bakery?"

Her bakery. Michelle loved the faith her mother had in her even with so many odds stacked against her. "I have. And I even talked about it with Todd."

"Good. So he knows this is what you want?"

Wanting was the easy part, but only a small portion of the whole. "I don't even know for sure that this is what I want. I mean, I know it is, just not if it's going to happen. The economy's in the toilet, and when am I going to find time for all the work involved when ten hours a day are eaten up at the office?"

Flour dusting her wrists and her apron, her mother opened the Gruyère for grating. "Put together your plans, then show them to us. Your father and I. We want to help you make it happen."

Was she kidding? Did she have any idea how often Michelle had dreamed of involving her family in whatever business venture she tackled? "I would love for both of you to be a part of it, but I'd want you to have a say, be true partners."

"It's your baby, Michelle. Your father and I talked about it that day after the baking class. We both know how long you've dreamed of owning your own bakery. We want to be a part of that dream, to help you in any way we can, but we want you to be the creative force. To bring it to life on your terms."

Michelle's throat swelled, her chest ached, her eyes grew misty. What had she ever done to deserve such a loving family? Their support, their generosity; it meant everything. "I don't even know what to say."

"Say yes."

"Of course I'll say yes!" She laughed, sniffed, reached for her mother and hugged. "But you can't be too silent of a partner. I want you to cook with me. It won't be as much fun if I'm doing it on my own."

"As long as by cooking you don't mean washing dishes."

Michelle held up a hand to swear. "Until we can afford to hire extra help, I promise I'll do the dishes."

Michelle's mother glanced around the countertop and island, frowning. "Check and see if I left the Dijon in the fridge. I swore I got it out, but I obviously should be swearing at losing my mind."

The mustard was on the door with the rest of the condiments. Michelle handed it to her mother and asked, "What do you want me to do?"

"Stir the onions, will you?"

While her mother put the tart shell in the oven and prepared the florets to follow, Michelle set about stirring the pan of onions browning in olive oil and butter. She felt as if she were walking on air.

To have not only her parents emotional support, but their financial backing? Their faith in her had never wavered, not once in her life, but this was more than she'd ever expected. She didn't know what she'd do without them.

Her dream was looking more and more like it might become a reality, though not without a lot of work. Inspections, licenses, permits. It overwhelmed her just to think about. One step at a time. That's all she could do. She'd start with a list of the lists she would need to make, and go from there.

And, of course, she was going to have to decide how to do it all and not screw up what she had with Todd.

"Onions stirred. What else?"

"The baby artichokes. There's a couple pounds in the fridge. You can prep those to go in with the red fingerling potatoes."

"And who's going to be eating all of this?"

"Your father and I for dinner, and you if you're still here. If not, you get to take home your third of the tart, and the potatoes."

With all the cheese, eggs, and cream added to the veggies, Michelle was pretty sure even one serving of the tart would be more than she could eat. The potato dish, however, she could feast on for days.

After cutting the artichokes near the base, she set about peeling the stems and getting rid of the bottom and tough outer leaves. Her thoughts drifted back to Todd and her bakery dreams, and the balance between work and romance.

If they were in a long-term relationship, she wouldn't think

THE ICING ON THE CAKE

twice about tackling a new business, but was it fair to put that much strain on the two of them so soon? What they had was new, exciting, and she had to admit that she saw great potential for a happily ever after ending.

But the bigger worry was starting a relationship concurrently with a business. A bakery would eat up hours and days and weeks, and create a deficit of time for them to spend together.

Even if he was a fan of her cupcakery idea, how would he feel when faced with the reality of having less and less of her attention, her focus? And how would she feel having less of herself to give him?

Making any sort of decision while he was away wouldn't be fair to either of them. Yes, she could weigh her options, make her lists, including one for pros and cons. But she owed it to herself to also explore this thing with Todd. She wanted both, a business and a family. She'd seen her mother make a go of it and knew it was not an impossible feat.

Even if Todd did not turn out to be *The One*, she'd have to face the same conflicts with someone else. Maybe the dual pressure of creating a home with a man and a career was going to be too much to deal with. Maybe she needed to solidify one, get a good foundation beneath it, before even considering the other.

But which to go for first?

How did anyone make such a decision?

"Michelle. You're supposed to get rid of the leaves and the this-tle, not strip out the hearts."

She looked down at the mess she'd left on the island. Oops. "I guess I should run to the market?"

"Yeah," her mother said, shaking her head. "I guess you should."

Fourteen

*Cookie MOMster: chocolate bottom with
almond Oreo buttercream top

THE WEEK AHEAD WAS GOING TO BE nothing but crazy. Crazy
with waiting for Todd to get back from Germany, crazy with
missing him, and crazy because Michelle decided that with her
parents backing, there was no reason not to work on the business
plan for her bakery while Todd was away.

She couldn't deny the economy was an issue, but that very
same financial state of the union wasn't making her future in real
estate marketing look very bright. The thought was to get the
basics put together. And she started just where Todd had suggested—giving her cupcakes their names.

Propped against the pillows in her very lonely bed, she booted
her laptop and pulled up a blank spreadsheet, titling it Cake
Babies, and saving it in a new folder she called Cupcakery. Next
came the column headers: Chocolates, Fruit-Flavors, Novelty,
Miscellaneous.

Under Novelty, the first description she typed out was for
the s'mores recipe she and Todd had baked together last night.
Dropping him off at the airport afterward had been painful,

and back in her car, she'd had to catch her breath before driving home.

Thank goodness she'd already planned to spend Sunday hanging out at her folks' house. Now all she had to do was find things to keep her busy for the rest of the week, things that didn't involve a lot of fattening food like today's cooking-palooza with her mom.

Still stuffed from the dinner feast of cauliflower and artichokes, she turned her attention to her spreadsheet. In the Fruit-Flavors column, she made a simple list: banana, strawberry, apple, lemon, blueberry, pumpkin, coconut, cherry, key lime, carrot.

She had recipes for some of the flavors, not all, but wasn't ready to rule out any possibilities until she'd tested several batches. Oprah's choice years ago of a key lime Bundt cake as one of her favorite things had Michelle pondering the possibility of tapping popular culture for ideas.

Though she'd just told herself to find something besides cooking to fill her time, trying out recipes would be the perfect thing to do this week while Todd was away. And unlike the veggies she'd cooked with her mother, the baked goods would end up at the office, not on her hips.

Tomorrow her coworkers would enjoy the rest of the s'mores batch still sitting in her kitchen. Last time she'd brought them in, one of the IT staff had said the flavors reminded him of family vacations spent melting chocolate and marshmallows around the campfire.

Campfire! A perfect name! She added the name above the description, wondering if Todd would approve. This was her dream, yes, but they'd had such fun last night cooking as a team. It seemed a natural extension to ask his opinion on what she was certain to think of now as his cupcake.

Then again, it was probably a better idea to keep her personal life separate from her work and her dreams—especially this early in the relationship game. Who knew what would happen when Todd returned? Or after her trip to the U.K.? She had great hopes, of course, but knew better than to count chickens before they hatched.

So what next? Apple. She leaned against the headboard, closed her eyes, pictured Jonathans and Fujis and Granny Smiths. Apple butter, apple fritters—her dad's Dunkin' Donuts favorite—apple dumplings, bobbing for apples, Johnny Appleseed, a bad apple, apple of my eye, apple pie. Or . . . Yes! *Why not both,* she mused, typing out Apple of My Pie.

Moving on, she considered one of her personal favorites, one she'd described briefly to Todd. The coffee-flavored cake doughnut bottom, not overly sweet or too heavy, with a mocha fudge buttercream top. A perfect breakfast, really. Like having a doughnut and a cup of Joe . . . which would make it a Joe-n-Dough! Of course!

Before she could name another, her cell phone chimed on the nightstand. An incoming text. She looked at the clock. It was midnight . . . Who in the world?

Early here in Munich. Hope I'm not waking you. Just wanted to let you know I hooked up with the guys and we're all good. Also, that I haven't forgotten about you. Yet.

She pressed her fingers to her lips and laughed, reading the note again through watery eyes. Oh, he made her laugh, but most of what he made her feel was amazing, joyous. She loved the teasing and the flirting and the threats to forget her. She especially loved that he was doing it from thousands of miles away—and that she could do it right back.

Watch out for the fräuleins! If you don't, I'll be the one forgetting about you!

Though that would never happen. He always gave her something to think about, a new angle, options she hadn't considered. As much as they bantered and played, talked music and movies, their deeper conversations—life, dreams, goals—left her feeling contemplative.

Even if whatever this was between them didn't grow into forever, she would never forget Todd Bracken.

On Todd's last day in Germany, his traveling buds left the hotel before the crack of dawn to make the first of several flights that would see them on their way to Ohio. Todd's flight out was scheduled for later, and before boarding for D.C., he was facing an overnight layover in London—twelve hours he was not looking forward to in the least. He wanted to be home with Michelle. He didn't want to spend another night abroad or have to cross the Atlantic to get there.

The delay aside, the vacation had been one of the best weeks of his life. From the first day of Oktoberfest on the Wiesn, when the group had been tossed out of the Hippodrome after a tagalong friend had thrown up on a fräulein's feet, to speeding down the Autobahn to see Salzburg and Vienna, which were ridiculously beautiful, to roughing it with amazing food and beer at a plush alpine lodge near Lake Königssee in the German Alps, he'd enjoyed every minute of the trip.

Part of him wished he'd taken it before meeting Michelle. Not that she'd been a distraction, but she had been on his mind. A lot. He'd phoned her from his bike near the Olympic Village on Monday, catching her as she was getting ready for work. He'd called her a second time from the hilltop in Königssee, thinking then how much he would love to show her the view.

They'd exchanged text messages throughout the week, his

enjoyment of her notes causing the guys to give him more than a few "what's up" looks. He'd mentioned he and Michelle were dating, but hadn't shared much about her, wanting to keep what they had private until he understood it better himself.

Even so, before ever leaving the States, he'd called his mother from the airport to let her know he was seeing someone. Someone who made him happy. Someone he liked a lot. And though he'd kept it to himself, someone he was thinking of bringing home for her to meet once he got back from Germany.

It was a good thing he was flying alone. His friends would've given him a buttload of grief over how miserable the return trip was making him. Even when he boarded the plane at Heathrow, after a restless night in a nearby hotel, he wasn't able to sleep or eat or pay attention to whatever in-flight movie played.

The whole disastrous adventure gave him too much time to think. He'd known Michelle Snow less than three weeks, and yet he'd let her so close that he couldn't get her out of his mind. He wasn't sure he was comfortable having her there. In fact, he was pretty sure he should be cruising rather than blasting forward at warp speed.

He hated chalking up what he felt to a crush, or to something as basic as lust, but anything deeper didn't make sense. Not after ten days in her company. He wasn't sure it would make sense after ten weeks. He wasn't looking to fill a void in his life. His life was pretty damned good. And he wasn't on the rebound; his last relationship was a couple of years behind him.

But while flying across the Atlantic, looking down at the endless expanse of water, the sun shining across the surface like rippling strings of light, it was all he could do to stay in his seat and not rush the pilot to floor it. He was ready to put his feet on the ground and his arms around Michelle.

Landing at Dulles was the first time in over twenty-four hours that his chest hadn't ached when he breathed. He told himself it was nothing but normal travel anxiety, wanting the trip home to be done. But as he waited for another agonizing hour to clear customs, he had to admit the truth. It was waiting to see Michelle that was making him crazy nuts.

Finally, he was free, and he walked out of customs expecting to see her. She wasn't there. He looked everywhere. She wasn't there. He headed outside. Nothing. She wasn't there. Where the hell was she? He went back to baggage claim, telling himself with one side of his brain that she'd show, the other knocking him upside the head for letting her get to him.

That was when he saw her, bouncing toward him, her hair wild, tousled, a sexy cloud of gold and brown. Her dress was a bronze-colored sun thing, and her heels were killer, her legs gorgeous as she nearly ran to meet him. And then she was in his arms, pressed close and tight, her heart pounding just as hard as his own.

"Oh, Todd, I have missed you so much," she said, the words muttered against his chest.

He couldn't take it anymore. He pulled back and brought his mouth down on hers, kissing her as if he'd been gone for years instead of days, as if he'd known her for years instead of days. Kissing her as if they weren't surrounded by dozens, hundreds of onlookers but were shut away behind the closed doors of her condo. He didn't think they could get there fast enough.

A very long minute later, he let her go, and laughing, she reached up to rub her lipstick from his face. "I made a mess of you."

He planned to do the same to her. "Don't worry about it. I'm low maintenance wash and wear."

She laughed again, a giggle, really, as if nothing in the world could've made her as happy as seeing him again. "Are you hungry?"

"Starving." It had been hours since he'd eaten, days since he'd had her.

"I thought you might be." She looped her arm through his as he slung his duffel bag over his shoulder. "I'm going to take you to lunch, though I guess for you it'll be dinner."

A bowl of cereal standing in her kitchen would do him just fine. "I was hoping you were going to take me home."

"Good things come to those who wait," she told him, hugging her body to his arm as they walked to her car.

Michelle glanced over at Todd as she drove. His head was back, his eyes closed. He was exhausted. Too late, she realized she should've thought about that before making plans. She'd had her car detailed first thing this morning, then spent the next few hours getting ready. Hair, dress, shoes, makeup. She'd wanted everything to be perfect.

She'd wanted Todd to take one look at her and remember Mon Ami Gabi and Mike's, the sushi from Raku, and the omelet from the Silver Diner. To recall texting about his laundry, baking cupcakes. To relive their first kiss, their first night, every night after. She wanted—

"What did I miss this last week? Anything good?"

Besides me? she thought about saying, but kept her hunger for him to herself. "I spent a day cooking with my mother—"

"Did you tell her about me?"

"I may have mentioned meeting someone."

He was quiet for a moment, then asked, "Did you bake more cupcakes?"

"I did, yes. And I came up with the beginnings of a menu. Played with some product names."

At that, he sat straighter in his seat and looked over, smiling. "Good for you."

She felt the thrill of his smile—and his approval—to her bones. "It's not much, but it's a start. And it was fun. The guys at work probably gained ten pounds each eating the test-recipe results."

"Fun is good. Fun is everything. Work should be fun. Life's too short for it not to be."

He was right. She hadn't had fun in far too long and was learning that being happy and content was only part of the picture. Todd had brought joy into her very days, making it easy for her to see that though her career came with its own rewards, personal fulfillment wasn't one of them.

That she had only begun to find by giving wings to her dream. And she'd always be thankful to Todd for helping her uncover that truth.

At her side, Todd read the road signs and chuckled. "You're taking me to Shirlington?"

"I am," she said, driving into the quaint little Virginia village and finding a spot to park. "I figured after a week of beer and sausage and spätzle, you might be in the mood for sushi."

"That, and a few other things," he told her, the hooded look in his eyes leaving no doubt as to what he had in mind.

A shiver ran through her, warmed her, and she allowed a private smile as they walked toward the restaurant hand in hand. She was equally ready to strip out of her clothes, but thought it best to keep that to herself for the moment.

They dined al fresco, enjoying their rolls, the gorgeous autumn air, and one another's company. Todd told her about biking through Munich with his friends, seeing the Englischer Gartens and the BMW Headquarters.

He told her about the backpacks he and one of the others had bought for the trip, thinking they might stay in hostels, when instead they'd dined on authentic Italian pizza in an outdoor café and swam in a heated pool in the Alps.

"It was good to see the guys, I gotta say." He stretched out his legs, sat back.

"I'm glad you had a good time. But I'm even more happy that you're back. I think I needed to see you again to know those days we had before you left weren't a dream."

"We had days before I left?"

She glared at him, her ferocious expression as much a tease as his words. "You know we're just as close to your house as we are to my place. I won't have a bit of trouble dropping your jet-lagged butt there and going home alone."

"Oh, yes you will," he told her, placing his napkin on the table and reaching for her chair to slide it close to his. "You nearly crawled inside my skin at the airport. That kiss told me exactly how much you missed me. So I'm kinda wondering what we're doing still sitting here."

She couldn't find her voice to answer. She couldn't move. She couldn't think. All she could do was stare into his eyes. His hunger took her over, stole her strength, her will. She didn't know why she'd thought they could wait when the welcome home she most wanted to give him was the one he most desired, and they needed privacy to make it happen.

She was the first to get to her feet. He stood more slowly, taking his time, as if teasing her with the thought of what was to come. As if he knew what the anticipation did to her. He probably did know. He probably saw it in her eyes. Hiding her emotions had never been a skill she'd mastered. She'd never seen the need.

They made it to her car in half the time they'd taken walking to the restaurant, and she had trouble going no more than ten miles over the speed limit on the drive home. Todd closed his eyes for the trip, but the tension between them remained. The only sounds she heard in the car were that of her breathing and an equally labored beat of her heart.

By the time she reached her condo and parked, her clothes were too hot on her skin. Todd took her hand, pulled her with him to the elevator, then pulled her into his arms. The ride up was endless, and her hands were everywhere—in his hair, beneath his shirt, laced with his own.

They ran down the hall once they'd reached her floor, breathless, laughing, no words spoken. She fumbled with the keys. Todd took them from her and opened the door. She shut it, locked it, kicked out of her shoes while she did.

He was already out of his shirt when she turned, and she reached for his belt buckle, then the button and zipper of his fly. He pulled the straps of her dress down her arms, baring her breasts. His hands were there, then his mouth. She closed her eyes, let her head fall back, and shimmied until the garment dropped to the floor.

Everything else they were wearing followed, discarded and scattered, and how they made it to the bedroom she didn't know. But they were there, coming together, loving, finding what they'd lost, no longer missing but learning, discovering, promising without words that even time apart would never come between them.

Fifteen

*Campfire: graham cracker bottom with milk
chocolate ganache & marshmallow top

"ARE YOU NERVOUS?" MICHELLE ASKED, walking with Todd through the mall as they window-shopped on their way to meet her parents for brunch. It was time. She and Todd had been together nearly a month. He was a very big part of her life now, and she wanted her parents to know him.

"Should I be?" He stopped, frowned down at her, his blue eyes going playfully wide. "Are your parents scary?"

Laughing, she reached back for him and dragged him forward without any kicking or screaming. "No more scary than me or you."

"Hmm. Maybe I should be nervous," he said, falling into step beside her. "You thought I was going to be a monster. The first night you met me. I remember you saying so."

Ugh, had she actually admitted her fears to him? That even having seen his photo, she worried he was going to be an ogre? "That's the trouble with blind dates. Like boxes of chocolates, you never know what you're going to get. Which is why I'm kind of hoping I'm done with that."

"Wait a minute," he said, pulling her to a stop and around to face him, creating a middle of the mall roadblock. "What's this kind of hoping business?"

Head cocked, she looked up. His frown caught her off guard. She'd thought they were teasing here, keeping the mood light. Even if he wasn't nervous, she was. She wanted brunch to go well. She wanted her parents to see for themselves how amazing Todd was.

But she didn't want him to feel pressured into something he wasn't ready for. She didn't want that at all, and she hurried to backtrack in case they weren't on the same page. "It just means that as well as things are going between us, I don't want to count my chickens before they're hatched."

He considered her for a long moment, his expression relaxing as he did. "And here I had my calculator ready."

Breathing easier, she put them both into motion again. "I know. It's hard to remember that we only met last month."

"Seems kinda soon to be taking the great parent test," he said, dragging his feet, though only metaphorically.

"It's not a test," she assured him. "They're just anxious to put a face to the name of this guy I keep talking about."

"It's pretty important to you, then. That we meet."

"It is."

"Then I should probably add a last-minute condition."

This time she was the one to stop in the middle of the walkway, causing the two women behind them to sidestep to the right. She apologized, then turned her gaze on Todd. If he was getting back at her, a tit-for-tat teasing, making her do some sweating of her own, okay. She could deal.

If he was serious . . . she didn't know what to think. "What is it?"

"You come to Ohio next time I go to visit my dad."

That was it? That was all? Here she was, sweating for nothing? "Of course! I would love to."

"I really want to introduce the two of you in case—" He paused, glanced into the distance as if needing breathing room, then shook it off and continued. "In case I don't get a chance to do it later. Plus, my mom is superanxious to meet you."

She didn't like hearing the sadness in his voice, or thinking about the possibility of him losing his father. Then she realized what else he'd said. "You've talked about me to your mom?"

"You've talked about *me* to *your* mom," he replied.

But she and her mother spoke every day and about everything, so his not coming up in conversation would've been strange. She couldn't help but wonder the circumstances that had him discussing her with his. "Is it weird that we're both talking to our parents? After only a month? I mean, we're not exactly teenagers here."

"Why would it be? Don't you tell your mom what's going on in your life?"

"I don't tell her about all my dates, no. Most I would just as soon forget."

"Good. Glad to know I rate."

He did, but she wasn't about to let on that he was the first man since her disastrous college break who'd made the grade. Giving him a quick wink, she said, "Don't let it go to your head."

"You mean I shouldn't assume the next step will be trading house keys?"

Ah, that. Though he didn't know it yet, she'd already arranged for him to have one as well as access to her garage. She was going down to let him in so often that it only made sense. But it was a big step for her, opening herself up, trusting.

She was saved from having to respond by a window display that caught her eye, and she tugged him toward the accessories shop where belts and scarves hung next to trees of funky jewelry. "Oh, look at that."

The trinket box sat on pewter feet, the sides papered in a yellow and white stripe, the top in black and white polka dots. A yellow silk rose trimmed in black and white ribbon sat on the lid, and a cabochon on the front finished it off.

"C'mon," she said, grabbing his sleeve. "Let's go in so I can see it up close."

"Ah, yes. The shopping vice."

Now *that* she did remember telling him. "It's not for me. I want to get something to send to Woodsie while we're here. Do you mind? We've got plenty of time."

"I don't mind, but I don't know anything about a Woodsie."

She stopped halfway to the door and looked up. "Really? I haven't told you about her? My childhood nanny?"

"Nope," he said, shaking his head. "Not a word."

How could she not have told Todd about the woman who'd been her second mother and her own mother's salvation? Who was as much a part of her life as her nuclear family? Who was family, if not in name or by blood?

An unbelievable oversight, but one easily remedied. "She lives in Carlisle. Where I grew up."

"Pennsylvania."

Michelle nodded and led him into the store. "When my mom was my age with three small children, Woodsie was a lifesaver. She took care of me and my brothers any time my parents' working hours overlapped. And we'd stay with her when my parents went out on the weekends."

"You're still close."

"Oh, yes. Very much. For some reason, I seem to bring the sunshine she needs. She's had a difficult life, emotionally, financially." Michelle left the explanation there, moving farther into the small store. It wasn't her place to reveal anything about the other woman's life, even to Todd.

She checked the price tag on a scarf, thinking the yellow pattern a bit too bright. "I try to visit every couple of months. My mother and I usually go together. We'll all have lunch, then Mom will go see old friends while Woodsie and I spend the day catching up."

"I'd like to meet her sometime. If, you know, the chickens hatch."

Introducing two of the most important people in her life? Michelle would love it, too, though she knew what a private person Woodsie was. Her own relationship with the older woman was made more precious for that very reason.

Still, Todd had always been a perfect gentleman. She had no reason to think he wouldn't respect Woodsie's boundaries. "I think she would love you. Chickens or no chickens."

He followed as she circled through the store, commenting on the pieces she examined. A tiny ceramic picture frame in the shape of the sun. A necklace of chunky amber beads. An antique broach in a lacy brushed gold with a yellow glass center cut to resemble a topaz.

Finally she returned to the trinket box she'd seen in the front window, admiring it as Todd asked, "Are you looking for anything in particular?"

"I usually find what I want when I'm not even looking," she said, realizing how aptly the sentiment applied to her finding him, too.

"Or in the most unexpected places," he came back, and she was certain he was reading her mind.

Smiling as she thought of Match.com, she picked up the box, opened it. The craftsmanship was gorgeous. "I know this is totally impractical, but it makes me think of her. She could put a sweater or shawl to much better use."

Todd took the box from her hands, turned it over, and examined it thoroughly before giving it back. "Or maybe something totally impractical is just what she needs. Something to remind her of you every time she sees it."

"Do you think so?"

"I do," he said, reaching into his pocket and handing her a small box wrapped in red paper. "Kinda like this."

"Todd?" Her pulse fluttering, Michelle set aside the trinket box and reached for the one Todd held. She peeled the paper free and opened it to find a pair of delicate sterling silver cross earrings on the cotton inside. "Oh, Todd. These are beautiful."

"You like?"

"I love. They're lovely. But you shouldn't have." Then she remembered what he'd said about a gift as a memento or keepsake. "Is this to remind you that I'm a good Catholic girl?"

He shook his head, his dimple a crescent in his cheek as he smiled. "They're to remind you how glad I am that you're not a nun."

Todd would've had no trouble picking out Michelle's parents from a lineup. Ann Snow was as petite and energetic as her daughter, and Jack Snow's eyes had the same warm twinkle. Todd shook his hand as Michelle made introductions and gave her mother a hug when Ann opened her arms.

"I've been looking forward to meeting you both," he said as the four of them took their seats, Michelle on his left, her father on his right. "Michelle's told me so much about you that it's hard to believe this is the first time we've met."

"She hasn't told us near enough about you," Jack said, and

when Michelle gasped, saying, "Dad, behave!" he came back with, "What? It's the truth. All we know is that he likes to run and eat sushi like you do, and that you've seemed happier the last few weeks than you have in a long time. I need to know more. Like if he's a Yankees or Red Sox man."

Jack's question had everyone laughing, and the rest of the brunch was spent in casual conversation, no grilling for hidden agendas or digging into Todd's past. Not that he wouldn't have dredged up whatever the Snows wanted to know—he had no secrets he wasn't willing to tell—but they didn't ask.

All the four of them did was talk. About politics and living in the center of it all, about the economy and the stress of the real estate market on Michelle and her job. About their favorite spots in D.C.—Todd loved the FDR Memorial—and the winters in Ohio versus those on the Atlantic coast.

What Todd did learn, that Michelle hadn't told him, was that she and her mother had talked about opening a bakery for years. He listened to the two women discuss recipes and desserts until no amount of his grilled chicken salad could stop his stomach from growling. Who knew he was such a sucker for sweets?

"Now you see what I've had to deal with for years," Jack said to him in an aside.

"You appear none the worse for wear," Todd responded, glad for the distraction before he booted his health kick to the curb. "You must hit the gym on a regular basis."

"Not as often as I need to, I'm afraid." Jack sat back, crossed his arms above his stomach. "Michelle says you're studying Krav Maga?"

"Yes, sir. For a couple of years now. It's more about neutralizing threats and preemptive attacks against violence than strict self-defense. I mean, I'm not out there kicking in anyone's teeth or anything," Todd hurried to assure the other man. Knowing he studied the martial arts form developed and employed by Israel's national intelligence agency might not sit well with Michelle's father.

But Jack didn't seem the least bit fazed. "Good to hear. But I still like knowing when Michelle goes running that someone's got her back."

The mention of her name caught Michelle's attention, and she looked from Todd to Jack. "Now, Dad, you know I've never been a fan of running alone after dark. And when I do go out at night, I stay off the trails and out of the woods."

Jack blew out a hefty puff of breath. "Who's talking about the time of day? I've never liked knowing you were out on the streets alone period."

"Well, now I'm not, so you can stop worrying and stop making Todd feel as if he's responsible for me."

Jack Snow glanced from his daughter to his wife before turning his gaze on Todd, and though when he spoke his words were for Michelle, the deeper meaning wasn't lost. "I'm pretty sure if he feels at all responsible for you, it's not because of anything I've said."

Grinning as Michelle and her father got into a friendly row, Todd concentrated on his salad, spearing his fork through the dressed greens and thinking that Jack Snow was incredibly perceptive.

And that his being so made him scary in ways that had nothing to do with monsters.

Sixteen

***Baba's Baby: carrot bottom with vanilla
cream cheese buttercream top**

TURNABOUT BEING FAIR PLAY, Todd made plans for Michelle
to meet his family a couple of weeks later. Unlike her easily
arranged trip to the mall for brunch, he had to see to airfare and
lodging—though the minute his mother heard he was coming
home and bringing her with him, she insisted they stay with her.
She had plenty of empty bedrooms, after all.

Neither he nor Michelle had been thrilled at the prospect of a
long weekend spent sleeping apart, but Michelle had no problem
respecting his mother's wishes. It was only three nights, and
they'd have their days together. Todd grumbled, but agreed, and
they left D.C. for Ohio on a Friday afternoon, both taking off
early from work to make the trip.

In the airport in Columbus, Michelle found herself more anxious than she'd thought she'd be as she and Todd walked from
their gate to where his mother was waiting in the terminal. She
wanted to make a good first impression; Todd's mother might
very well end up being a permanent part of her life.

But the minute the other woman opened her arms for her son, Michelle's worries vanished like mist in the air. Todd's mother was all smiles, warm and welcoming, and so obviously glad to see her youngest child. Michelle stood to the side and gave them their time, enjoying the public display of affection.

Not that she was surprised. Todd was equally demonstrative with her, holding hands as they walked, sitting close as they dined, even kissing her without worrying about onlookers. He was spontaneous, and she liked that. Liked, too, that he hadn't let distance come between him and his family.

The idea of living so far from her parents and brothers left her feeling adrift. Her mom and dad were her anchors, Brian and Michael, too. She couldn't imagine not seeing them as often as she did, and admired Todd all the more for the strength of character that allowed him his independence.

Finally, he released his mother and looked over, a beatific smile on his face. "Mom, I'd like you to meet Michelle Snow. Michelle, this is my mother."

"I'm so happy to meet you," the older woman said, pulling Michelle close. "I've been dying to ever since Todd called me on his way to Germany and told me about you."

"He did?" She glanced at Todd, watched his dimple deepen as his mouth quirked mischievously. "I knew he'd spoken to you about me, but I didn't know that was when he called."

Todd's mother hooked her arm through Michelle's, leaving Todd to haul their carry-ons as they headed for her car. "He did, and I can't remember ever hearing him so excited about having met someone. I was beginning to wonder if he was even dating or was too busy with work and his martial arts."

Michelle searched out and caught Todd's gaze. He gave a careless shrug, as if his enthusiasm in telling his mother about her meant nothing, when to Michelle it was everything in the world.

He'd taken his trip ten days after their first date. Ten days, and he'd phoned his mother to tell her they'd met. Yes, Michelle had mentioned Todd to her mother the same weekend, but the confession had come out in the course of conversation while she and her mother had cooked.

The fact that Todd had wanted his mother to know about her and that his feelings had been obvious—and so soon after their first meeting—melted Michelle's heart. She listened as the other woman explained the plans she'd made for their weekend stay, but the details of the family dinners and football game tailgating party barely registered.

All Michelle's thoughts were for the man she was coming to love.

Todd didn't think Michelle could've fit any better into his family had she grown up next door, walked with him to school, and eaten dinners at the Bracken's table. His mother loved her, his sister loved her, his brother loved her, as did all of his siblings' kids.

If anyone was uncomfortable with the visit, he was, and he couldn't say why except that Ohio hadn't been his home for a very long time, and he felt more at ease with Michelle in D.C. This was his history, she was his here and now, and the mix didn't sit as well as it should have.

Watching her now engaged in conversation with his mother, sister, and sister-in-law, as around them car horns blared in the stadium parking lot and radios blasted the Buckeyes pre-game show, he told himself he was being ridiculous. This was what family was about, getting together, enjoying one another's company, catching up on news, plans, and hometown gossip. Which might've been the problem.

As much as he wanted to have Michelle meet his family and see them himself, he hated being away from their life, their world. Hearing what was going on in the place that meant the most to them. Spending time enjoying their city, the running trails, the restaurants.

Having grown up in a loving home, even after it had broken, he wouldn't have thought he'd have felt this way. He'd been close to his siblings, he and his brother throwing things back and forth at the dinner table, keeping the mood light and their mother's mind off the divorce.

They'd competed to see who could be funnier, his brother's style that of an early, edgy David Letterman, his own goofy sense of humor more in tune with the *Saturday Night Live* years of Adam Sandler and Chris Farley.

He'd loved his life here, his friendships with Scott Tucker and others, playing lacrosse and all those state wins. But he couldn't deny that his life was different now that he'd met Michelle. That even though they had no legal document making it so, she was his family, his every day, his time to come.

She was his home.

He shook off his musings, listened as his brother and brother-in-law discussed player stats, coaching styles, offensive game plans, and defensive strategy like only true college fans can do. The grounds outside the Horseshoe were awash in a sea of red . . . flags, banners, T-shirts, jerseys, coolers. He'd seen the same on the morning's drive through Columbus, the town showing support for their team.

Since he and Michelle didn't have tickets to the game, they'd be on their way shortly to visit with his father for the rest of the day. Then after dinner at J. Alexander's, with his mother, his siblings, and their spouses, they'd have one night to spend here before returning to D.C.

He was ready. He hated admitting it, but except for his family and the few friends from school who had stayed here, Ohio was a part of his past. A good part, but the past still the same.

Michelle stood just inside the doorway of the room that had been hers for the duration of their stay. Todd stood just outside in the hallway. She cocked her head to one side, looking for any resemblance between him and the members of his family. He shared his sister's smile, his mother's bone structure and dimples. They were a beautiful family, the Brackens.

And his father. Now she understood Todd's sense of humor. Father and son were an unstoppable team. "I loved meeting your dad this afternoon."

"He enjoyed you, too." Todd waggled both brows. "He called you hot. Told you he was a ladies' man."

"He is totally larger than life."

"You should've seen him back in the day. Large isn't even big enough to describe him."

"You must be proud to think of all the lives he's saved."

"I am." He reached up, stroked a finger down her cheek to the hollow of her throat. "It's tough seeing him as weak as he is, though he did look good today."

She hated what the family was going through. She couldn't think of anything worse than watching a loved one's decline and being helpless in the face of the disease. "Are you going to be okay sleeping alone? It's just one more night."

"No, I'm not going to be okay," he grumbled. "And I'm probably not going to sleep either."

"Poor baby." She reached up, cupped a hand to his cheek, shivering as his late-night stubble scraped her inner wrist. "Hard to believe there was a time when we didn't share a bed."

"We should've stayed in a hotel."

"I don't think your mother would've allowed that." She let her hand stray, down his neck, to his throat. She raised up on tiptoes and kissed him there, a tiny brush of her lips, and felt the thump of his heart when she did. "Just think how much you have to look forward to."

His brow arched wickedly. "Why don't you come out here and remind me?"

Out here, the safe and public space where nothing could happen. Or so he thought. She took him up on his dare, wedging one of her legs between his, draping one hand over his shoulder, keeping the other between their bodies to play.

He grinned, his dimple a deep and devilish half-moon, and brought his mouth down on hers. She opened beneath him, slid her tongue along his, pulling away to nip at his lower lip as she worked her hand behind his belt buckle.

"You are a wench," he whispered.

"You love it," she whispered back.

And then he was kissing her again, his mouth pressing, his skin feverish when she tugged his shirttails out of the way. He swayed, then straightened, and took a step to brace his shoulder against her door. She leaned harder against him, making him sweat, making him groan.

"Not so sure this was a good idea," he pulled free to say.

"And here I thought we were having fun."

The sound in his throat was husky and raw and full of promises he intended to keep. "We are, but you've got me in the mood for more."

"I noticed," she said, skimming her fingertips over the tip of his erection. "Just pretend we're in high school and trying not to get caught."

"If this reminds you of high school, you had a better time of it than me," he said, pushing into the cup of her hand once, twice.

Dare she confess what a good little Catholic girl she really was? That he brought out the wicked in her? "If you'll kiss me goodnight, I'll stop teasing you."

"Or we could go inside and close the door and you could tease me goodnight."

She shook her head, then shook a finger. "No boys allowed. House rules."

"Hmm. I don't remember that being a rule when I lived here."

"Because your rule would've been no girls."

"Both rules are cramping my style," he said, the words coming out on a strangled sort of grunt.

As much as she loved teasing him, she, too, had had enough of the torture. She wanted to be home, in their bed . . . Oh, but she loved the sound of that. Their bed. "Then kiss me goodnight and go to sleep and we'll be that much closer to flying home and setting our own rules."

He seemed to consider that, bringing up a hand to cradle the back of her head. "Rule number one. No more of your hands in my pants if I can't get mine into yours."

"I like that one," she said, tilting back her head and waiting.

"Rule number two. No more meeting friends or relatives until next year. Or at least until Thanksgiving." He brought his mouth to hers, brushed his lips against the corner of hers, tiny little kisses that were barely more than a breath.

"That's a good one," she said, willing him to hurry. She wanted more of him than playful nips and bites.

"Rule number three. Any future traveling we do will involve a hotel room with a king-size bed."

"Even if we're not staying the night?"

"Even if," he said, and then he kissed her fully, opening his mouth and asking her for the same.

Willingly, she gave him what he wanted, her tongue stroking his, her lips pressing. She scraped her nails over the skin at his nape and he groaned, a rumbling vibration that tickled its way through her, settling in the pit of her stomach and building to a roar.

She loved this connection between them, the ferocious need each shared for the other, the way neither was shy about showing it. For now, however, she decided they'd done enough showing. She pulled from his embrace with great reluctance, smiling as she looked up into his eyes.

"Good night, Todd. Sweet dreams."

His sigh was heavy, disappointed, and broke her heart. "See you in the morning. Assuming I survive the night."

"You'll survive," she said, and since he wasn't moving, she pushed against his chest.

He feigned stumbling backward, his hand coming up as if to cover the wound she'd inflicted. Then, as she laughed softly, he pulled himself upright and stumbled down the hall, making enough noise that she shushed him before he woke his mother.

Though, she supposed, closing her own door behind her, at least his mother would know they were in separate rooms if he did.

Seventeen

*Autumn Luv: spice bottom with almond buttercream top

The Birds & The Bees
(yes . . . Eileen & I are The Bird and The Bee)
are having a mini Monster Mash chez Snow to kick off
the Halloween weekend. Join us for sweets, treats, Jell-O shooters,
and a lesson on The Birds & The Bees (just in case your
parentals never gave you The Talk). My place is itty-bitty,
teenie-tiny but there is plenty of room for big wigs,
as **COSTUMES ARE REQUIRED!**
We'll get the par-tay started here and take the madness
to the spooky streets of Bethesda.

"ARE YOU SURE WE HAVE ENOUGH CUPCAKES?"

At Eileen's question, Michelle looked at the four dozen cup-cakes lined up on her bar. She'd baked them after work, stored them overnight, then today piped the edges with a ring of rich buttercream icing, placing miniature candy bars in the center to complete the Halloween treats.

Since said treats were for the guests attending their mini Monster Mash rather than costumed kids toting pillowcases, and since she'd received only twenty RSVPs, well . . . she counted again to be sure.

With the table set up as a tapas bar—Eileen's menu included herbed Marsala meatballs, butter-leaf lettuce wraps, Portuguese crab cakes, shrimp and avocado feta rolls, and stuffed mushrooms—and at least two cupcakes per guest, she couldn't imagine anyone going hungry.

Unless, of course, word of the feast got out and their party had crashers. She shook her head. She couldn't worry about that now. "We'll have plenty. In fact, we'll have leftovers, and I'm counting on you to take most of them home."

"As if you had to ask. You know how I feel about the things that come out of your kitchen."

"I do know, but since you did as much cooking as I did today, the credit for tonight is as much yours as mine."

"Ah, but I didn't bake the cupcakes."

A minor detail. "But you made the shrimp and the meatballs and the crab cakes and the lettuce wraps. All I did were the mushrooms. That counts for way more."

Eileen flipped her hair back over her shoulder and posed. "Does that make me the hostess with the mostest?"

"At the very least," Michelle said, grinning, then looked at the clock on her stove and took a deep breath. "I think we're ready."

"I'll slip into my wings, then man the door while you get your buzz on." Laughing, Eileen scurried down the hall to the bedroom, popping back around the corner for a quick, "I can't wait to meet Todd."

Caught in a crazy flux of emotions, Michelle rolled her eyes, grinning as she shooed her best friend on her way. She was excited about the party, nervous about what she might be forgetting, eager to get outside and see what crazy fun they'd find on

THE ICING ON THE CAKE 173

the streets. But most of all, she was anticipating her friends' reactions to Todd.

Tonight would be the first time most of them would meet the man she'd been talking about for the last month and a half. She'd known from their second night together at Mike's that Todd wasn't going to be a short-term fling, but she still hadn't been ready to share him.

Taking their relationship public opened it to questions and criticism as well as congratulations. Her family loved Todd. His family loved her. Her best friends were going to adore him as much as she did. But there were always one or two voices in every crowd that just didn't know when to be quiet. And those were the voices she wanted to avoid.

She didn't want to hear that a month and a half meant nothing when she knew it meant everything. She didn't want to hear that she was listening to her biological clock instead of her heart. Yes, she wanted children, but she'd been resigned to living her life as a doting aunt before Todd came along.

She didn't want to be asked if she'd checked his credit report, if he had health insurance and a retirement plan. What she wanted was for her friends to be happy for her, to trust that she knew herself and what she wanted. She didn't want to have to choose between the man she was coming to love and those who'd been such a big part of her life up till now.

Todd was her future. They hadn't made plans or talked marriage, content to live one day at a time. But she knew in her heart of hearts the days ahead, the weeks, the months, the years, would be the brightest she'd ever known.

An hour into the evening's festivities, Michelle realized she needn't have worried. Todd was a total hit. He was engaging, charming, funny when jokes were called for, capable of intelligent conversation when things got deep. Not bad for a guy dressed as Chicken Caesar.

While she was the yellow and black bumblebee to Eileen's brightly plumed bird, Todd wore a toga, a laurel wreath, and ruled with a rubber chicken instead of a scepter. He was the most delicious Chicken Caesar she'd ever laid eyes on. And she thought more than a couple of her friends thought so, too.

From a quiet corner of her kitchen where she'd retreated for a bit of breathing room, she watched as two unattached females hung on his every word. He was a perfect gentleman, listening as they talked, responding when spoken to, laughing in appreciation of what was said.

What he didn't do was flirt. Even from here she could see there was nothing untoward in his behavior, nothing to make her doubt him. She liked that. Liked that he treated all her friends the same, no matter that a couple of the women she knew were showing their true colors by flirting aggressively with him. Obviously not the friends she'd thought they were.

Catching her staring, he extracted himself from the small group near the front door and made his way to the kitchen. She'd finally managed to sneak away for a bite to eat, but her appetite fled in the face of the cartwheels her stomach was doing at his approach.

"Nice party." He didn't stop, backing her into the refrigerator and out of sight of her guests.

She attempted a curtsy, her antennae bobbing, her wings catching on the refrigerator door. "Thank you, my lord."

"Hmm. I like the sound of that."

"I wouldn't get used to it. Holding court with a rubber chicken isn't going to earn you a lot of respect."

"That coming from a bee?"

"Lucky for you I wasn't the bird since that thing on your head looks like a nest."

"No," he said, waggling his brows, the wreath waggling, too. "Lucky for me you weren't a nun."

Oh, the cartwheels, and the dizzy spinning things he did to her head and her heart. She was infatuated, insane with it, loving the way he made her feel like she was the only woman in room. Like they were the only couple, the kitchen an island in the middle of the music and the conversation.

She wondered how long they could stay marooned here. How soon someone would come to rescue them when she didn't want to be rescued. "I have something for you."

"As long as it's not chocolate, because I've already eaten like three cupcakes. Including every bit of the icing. And the candy bar tops," he said, puffing out his cheeks as if ready to explode.

That was okay because three months from now, he'd be over it. "There might be chocolate involved. Hot chocolate. A roaring fire. Lots of cold snow. Skis."

His eyes perked up at skis. "You've traded your trip to the U.K. for one to Bavaria?"

"No. I let you go to Germany, so you're stuck with me going to London." And she was stuck allowing another week to come between them. This gift should make up for it, or at least make the separation easier to forget.

"I was afraid you'd say that."

Her gaze on the plate she held, she twisted a meatball on its skewer, praying he wouldn't say no to her invitation. "But I have reservations in February at a lodge in Park City, Utah."

"You and Eileen have reservations, you mean."

Had she told him about the trip, or was he guessing? It didn't matter. Plans had changed. She looked up, her gaze firm, insistent, her heart pleading. "Not anymore."

"What?" He drew out the word, curious, a many-layered question.

She answered the easiest one first. "It's a trip my company arranged. Eileen was going to go with me, but she suggested I take you instead."

"Good friend you've got there."

She was. Michelle would be lost without her. "I missed getting you anything for your birthday, so I'd like this to be my gift to you."

He took the meatball from her hand, popped it into his mouth. "You make it hard for a guy to say no."

"Then don't say it." *Please, please don't say it.*

A roar of laughter went up in the main room, and he waited for it to die down before he said anything at all. "You also make it hard for a guy to top something like that."

"Then don't try. This isn't a competition." He'd given her a trip to Ohio. He'd given her earrings. He'd given her nights she would never forget, days she relived when she missed him.

"What is it then?" he asked, his voice soft, tender.

"I'm hoping it's a relationship." It was for her. No matter how many times she told herself not to count unhatched chickens, she couldn't deny that she'd committed herself to him the night they'd shared sushi on her balcony and much more in her bed.

Reaching up, he tucked a loose strand of her hair behind her ear. "We could call it that."

Did that mean he was willing to stick a name on it but not define it any further? And why had she even brought it up? The time was wrong, the situation even more so for the sort of con-

THE ICING ON THE CAKE 177

versation they would need to have to make sure they were on the same page.

This would be such a great time for a do over. "We don't have to call it anything. I mean, it's really too soon—"

"No. It's not," he said, sliding his lingering fingertip around the shell of her ear.

Eyes closed, she took a deep breath, hoping to calm the flutters of pleasure his words set off in her chest. "I wasn't trying to pressure you—"

"Into what? Admitting we've got something going here? That I'm not going anywhere? That I'm not going to let you get away?"

"Yeah. Something like that." It was all she could get out. Her throat had swelled tight with emotion. The things he made her feel . . .

He leaned in closer, blocking her view of everything but his face. "I don't have to be pressured into admitting any of that. It's as easy to say as is my own name."

She couldn't think, couldn't breathe, knew nothing but Todd, the way he felt like forever, and then another round of party noise brought her back to the present. Things were getting way out of hand, and so she gazed up at him blankly, and asked, "What is your name, by the way?"

He chuckled, stepped back and leaned against the counter's edge as if he, too, needed a jolt back to reality. "I'm not sure. You kinda make me lose my mind."

"That's probably the cupcakes. And the candy. How many did you say you ate?"

"Enough that I can't be held responsible for anything I say or do."

"No, no, no. You're not going to get out of this relationship that easily."

He held her gaze, his certain, confident. "So you're good going there?"

"I am." He'd made it easy for her. She tucked a finger into the folds of his toga and tugged. "Besides, I don't let just any Roman emperor put his hands on me."

"I thought that was one of the perks of being Caesar," he said and caught her hand to his chest.

"No, but it's a perk of being Todd Bracken." She had a thought, trailed her finger to his waist before reaching for her drink and asking before she sipped, "You are wearing something under that sheet, aren't you?"

"What if I'm not?"

"You're going to get awfully cold when we hit the streets."

"All the better for you to warm me up when we get back."

That she could do, but first to settle the other issue of her belated birthday gift. "So you'll come with me? Skiing in Utah?"

"Of course, I will. Are you kidding?"

Whew. "I was afraid you would think me presumptuous. You know, planning something that far ahead."

"It's you and me, time away. Be as presumptuous as you'd like."

Oh, she liked this man so much. "It's in February. Can you take the time off?"

"Give me the dates. I'll let the big guys know on Monday."

"No asking permission? Just telling them that's how it is?"

"One of those perks of being Todd Bracken," he said with a swing of the rubber chicken.

She smiled, then shook her head. "I'm just happy this is a company-sponsored trip or I might not get the time away. Especially since I'll be out a week next month for the vacation with Eileen."

"Tough to be in real estate these days."

"You don't know the half of it."

"Guess it's a good thing you're looking ahead to the cupcake business."

He had to know a venture of her own was going to be just as tough. "It'll eat up tons of my time."

He shifted a step away from her and closer to the main room. Whether he was making a self-protective statement with the space or just moving to see her better, she couldn't tell. His expression hadn't changed. His focus on her hadn't wavered.

"It'll be worth it," he finally said. "Any dream is."

She hoped so. "Even if it will mean giving up Halloween parties? And ski trips?"

"Will it mean giving up running? And sushi dinners? And concerts?"

She cocked her head to the side. "We haven't gone to any concerts."

"Not yet. But we will. You need more music in your life than opera and Bach," he told her, as if handing down an edict.

"And I suppose you're the authority who'll make it happen?"

He laughed beneath his breath, his dimple a deep half moon. "If you only knew."

"Knew what?"

"Back in high school? I carried a library of music in my car. Like five hundred cassettes," he said, gesturing with an expansive sweep of one arm. "And I knew where all of them were. Passenger side, backseat door pocket, right next to the mix tape that had 'Jane's Addiction' on the B side. Everyone knew I was the go-to guy for new stuff."

Cute. "And now? You have hard drives full of MP3s?"

"Your vice is shopping. Mine's music. What can I say?"

"That first night I came over. What were you playing then?"

He frowned, thinking. "Maybe The Fray?"

"Have you seen them in concert?"

"No, but they'll be at the Nine-thirty Club in January. Want to go with me?"

"I would love to." And she spoke the truth with not a single regret.

"I'll get the tickets, then."

"Hey, Michelle." At the sound of Eileen's voice, Michelle turned to see her friend pointing toward the door. "We're heading out. Are you guys coming?"

She looked up at Todd. "Ready to take this show on the road?"

"I came, I conquered. I'm ready to cluck," he said, swinging the chicken again.

Michelle wasn't sure which of them groaned the loudest.

Eighteen

*Skinnimint: chocolate bottom with peppermint
vanilla buttercream top

OVER THE NEXT FOURTEEN DAYS, Todd found himself preparing for his week alone while Michelle went on her vacation. He'd been staying at her condo most of the time and ignoring his shack of a house. He was determined to make some progress there while she and Eileen were gone, and he would—as long as missing her didn't get in the way.

He didn't know why he was having so much trouble accepting the speed at which things were moving, how they'd gone from being strangers to intimates within a matter of days. They never argued. They rarely disagreed. They each gave deference to the other rather than insisting on getting their way.

It just wasn't . . . normal. What he'd known. What he was used to. Michelle was like no woman he'd ever dated, their fit too comfortable for words.

Running beside her now as they made their Friday-night trip along the Capital Crescent Trail, he thought how easy it was to be with her. Maybe that was the problem. Their relationship required no work. It just was, as if it had risen fully formed, an entity with a life of its own. That was a crazy way to look at things, but it was what it was.

He'd never known of any relationship that didn't require work, whether romantic, business, even friendship, and often family. There was no give and take with Michelle; it was all giving, caring. There was generosity and kindness, but nothing he could call sacrifice, at least not on his part.

What he feared was that she was the one sacrificing to be with him. Yes, she talked about her bakery. Yes, she baked test batches of cupcakes and employed him as her taster. Yes, she kept notes on the things she needed to research—everything from baking supplies to baking equipment to licenses allowing her to sell her baked goods.

What he hadn't seen were applications for said licenses, or research on the square footage she'd need for her space, or quotes on the cost of a lease to fit those needs. Either she hadn't done the work, or she was keeping it from him. He wanted to ask, but he wasn't sure he wanted the answers.

If their relationship was an impediment to her dream, the guilt would be a hell of a burden to bear.

"You're awfully quiet over there," Michelle said, matching his pace step for step.

That always amazed him, how they were such a perfect match when he was a good nine inches taller. He took a moment, breathed deeply of the cool autumn evening, frost in the air, foliage turning to earth, what birds that remained sadly silent. "You know you can use my brain any time you need to."

"What do you mean, use your brain?"

"I'm organized, more than a bit OCD, give great ideas. Am happy to brainstorm."

She laughed, stepped behind him to allow a cyclist to pass. "I'll keep that in mind should I need another lobe or two."

"I thought you might need it now."

"Why's that?"

She was still in a good mood, her tone light-hearted, her steps sure rather than plodding. She'd be leaving for her vacation in a couple of days. He didn't want to drop a big downer on her, but he'd been worrying this back and forth and needed to unload no matter how badly the timing sucked.

"For the bakery. If you wanted to hash out pros and cons of locations, or have me help vet suppliers. You've obviously got the best contacts for real estate, but—"

He stopped, realizing he didn't hear the rhythmic fall of Michelle's footsteps or her breathing. Turning, he found her standing on the trail, her hands at her hips, a frown where moments ago her smile had been.

Yeah, he'd been afraid of this, her thinking he was butting in where he had no business or thinking he didn't know what the hell he was talking about. He walked back to where she stood, taking his time so she'd use the same to cool down.

"I have a brain, thank you." A succinct response.

"Never said you didn't," he came back, just as terse.

"No, but you implied I wasn't using it."

"Did I? I thought I was just offering you the assistance of mine."

She crossed her arms, her stance wide, her brow a furrow of frown lines. "That's not what it sounded like."

He knew what he'd said. The words he'd used. He'd chosen them carefully, hoping she'd take them in the vein they were intended. Then again, that's just what she'd done, hadn't she? Read between his not so subtle lines to the subtext.

He'd called her on giving mouth music to her dream. He deserved whatever she doled out. "I didn't mean for it to sound like anything but me offering to help you get this thing going."

"Because I'm not moving fast enough for you?"

Now or never, dude. Now or never. "Because I haven't seen much movement at all."

She looked away, her jaw set, said nothing.

He took a deep breath and another step toward her. "Look. Either you want to give this a go or you don't. I'm fine with whatever you decide."

"As long as I do my deciding on your timetable."

Aha. "So you haven't decided."

"It's not that simple, Todd. The amount of time and work it's going to take to make a success of a business in this economy? Something else is going to have to give. I like my life. I love my dream. But I'm not sure if I'm ready for such a monstrous upheaval." She walked away from him to one of the benches at the edge of the trail and sat.

He followed because he wasn't about to leave her alone, and sat beside her, leaving distance he'd let her be the one to close. "It's not going to be easy. But don't you think living your dream will be worth any upheaval?"

"Even if it cuts into the time I have to spend with you?"

Was that what this was about? Had their two months of constant togetherness put a damper on her enthusiasm? "I'm not going anywhere, Michelle."

Her hands pressed together between her knees, she looked down, scuffed a sole over the dead leaves and gravel at the trail's edge. "I don't want to have to choose between having you and having the bakery."

Now he was confused. "Why would you have to?"

"Because I'm a one-hundred percent kinda girl."

And she couldn't give one-hundred percent of herself to both a new relationship and a new business. He got it. "Then it's a good thing I'm a one-hundred percent kinda guy."

Her chin came up, but she looked off toward the trestle in the distance, not at him. "A relationship takes two people both giving it their all to work, and I'm not going to ask you to take on the burden of a startup."

"You didn't ask me to. All I did was offer you my brain."

"I know you did. And that means everything to me."

"But you still think you have to go it alone. The bakery, I mean." Because his being here for the relationship wasn't even a question.

"I've been cooking with my mother forever. I grew up helping her, learning from her, enjoying the extra effort she went to because of how special her doing so made everyone feel."

She'd told him all of that at some point. None of this was news. But since he had no idea where she was going, he sat and waited instead of trying to fix whatever it was that had broken. He didn't like seeing her sad.

Michelle pulled in a breath, blew it out, swung her legs back and forth. "The minute I started thinking about the bakery, I knew it would require taking that same effort to another level to achieve what I want."

"The cupcakery where everybody knows your name," he said, and heard what sounded like a laugh, but might've been nothing but a sigh.

"Something like that. And I'm really trying not to be a control freak, but to make things happen the way I see them, I've got to be the one to put in the time and effort."

"Accepting help won't make it any less yours. Whether it's mine or your parents."

She turned to him then, her eyes filled as much with uncertainty as anything else. "But I don't have to worry about screwing things up with my parents. They're stuck with me, whether I lose all our money or make us a fortune."

"You think I'd hold a failure against you?"

"I don't know what I think except that I don't want to take on a venture that will get in the way of you and me. Whether it's time, money, you offering suggestions that I reject . . ."

He really didn't think his feelings were that easily hurt, but she was clearly concerned, and he was pretty sure convincing her she had nothing to worry about was more a matter of time than words.

"Michelle, baby. I'm not going to let any part of your bakery get in the way of you and me."

"You say that now—"

"And I'll mean it later. Seeing you excited over this, knowing how happy it will make you . . ." How could he assure her this wasn't an issue? That this was where the for better or for worse started? He reached over, took her hand, laced their fingers together and waited for her to look up.

Dusk had settled, the headlights of cars as they passed over the nearest bridge throwing shadows along the trail and into the trees. Todd knew Michelle wasn't a fan of running in the dark and didn't want the physical distance between them to add to her discomfort.

"I couldn't be happier that you're making this leap of faith had it been my idea."

She gave him a soft smile. "A whole lot of it has been your idea. At least the putting it into motion part."

"Then do it, and don't worry. I've been here through your late hours at work. I'll be here while you're off trotting through the U.K."

"I told you," she said, her eyes narrowed as she fought the smile now taking over her face. "I do not trot."

"You've stuck with me through my house mess, my work hours, and my Krav Maga class schedule, not to mention my trips home to see my dad." He'd been taking them even before meeting her, had accompanied him to an out-of-state clinic for treatment, but had only taken Michelle with him the once.

"I want you to see your dad. You need to see him. That's not even a question," she said, squeezing his hand.

She had no idea what it meant to have her in his corner when he was facing something so dire. But he pushed that thought aside to settle things with her.

"Your bakery isn't a question either. I know it's not a comparable situation," he hurried on with, sensing the interruption on the tip of her tongue. "But it is about life. Your life. So promise me you'll use my brain or my brawn if you need them?"

"I promise," she said, leaning her head on his shoulder, neither one of them moving again until long after dark.

After four days, Michelle and Eileen left London behind for the Emerald Isle. The second leg of their trip took them across the Irish Sea, putting her that much closer to Todd. Yes, she was enjoying the vacation. Oh, but she was enjoying the vacation. She should've taken the break months ago and booked twice the time away. Her sanity was ever so grateful.

And, no, she wasn't spending the time mooning over Todd, though she did miss him. He was on her mind a lot—a whole, whole lot—and had been since her first call home after landing. He was booked on the next flight to Ohio. Due to a weakened immune system, his father had developed a massive infection and fallen into a coma.

It was hard to find the same enthusiasm for fun after hearing such devastating news, but even with her worries about Todd and his father, she'd loved her time in London. Traveling with Eileen was like going it alone only better. They were both spontaneous, hating planned excursions and preferring to sleep in, eat when and where and what they wanted—even clotted cream and scones at every meal if they chose.

The weather had not been the best, typical autumn fog and miserably cold drizzle, but the London Eye had given them an amazing view of the city anyway. They'd lunched at a pub near Piccadilly Circus, shopped at Harrod's, taken trips to Hampton Court Palace, Tate Modern, and the Tower of London. Growing up loving Princess Di, Michelle was bummed their last day to find Kensington Palace closed, but there'd been so much to see and do that the disappointment was only a blip.

It was their jaunt to Ireland that began with a disastrous mix-up of signals. They'd boarded the bus at the airport for their hotel, only to disembark at the wrong location. In a torrential downpour. With no way to reach the place they were staying without an hour's walk in the rain.

Fortunately, both were able to laugh off the adventure and make the most of the next two days. They soaked up everything Dublin, touring the Guinness Storehouse, Trinity College, Dublin Castle, shopping on Grafton and Henry Streets, downing Guinness and eating at all the pubs in Temple Bar.

On their last night in country, they were treated to a true Irish experience. The pub where they went for dinner was a raucous as Michelle had expected. She could barely hear herself think, much less make out what Eileen was shouting at her over the din. All she could do was grab the other woman's arm and let her friend lead her through the throng.

The room smelled of wood smoke, hops, fried fish, and potatoes, and the cool bite of deep autumn clinging to wool. Beer sloshed from glasses raised in toasts, and voices rose even higher. Eileen found them a small table near the wall and a ruddy-faced server stopped as they sat.

He planted his meaty hands on the table and leaned forward. "What'll ye be havin', lassies?"

"What everyone else is having would be great," Eileen told him. "Your fish and chips seem to be the thing to guarantee a good mood."

The server gave a rowdy laugh, his eyes crinkling at the corners when they narrowed. "Moods of any other sort get checked at the door. Be right back with your pints."

Michelle leaned toward Eileen, laughing as she nearly shouted, "After all the Guinness I've downed the last two days, I'm not sure I can drink a whole pint."

"I'm happy to finish what you can't."

"Thanks, I'm sure," she said, sitting back and suddenly ready to collapse. "Wow. I think I'm suffering vacation exhaustion."

"But it's a good exhaustion," Eileen said. "The exhaustion of nonstop fun and good food. Or mostly good food."

Michelle picked up the mug their server had set in front of them on his way to put out another customer fire. "Cheers and a safe trip home."

Eileen lifted her mug to Michelle's, downed a swallow. "I guess you're ready to get back to Todd. Any word on his dad?"

"Nothing new since we last talked. He said he'd be at the airport to pick us up, though."

"So he came home?"

Michelle nodded. "He'll go back next weekend, after the holiday."

"Is he coming to your mom's for Thanksgiving?"

"He is, and you are, too, yes?"

"Are you kidding? Your mom's turkey dinners are the best." She ran her finger around the rim of her mug, gave Michelle a hopeful look. "Though getting back so late I guess you won't have time to bake cupcakes."

"Wonder what jet-lag cupcakes would taste like? Cardboard bottoms with tired tasteless tops?" Laughing, she moved her mug to make room for the platters of fish and chips.

"Here ya go, lassies. No tasteless cardboard. Eat up or I'll be back to make sure that you do." Their server set down a shaker of salt and bottle of malt vinegar, cursing loudly and running off as down the pub fisticuffs got out of hand. Eileen and Michelle both flinched at the sound of a chair breaking, and the band playing louder to cover the noise.

"Who knew we'd have this much excitement on our last night?" Michelle said squeezing her lemon half over her fish.

Eileen did the same. "It can't have been easy to be here, knowing what Todd's been going through."

It hadn't been, but she'd done her best not to let it put a damper on things. "Even if I was home, I wouldn't be able to do anything, or even be with him since he's spending the week in Ohio, so please don't think I haven't had a good time."

Chowing down on her chips, Eileen shook her head. "I know you've had a good time. I've been with you every day, remember?"

"Do I have to remember walking an hour in the rain?"

"Yes, because it will give you and Todd something to laugh about. I imagine he could use some laughter right about now. Not to mention some good loving."

"Trust me. I'll make sure he gets plenty the minute we're home."

"As long as by home you mean your condo, and not American soil," Eileen said, reaching for her mug, the look of horror on her face giving Michelle the best laugh of the day.

Nineteen

*Apple of My Pie: apple spice bottom with
vanilla caramel buttercream top

THE HOLIDAY SEASON FLEW BY with office parties, family gatherings, a Thanksgiving dinner to die for, and gifts exchanged with good friends over intimate dinners or drinks. Though his father's condition remained unchanged, Todd returned to Ohio a couple of times before the end of the year to deal with his obligations there.

Michelle wanted badly to do more for him than offer a willing ear and a shoulder to lean on, but knew that was the sort of support he most needed from her. She was his island in the middle of this horrible, ongoing storm.

To ring in the new year, he surprised her with a trip to Manhattan. New York was her favorite city in the world and to visit it with Todd made it that much more special—even if they didn't see much of anything but the inside of their borrowed Gramercy Park condo the first couple of days.

This morning, however, Todd had told her to be bundled up for a day on her feet instead of her back. He'd said it while she'd been half asleep, her awake half wondering what he was doing on his laptop in the bedroom's chaise lounge instead of curled up in bed beside her.

When she'd told him to come back, he'd replied they had places to go and people to see. And that was the only reason she was up long before she was ready to be, getting dressed for a day of more walking than she was in the mood for.

"What do you mean, no breakfast?" she asked, tugging her knit cap over her ears. "How am I going to walk all these miles you've mapped out without a warm bagel and jelly first?"

Todd checked his notes, calculating. "It's a lot of blocks, not so many miles, and we've got seven stops to make so plenty of time to rest your tootsies. We should be back here before five, and by then we'll probably be more than ready for dinner."

Wait a minute. What? She looked up from checking her boot laces. "We're not going to eat until dinner?"

His blue eyes sparkled, a bright tease of mischief. "Oh, we're going to eat. That's what the stops are all about."

Seven stops sounded like way too many meals, unless he was planning for her to eat only a couple of bites each time. She supposed it was a good way to try out a lot of the hidden gem eateries the city offered. But still. She would've been more than happy to eat in.

"Am I even going to want dinner when we get back?" she asked, making sure her gloves were tucked into her coat pockets.

Todd laughed, tugging the brim of his ball cap down low. "Yeah. You will. Trust me on that."

Now she was really curious. But she was also suddenly excited. Todd had put a lot of thought into their outing, and being a big fan of surprises, she couldn't wait to find out what was in store.

The first leg of their walk took them twenty blocks east, or so she estimated; she'd stopped counting at fifteen. They held hands as they walked, bumping one another on purpose, laughing as they teased, pointing out sites they recognized, people watching and soaking up the atmosphere.

After spending the first two days of the new year alone, it was great to feel the energy of Manhattan. The air was crisp, Michelle's lungs burning when she breathed it in, but seeing the city with Todd was like seeing it for the first time. In his company, everything was more vibrant. The colors and the smells, the sounds and the neighborhood flavors, they all burst to life just like she did in his company.

"Here we are," he said, holding her elbow and guiding her across the bustling sidewalk to a small Bleeker Street storefront. "Stop number one."

She looked from the curtains tied back in the windows to the awning, read the words there, and glanced up to find him waiting for her response. "You said you hadn't watched *Sex and the City*."

"Don't have to watch to hear the scoop. Especially when my office watercooler's as busy as anyone's."

She looked up again at the sign. The Magnolia Bakery. She couldn't believe it. Were the rest of their stops famous television landmarks? Or restaurants at least? Wait, no. He'd brought her to a bakery.

Oh my gosh! Really? She turned to him, expectant. "Are you taking me on a bakery tour?"

"I knew you were a smart cookie when I met you," he said, dropping a kiss to her nose before ushering her inside.

Oh, the aromas. Sugar and vanilla and rich buttercream. Cinnamon and ginger. Chocolate and coffee. Sweet berries and mellow bananas and tart pears. She breathed in every one, drowning, growing intoxicated and dizzy and hungry all at once.

She chose a red velvet cupcake, peeling back the paper as Todd paid, scooping her finger through the edge of the icing and licking it clean, letting the dollop of airy bliss dissolve in the bowl of her tongue. It wasn't until they walked outside that he hadn't bought anything for himself.

"You don't want one?"

"I'm planning to eat half of yours," he told her as they crossed the street to the Biography Bookshop. "Unless you think you can down all of that and keep walking."

Little does he know, she mused, savoring the texture that was moist without being spongy, the hint of chocolate as subtle as the vanilla, the whipped icing lighter than that made with cream cheese.

While Todd browsed the titles on the carts lined up on the sidewalk, she turned her attention to the cupcake, breaking off pieces from only one side. Breathing deeply of each, she let them melt in her mouth, then handed him the rest when his shopping was done.

"Good girl," he said, giving her a wink as he bit away most of the remaining portion in one bite.

"I'd ask if you liked it," she said, slipping her arm through his. "But you can't taste anything when you inhale it like that."

"That's what you think," he said, finishing it off and licking the crumbs from his fingers. "Mmm, mmm, mmm."

Several blocks later, they reached the Milk and Cookies Bakery on Commerce Street. There, Michelle chose a whoopie pie, the cream cheese frosting sandwiched between two chocolate cookies, which turned out to be crunchier than the traditional cake style she'd expected. Still, she couldn't fault the combination of flavors.

As she had with the red velvet cupcake, she broke this treat in two. Todd bit into the piece she handed him, closing his eyes and enjoying the mesh of flavors and textures. Turning a whoopie pie into a cupcake . . . sure, it could be done. A chocolate bottom, though she'd go with a marshmallow rather than cream cheese filling, and a whipped ganache top. Pure, edible nostalgia. Her mother would totally love the idea.

Another nine or so blocks saw them at Jacques Torres Chocolate where she bought a small box of homemade chocolate marshmallows dipped in a delicious dark chocolate coating. Those she stuffed into her pocket for later, thinking it a good idea to not eat on at least one of the seven stops.

For the next stretch they took their time, and a leisurely twenty minutes later brought them to Billy's Bakery. Michelle was in heaven. This time she ordered a slice of key lime pie with a gingerbread crumb crust. She remembered thinking about key lime cupcakes, and realized as she dug into the dessert how perfect a complement the gingerbread was.

"Here. Taste this," she said, feeding Todd a bite. "Can you imagine this combination of flavors in a cupcake?"

"It's your job to imagine. It's my job to eat."

Shaking her head, she handed him the rest, which he polished off in seconds. The man was typical of his gender, a bottomless pit who she doubted would put on an extra ounce of fat by the end of the day.

It was a mile between Billy's and Babycakes where most of the baked goods were vegan. Michelle had a gluten-free carrot cupcake, sweetened with agave nectar and topped with creamy vanilla frosting. If she hadn't read the menu, she'd never have known the cupcake included no soy, no eggs, and no dairy.

She liked the idea of providing products for those whose diets prevented them from indulging in most desserts. Especially since Erin at Babycakes had proved sweets didn't have to be filled with refined sugar to be delish.

From Babycakes, they headed to sugar Sweet sunshine with its cool pink and yellow sixties vibe. Michelle had Todd choose, and he went for their *Black & White . . . Just Right*—a chocolate cake bottom with vanilla buttercream icing. Michelle ordered a coffee, and they sat and relaxed for a few minutes.

"This is so much fun," she told him, meaning every word.

"I knew it would be," he answered, a man well pleased.

Crumbs was another mile and a quarter and coffee or not, Michelle was beginning to feel it. Not the walking, but the walking fueled primarily by simple carbs. But, oh, the selection inside. Caramel apple cupcakes. Cappuccino cupcakes. Tiramisu and grasshopper and cookie dough cupcakes. Here, the owner donated proceeds from celebrity cupcakes to their chosen charities. Another idea Michelle loved.

What she wasn't loving was the total lack of nutrition in the day's food intake, but suffering the dizziest sugar high ever didn't stop her from ordering one of Crumbs' signature coconut cupcakes. Or from enjoying the story that went along with it—how Mia had baked them for Jason, and their love blossomed, as had their idea for Crumbs.

It was the final stop on Todd's bakery tour, and Michelle wondered if he'd known of the love story that had brought the bakery to life. Or if it had been a coincidence that he'd chosen to end their day here. But as much as she longed to know, she didn't ask. She didn't want to risk ruining an amazing day with such a leading question.

The trip from Crumbs back to the condo took a long twenty minutes. It was time for protein, vitamins, minerals, and complex carbs, not to mention a hot shower. Todd was feeling the drain of energy, too. He walked beside her, silent, his steps not as peppy as they'd been when they'd started out this morning.

After cleaning up and changing clothes, they ventured out again, ending up at a neighborhood pizza joint where they shared a plain four cheese pie. Both were dragging and too tired to talk, but that was okay. It was enough to spend the evening in Todd's company. His eyes, his smile . . . Michelle didn't need conversation when she had him.

"I've got something for you," he said moments later and out of the blue, reaching into his jacket pocket and handing her a light aqua box from her most favorite store in the world.

"Tiffany's?" The box was too large for earrings, too small for a necklace, and what she found when she opened it had her eyes tearing up, her throat swelling, her chest aching with so much emotion she couldn't get out a single word.

The charm bracelet was similar to her grandmother's which she'd worn months ago when she and Todd had brunched at the Silver Diner. Though he'd asked about the charms and listened as she'd told the stories behind them, she hadn't expected him to pay the sort of attention he obviously had.

It had been their third date. They'd met only three days before. And yet he *had* paid attention, to the bracelet, to the association between the charms and two people she loved. To her words as she'd spoken. Thinking back to that day . . . she'd had no idea he'd been so observant, hadn't known him well enough to understand the trait was part of his character.

She lifted the bracelet from the box, saw that it had a single dangling charm: a sterling silver oval with the letters NYC in a blocky black font. "Oh, Todd. You're so sweet. I absolutely love it."

"Put it on," he said, taking it from her hand and wrapping it around her wrist, working the clasp himself.

"I can't believe you did this." She turned her wrist this way and that. "I have loved seeing New York with you. I've been here a gazillion times since my parents are both New Yorkers, but the cookies and the cupcakes and the candy and the key lime pie . . ."

He picked up where she left off. "Not to mention the condo, and seeing the ball drop on New Year's Eve without having to face the crowds."

"I've probably gained five pounds today alone," she said, though she reached for another slice of pizza without feeling an ounce of guilt. The bracelet slid down her arm, the charm tickling. She loved feeling it there, the barest of weight but with such meaning. "I'll have to put in a few extra miles once we're back home."

"Who said anything about going home?" he asked, sitting back, legs outstretched, hands behind his head, all king-of-cool relaxed. "I kinda like this eating what and when we want, walking the city, staying in bed for days at a time."

"I'm sure you do," she said, laughing. "But we're going to have to because if I don't open my bakery after this, the trip won't count as a tax write off."

"This one's on me. My gift to you." He leaned forward then, laced his fingers through hers. "I have so much faith in you, Michelle. So much faith. You've got an amazing head on your shoulders, and a knack for details like nothing I've ever seen. With your mom and dad behind you, how can you fail?"

What about you? she started to ask, but kept silent. She knew she had his support. Look at the day he'd just given her! It had been as much of a gift as the bracelet. The thought he'd put into the bakery tour was nothing short of incredible and was so reflective of the thoughtful man he was.

If her business took off, the credit for its success would be as much his as hers. Did he not want to be a part of what she'd thought they were building? Was he afraid she didn't want him involved? Or was he waiting for her to invite him in as an invested partner?

The thought gave her pause. She couldn't ask him to take on any part of the financial risk. She just couldn't. If she failed, she would bring him down, and the guilt would be unbearable. This was her leap from a very tall cliff into the unknown.

That didn't mean he wasn't a vital piece of the whole.

Twenty

*Lemon Frost: lemon bottom with lemon buttercream top

OF ALL THE THINGS Todd and Michelle had in common, musical taste wasn't one of them. They shared a playful love of The Beach Boys, and an admiration for Ben Folds. But while Todd's iPod was filled with works by artists such as The Ting Tings and The Shins and Rilo Kiley, Michelle gravitated toward the classical works she'd grown up with.

Thankfully, she loved getting to know the bands he listened to, and tonight found them at the 9:30 Club in D.C., waiting to hear The Fray. It was dark, street lamps and lighted signs from surrounding buildings providing the only illumination as the cloud cover blocked the moon and the stars. It was also cold as hell, and damp, a fine mist clinging to their skin, their clothing, their hair.

In line waiting for the doors to open, Todd held Michelle in front of him, tight to his chest, his open jacket around her shoulders warming them both. Still, she shivered, the vibration rattling him. Bundled against the cold or not, she was a little thing and probably feeling the chill worse than he was.

He leaned forward, his mouth to her ear. "Do you want to go home? We don't have to stay."

She shook her head, tendrils of her hair catching in the scruff of his beard stubble. "You've been looking forward to this for weeks. We'll stay."

He had been, but it wasn't like this was the final leg of their final tour or anything. He could see them later in the year at another venue. "Yeah, but I wasn't looking forward to you freezing your butt off."

"I'm fine. I've got you and the body heat from hundreds of strangers to keep me warm." She snuggled against him, tucking her head beneath his chin.

It was hard to feel cold when she was so close, her hands wrapped up in his, her hair a damp cloud smelling of her shampoo, her skin so soft when he pressed his lips beneath her ear to kiss her.

She turned her head, but instead of kissing him in return as he'd hoped, she said, "You know you owe me one opera and one night at the symphony now."

He groaned. He didn't know she'd been keeping track of his music versus hers. "But that means dress clothes and sitting in real seats."

"What's wrong with real seats?"

"It's too hard to cuddle."

She shivered again. "Says the man who has yet to sit through an opera with me."

He liked the sound of that. Liked it a lot. "Then it's a date. And now that I think about it, I do like the idea of you getting all fixed up and me getting to make a mess of it."

She brought up a finger, tapped it to his nose. "That's because you have a one-track mind when it comes to me and my hair and my clothes."

"I wouldn't say that. I love seeing you in them as much as out of them."

"That's the one track I'm talking about."

"I'm a visual creature. What can I say?"

"Visual?" she asked, blowing out a snort. "You with your hands on and all over."

"You're not exactly the hands-off type yourself, Ms. Snow." A fact which he thanked the stars for on a regular basis.

She bound herself more completely into the circle of his arms. "Sorry. I'll work harder on my manners."

"Oh, no need to be mannerly on my account," he said, though he got a sense she had something more than their physical relationship on her mind. "You sure you're not cold?"

She sighed, the tension he'd sworn he'd felt slipping away, then returning to tighten the set of her shoulders. "Don't worry about it. Nothing else matters when you're here."

Hmm. He didn't like the sound of that. "I don't mind being your worry-free zone, but if something's going on that you haven't told me about . . ."

He let the sentence hang, hoping she'd open up without his having to pry. He couldn't help make things right without her letting him know where to start—a problem when she was so used to depending on no one but herself.

"Is this about my foul mood?"

Ah, so there was something bugging her. "I didn't say you were in a foul mood."

"Not in so many words, no, but I'll get over it."

"Michelle?" He pulled back, turned her in his arms. The night's mist clung to her lashes, wetting her eyes. "What's going on?"

She looked down, chin tucked to her chest. He nudged a finger beneath her jaw, forcing her gaze to his. "Michelle? Baby? What's wrong?"

"The lease on the bakery space fell through," she said, still not looking at him.

"What? When?" He knew how much she'd been counting on the location. The rent was right, the traffic exactly the demographic she was hoping to reach. "What happened? When did you find out?"

"Yesterday."

"And you didn't tell me?"

A soft grin lessened the sadness on her face. "I just did."

He took a deep breath. He didn't want to bitch. "Baby, these are the things you're supposed to share. How can I fix things if you don't tell me they're broken?"

"You don't have to fix things, Todd. Just being here is enough."

For her, maybe. "I know you were counting on getting that space. I'm so sorry."

She gave a little shrug. "Life goes on."

"I hate it when you do that, you know. Act all überindependent and don't ask for help."

"There's nothing anyone can do. I just have to grieve for a day or two, then pick myself up and find another place."

"And you'd rather do all that alone."

"It's not like you can grieve for me."

Was that really how she felt? When she'd been there for him while he dealt with his father's decline? "You don't think I hurt when you hurt?"

"Well, yes, but I can't unload all my business woes on you with all you've got going on. That's hardly fair."

Fair? "So, me unloading all the woes about my money-pit house is fair? Not to mention things with my dad?"

"Your dad is not the same thing. And you rarely say anything about your house anymore."

"It's exactly the same thing, no matter whether it's family or work or home or whatever. It doesn't matter. You're here for me.

I'm here for you. It works both ways, for everything, or it doesn't work at all."

She moved away, bumping into the person in front of her. Todd waited as she made her apologies, the streetlamps reflected in her eyes, the mist creating a haze between them. It felt like a barrier, one too ethereal to breach.

The crowd began to grow louder, signaling movement near the front of the line. Instead of responding to what he'd said, she crossed her arms and faced away, leaving him to wonder if anything between them would ever work again.

The doors opened then, and the queue began to snake forward. Behind her, Todd muttered, "Finally," but Michelle was stuck on what he'd said and couldn't respond.

Was he right? Had her song about wanting a partnership been nothing but mouth music? Surely she wasn't that clueless, and yet . . . every step of her mother's career, her father had taken with her. Every fall her father had suffered, her mother had ached from, too.

If she and Todd were going to have a future, wasn't it time to let him in to those places she still kept close?

Logic said yes, for the reasons she'd just given herself and more. But emotions . . . she reached up, shoved her damp hair out of her face. It was hard to think of someone she loved—and she loved him, she knew that she did—risking his money, devoting his time, pouring his energy into something that might very well fail.

Why should both of them have to go through that when the bakery was her dream? He wouldn't even be in the position to offer himself up for the taking if not for her. She didn't know if it was guilt that she was feeling, or something akin to regret. Whatever it was, she was uncertain what to do with it. She didn't like the way it itched.

Once inside the club, Todd hooked his arm around her shoulders, keeping them from being jarred apart. It was that crowded, a crushing mass of cold, wet bodies smelling of perfume and damp hair, the air in the club redolent with the scents of musty concrete and stale beer. Dim lights made navigating through the mob as a couple an iffy proposition.

And yet Todd made it happen. He never let her go. Even when a shoving match broke out to her right and a man three times her size fell against them, Todd was the one to take the brunt of the blow, turning and using his body as a shield.

Once past that fracas, they found a spot with a decent view of the stage, and Todd stood behind her, his arms around her middle tucking her close. He leaned his head forward, his mouth near her ear, and asked, "Can you see okay?"

She was shorter than him, shorter than a whole lot of the crowd, but she'd be able to see enough. Besides, they were here to listen, and she could do that with her eyes closed, leaning into Todd's warmth.

She was overthinking everything. She knew that, and yet she didn't seem to be able to turn off her worries. All of her life, she'd prided herself on setting goals and seeing them through with her own blood, sweat, and tears. So why was she finding it so hard let Todd in?

As she stood in his arms, their bodies pressed close, the music flowing through them, beautiful but so hauntingly sad, it hit her, a big crushing ball on her chest. Her dream. It was too big for her to manage, too large to be a one-woman show.

Though she was starting small, creating an intimate, cozy setting, a comfortable home away from home, the work involved in seeing her bakery from dream to reality was too much to tackle alone. She had her parents backing, and her mother would spend as many hours baking as she would, but she needed Todd.

She needed Todd.

He gave her strength when her own was flagging. He lifted her spirits when they sagged. With just a smile, that comma of a dimple, those flashing blue eyes, he brought her out of whatever funk was dragging her down.

He was there for her every minute of the day. Why had it been so hard to see that without him to share it, her dream would never bring her as much pleasure as it would if he were involved, at her side, her equal?

With a soundtrack of evocative piano notes driving her, she turned, wrapping her arms around his neck and pushing up on her toes. He looked down, frowning, bowing his head so she could whisper in his ear.

Instead, she kissed him, her mouth wordlessly speaking of her need that was more than physical desire. He pulled her tightly against him, and she nodded her agreement when he moved his lips near ear and said, "Let's go home."

Twenty-One

*'Nilla 'Nilla: vanilla bottom with vanilla buttercream top

THOUGH THE SKI VACATION TO THE RESORT at Park City was only sponsored by Michelle's employer, the fact that her boss and a few of the partners were along for the three-day weekend made it seem like a work trip instead of the romantic getaway she'd wanted to share with Todd.

She knew she had no reason to be nervous about bringing him or to guard her behavior, but as they arrived in Salt Lake City, she couldn't help feeling that the weekend would be spent walking on eggshells. Todd quickly set her at ease.

He fit in as he had at her Halloween party, charming and impressing her coworkers while never calling attention to himself or to her. He was the complete gentleman she knew him to be. She loved that about him, how he could size up a situation and the people involved and step seamlessly, even effortlessly into his role. He truly amazed her. She'd never known anyone so at ease in his own skin.

After sleeping in Saturday morning, they enjoyed a leisurely breakfast at their hotel before taking the shuttle to the resort. The rest of the group had gone earlier, leaving her and Todd to make this time away as much of a private event as they could.

Once outfitted for a morning spent on the mountain, they rode the lift to the top. Though Todd had done a lot of skiing out west with his father, this was Michelle's first time in this part of the country. The majesty of the view blew her away. She was used to winters in the northeast, slopes in the Adirondacks, getaway spots in the Shenandoah Valley.

The Rockies were breathtaking, the scenery as the lift climbed brilliant beyond belief. She leaned her head on Todd's shoulder and inhaled the intoxicating scents of pine and cold earth and frost-filled air. The sky was blue, the peaks purple and pink in the distance, shadows of faraway clouds playing games with the sun on the snow.

It was on their first run down the mountain that she realized what an expert skier Todd was. He made her look like a rank beginner. She was perfectly comfortable and had no trouble at all on the slopes. But, wow, Todd was amazing to watch. She shouldn't be surprised; he was an athlete. She knew how fit he was, how much work he put into having fun—whether running, lacrosse, or Krav Maga.

More than once on the morning's trips down, they stopped to take in the view. Todd was as captivated as she was, though she was certain a lot of his joy was in seeing the fun she was having. She had less fun the second half of the day when they both tried snowboarding for the first time.

And it wasn't so much that she didn't enjoy embracing her inner Shawn White as that she fell more than she was comfortable with, hitting her head way too often. The last straw was seeing a helicopter airlift a fallen skier off the mountain. At that, she picked up her board and walked the rest of the way down. Enough with the playing daredevil.

Now sitting in front of a roaring fire in the lodge, she looked up as Todd walked toward her, two steaming mugs of marshmallow-topped hot chocolate in his hands. She took hers, and eyes closed, breathed deeply of the sugar and cocoa and cream before she sipped.

"Mmm. Thank you," she said as he squeezed into the oversized and overstuffed chair beside her. "I've been looking forward to this all day."

"Which part?" he asked, giving her the eye as if there was only one correct answer. The drinking cocoa in front of a blazing fire-place or sitting squished up all cozy like with me?"

"Since I sat squished up against you in the ski lift all morning, I'll have to go with the cocoa and fireplace part," she said, hiding her grin as she sipped.

To protest, he nudged her with his elbow, but not so much that either of them spilled their drinks. "This is good stuff. Maybe you could add a hot chocolate and roaring fire cupcake to your menu."

She set her mug on the side table, pulled her knees to her chest, watched the flames leap and lick at the logs. "The chocolate part would be easy. Not sure how I'd incorporate the roaring fire."

"Soak it in rum and light a match?"

Now that would be a sight. "A cupcake flambé? I doubt I could afford the insurance to cover that."

"Did I tell you? I saw a website the other day for a bakery that sells booze-soaked cupcakes."

"Seriously?"

He nodded, reached for her legs and draped them over his lap. "It was billed as a man's answer to pink girly cupcakes."

Girly cupcakes? "What was on the menu?"

"Let's see," he said, leaning his head against the chair back. "They had one filled with a Bailey's Bavarian cream. One soaked in brandy. A chocolate beer cake with crushed pretzels in the icing. Another was maple with crumbled bacon on top."

She couldn't even imagine. A chocolate beer cake? Bacon? "I'll stick to my menu for now. You can be in charge of branching out into bacon and booze."

He looked over as she reached for her cocoa again, and she met his gaze. "What?"

"Are you thinking of branching out?" he asked, his tone laced not with judgment or assumptions but an invested curiosity.

His interest inspired her. He inspired her. "Since I haven't even opened my flagship yet, it's rather soon, don't you think?"

"Not really. I'm sure you have a five-year plan, maybe even a ten."

Ten. It seemed like so many years, but she knew it was nothing in business. She would love to be the next Sprinkles, to become a household name in the D.C. area and take her bakery nationwide. But that was a pie-in-the-sky dream. And she thought it best to focus on getting her launch done right.

"I do, and it includes adding new products, retiring those that don't sell well. Maybe bringing them back as new and improved for a limited time only. That sort of thing."

He let that sink in for a moment, came back with, "But no steak cupcakes with mashed-potato filling?"

She shook her head, shuddered. "That's wrong on so many levels. I don't even know where to start."

His arm draped across her thighs, he gave a sigh that sounded a whole lot like relief. "Good, because I think I'd do a lot better selling memberships to a Krav Maga gym than any booze-soaked man cakes."

Now this was news. "Really? Have you thought about opening a gym?"

He answered with a shrug. "It's a long way off, but you've motivated me to put it on my to-do list. I guess we'll just have to see what happens."

Back at their hotel, she pondered that as they dressed for an evening of hors d'oeuvres at the ski home of one of her company's partners. And she continued to think about it as she and Todd ate dinner later at a funky barbecue joint. They talked for hours, and always on her mind was the thought that going for her dream had encouraged him to go after his own.

It thrilled her to have been able to give that to him. With all that he'd given her, she often felt selfish. She knew Todd loved the plotting and planning for the bakery as much as she did, but she wasn't used to putting her own interests ahead of others. This twist made the time they spent together on her dream less of a burden.

They devoted most of the next day to skiing, exhausting themselves with several long runs down the mountain. Being that tired made the evening's ninety-minute Swedish massages a much appreciated indulgence. Topping off the night at the Blind Dog Grill, where they watched the sushi chefs prepare their selections, left them sated and ready for sleep.

Their final morning in Salt Lake, the air was crisp and clean, smelling of ice and pine, and the gorgeous view of the mountains nearly stole Michelle's breath. She and Todd took a cab from their hotel into town, walking and shopping and ending up at an adorable little bakery for a late breakfast.

While taking notes on the equipment and menu, Michelle said, "You know you can use my brain whenever you want to."

Todd stopped with his coffee mug halfway to his mouth. "Uh-oh. What did I do now?"

"You didn't do anything," she hurried to assure him. " I'm just making a preemptive strike."

At that, he grinned, his dimple a deep comma of cute. "Going all Krav Maga on me, are you?"

Boy, did she love that dimple and the twinkle it brought to his eyes. "No, I'm going all Todd Bracken on you."

"Ah, right. I wondered when that brain thing would come back to bite me."

She tucked her pen and notebook into her purse. "You've done so much for me. I'll never be able to repay you—"

"I'm not asking to be paid for anything."

"I know you're not," she said, pinching off a bite of an apple fritter she knew her father would love. "It's just that we're always talking about the bakery. Here we are on a romantic getaway and where are we? In a bakery. Checking out how they do things. Our New Year's trip to New York. What did we do? Ate ourselves sick on cupcakes."

"We ate more than cupcakes. And we did a lot more than eat."

A blush rose to heat her face. "I know, but it's always, always about me."

"And when it's my turn to sell gym membership or man cakes, it'll be all about me."

"Are you sure?"

He crossed his forearms on the table and leaned as far as he could into her space. "Baby, I wouldn't be here if I wasn't sure."

"Okay," she said, wanting nothing more than to lean forward and kiss his dimple before moving to his mouth. How in the world did she get so lucky with this one? "But promise me you'll tell me if the cake talk gets to be too much."

"I promise. I swear," he said, raising his mug to his mouth.

"And," she went on, because this was the most important part. "Promise you'll never again speak the words *man* and *cakes* in the same sentence."

At that, he sputtered coffee across the table, and Michelle gave herself permission to enjoy the rest of the day.

"I'm going to be gone for a couple of days. I need to go see my dad."

From their row's center seat as they flew back to D.C., Michelle glanced toward Todd where he sat next to the aisle. His gaze was trained at the floor, his frown etched deeply.

She reached over and took hold of his hand, left their laced fingers on his thigh. "Do you want me to go with you?"

"No. He won't know you're there."

"But you'll know."

"I'd rather know you're safe at home," he said, turning his gaze on her. "The weather says there's a massive blizzard on the way. I'd like to get there before it hits."

"So you're going to turn around and go right back?"

He shrugged one shoulder, then shrugged both. "I thought about booking a flight as soon as we land, but I'd probably better go home and shower, get some clean clothes, check on . . . things."

There was nothing he needed to check on. "Or you could book the flight, get to Ohio, have the hotel laundry wash what you have."

"I thought about that, too."

"Then you should do it." It made the most sense. "I can get home on my own."

His expression softened, his eyes growing sad. "I hate asking—"

"You're not asking." If she could stand, she'd put her foot down. On this, she would not take no for an answer. "I made the suggestion. You're timing's critical. I'll be fine."

"I don't know what I'd do without you." He reached up to

stroke a finger down her cheek, his smile tender and melancholy and breaking her heart.

She knew how much he was hurting. "I like to think I'm indispensible, but you'd do fine. You did fine before we met."

"I managed." He dropped his head against the seat back as if too exhausted to sit straight. "I'm not so sure I'd call it fine."

She leaned her head on his shoulder. She knew exactly what he meant. She'd been happy, alone but not lonely, content as Single Snow. Or so she'd convinced herself until Todd had come along and changed her mind.

Two days later, Michelle picked up the phone. "Hey, Sweetie. How're things?"

"Not good," he told her, his voice gruff, strained, the emotion in those two words telling her what had happened before he spoke the next, and she'd barely drawn a breath before he added, "He's gone."

Twenty-Two

*Choc-a-lot: chocolate bottom with chocolate fudge top

MICHELLE CHECKED THE CLOCK on her nightstand. Five whole minutes had passed since she'd last looked. How could it have been only five minutes? The wait for Todd was growing interminable. He'd called to let her know his flight from Ohio had landed and that he'd be to the condo soon. Their return flight left later this evening.

She'd packed all of her things and most of his. She'd let the office know she'd be out a few days for a family funeral. She'd double-checked that the balcony door was locked, the alarm set, the iron, coffee pot, and oven turned off.

What she hadn't yet done was pick up the phone to give her parents a call. She did that now, hating to break such tragic news over the phone, but the timing didn't allow for a visit. Her father picked up on the third ring. "Hello?"

"Hi, Dad. It's me."

"What's this? A middle of the day phone call from my girl?" he asked, and then as if realizing the import of what he'd just said, sobered. "Is anything wrong?"

"Yes," she said, trying to clear the emotion from her throat before her voice started breaking. "Todd's father passed away last night."

"Oh, Michelle. I'm so very sorry. What can we do?" And then she heard her mother in the background, listened as her father relayed the news.

Her mother's was the next voice in Michelle's ear. "Shelly? How is Todd? When is the funeral? Are you going to Ohio?"

"He's on his way here now," Michelle said, walking to the balcony doors and staring out. How could everything look the same as it had yesterday when nothing was the same at all? "We're flying out this evening. The service is the day after tomorrow. And as far as how Todd's doing . . ."

They'd had so little time to talk. He'd given her the news, told her when to expect him, then hung up to take care of things on his end. She'd scurried around to take care of things on hers, but until she saw him again . . .

"I really don't know how he's doing," she told her mother. "As well as can be expected, I suppose. I'll know more when he gets here."

"The minute you find out the details on the service let me know so your father and I can send our condolences."

"I will, Mom," she said, the words robotic and falling flat, as if she'd cut off all emotion, because doing so was the only way she knew to get through.

"And Michelle? Todd's going to need you now more than he ever has. He won't want to admit it. Men never do. They hate to seem weak, but mourning isn't weakness. You make sure he knows that. And knows you're there for him."

The tears began to flow then. She'd done such a good job of holding them back, doing what needed to be done. But thinking of Todd hurting was more than she could bear, and if not for the sound of his key in the front door lock, she feared she would've broken down completely.

"He's here, Mom. I'll call you as soon as I know about the arrangements. I love you," she said, hearing her mother echo the sentiment seconds before she hung up.

She tossed the phone to the sofa and ran to him, wrapping her arms around his waist, pressing her cheek to his chest. Words failed her. All she could do was hold him and tell him with her heart and her hands how much he meant to her and how very sorry she was.

He remained still longer than she'd expected him to, still and silent as if lost. She listened to the beat of his heart, to the breaths he pulled in and blew out. Finally, he brought up one hand to cup her head and placed the other between her shoulder blades, holding her close.

They stood like that for the longest time, a wordless giving and taking, an understanding that came from a bond forged by the joining of bodies and the mating of souls. If this was all she could give him, it was enough.

The day had been the longest of Todd's life, and he didn't think getting through the next few hours was going to be any easier. The only thing keeping him upright was knowing he didn't have to spend them alone. He would survive the night just as he had the day's funeral. With Michelle at his side.

Still wearing the black dress, sweater, and heels she'd had on since this morning, she reached for his suit coat as he shrugged it off. She had to be as ready to get out of her things as he was. It was almost midnight. And funeral clothes always seemed a tighter fit than they really were.

"Let me hang this up. And your tie."

He worried the knot loose, tugged it like a noose over his head, went to work on his shirt buttons as Michelle walked to the hotel room's closet. He'd been so relieved to have her near, so proud. She'd consoled his family members as if they were her own and had graciously accepted condolences. He hadn't known he would need the crutch of her presence. He had.

Even now, as memories of his childhood flooded back, he was so glad not to be alone. He scrubbed his hands over his face, groaned as if doing so would help bottleneck his emotions. "I keep thinking about how hard Dad tried to get to my lacrosse games. He worked sixty-, seventy-hour weeks. He was still working them when he got sick. He never made as many as he wanted to, but knowing he tried . . ."

"I'm sure he would've loved to have seen every game you played," she said, brushing back his hair with her fingertips, massaging his scalp, drawing away his pain in slow, measured, hypnotic strokes.

Todd felt as if he was stuck on autopilot, going through motions, a zombie. "He was born to save lives. That meant days and nights in the OR. I can't fault him for that."

"And you had your ski trips."

He nodded. While in Utah he'd told her about skiing with his dad, their friendly competition to best each other with each run, the less friendly competition they'd had with the unforgiving and unyielding mountains. "Man, but those were some incredible times together. Just the two of us at the mercy of God's country."

She picked up his shirt and draped it over the back of the desk chair, then sat beside him on the foot of the bed, one leg crossed and tucked behind his. "I'm so sorry you didn't have more time with him growing up. I know you were happy, but that still had to be hard."

"It was what it was, but yeah. I missed him." He leaned forward, emotion a cloud rolling over him, heavy and gray and pressing him down. He shook his head, hoping to dislodge the grief, but it stayed, it grew, it became a monster, choking him. "I'm so going to miss him."

When Michelle wrapped her arms around him, he let go and cried, sobs that burned like brimstone in his chest, that tore at his throat like talons, that fought him with switchblades when he tried to breathe. He buried his face in his hands, hiding the tears, though he didn't know why. He had no need. The tender touch of Michelle's fingers on his back gave him permission to grieve.

And so he did, for the little boy who'd wanted to share his jokes with his dad, for the teen who'd glanced at the stands to see if this time his father had been able to get away. For the adult who would never again sit across the table from his old man and enjoy a Chinese dinner, for his own children who would know only the legend of their grandfather.

It was agony, to remember, to accept, to rage against his loss. He didn't think anything had ever shredded him with such force. He was spent when they crawled into bed, his body limp, his bones aching, his brain numb. He felt as if he'd run a marathon. He was completely wiped out. Michelle swathed herself around him, her head on his shoulder, an arm across his chest, one leg draped to wedge between his.

He breathed her in, her shampoo, her skin, and soaked up the warmth she gave him. They lay like that for what seemed like hours, neither one sleeping, neither one speaking. The quiet and the dark enveloped them, the only sounds were those of their breathing and their hearts beating softly.

It was the first peace Todd had known in days.

Twenty-Three

*Cookie MINTster: chocolate bottom with
mint cookies-n-cream buttercream top

IF TODD HAD LEARNED ANYTHING over the last few months
it was that he refused to waste a minute of his life and that he didn't
want to see Michelle doing anything but living hers to the fullest.

Their New Year's trip to New York and their walking bakery
tour had been an unbelievable experience. Just seeing Michelle's
expression when she realized what he'd planned had been worth
the sugar buzz and ridiculous calorie consumption.

In fact, until they'd made his belated birthday visit to Park City
in February to ski and snowboard, he wouldn't have thought anything could top that day of cookies and cupcakes. But neither
spot would've been as magical if he hadn't shared the fun with
Michelle.

And then his father had passed, causing Todd to reflect on
where he was headed. His personal renaissance wasn't enough.
The getting in shape, the self-examination, the taking stock—it
was all too insular, too selfish. It was all about him when he
wasn't an island.

Michelle was a part of his life and had been since the first night they'd met. The decisions he made now had to include her, to be theirs, not his alone. He wanted to be involved in her choices, too—not those of a personal nature, but the ones that would have an impact on the two of them.

If they were going to have a future, if they were going to be the couple he thought of them as, that he knew they were, they had to look forward together. And that included the plans for her bakery. Which was why he'd told her he was taking her out tonight for a two-part surprise.

"Okay. What's this all about?" she asked once they were seated at their table in the D.C. sushi bar and their orders placed in front of them. "You know how much I love your surprises, and this place is a nice one," she added, looking around. "But I can only take the suspense so long."

Todd reached for his chopsticks, hoping the restaurant lived up to the recommendations he'd gotten. He wanted tonight to go well. "That's because you're always the one on the giving end, making the rest of us wait."

"I do not—"

He cut her off before she got out anything else. "You do, too. All the time. But since you're the most generous person I know, your gifts are worth it."

"When have I made you wait for anything? Besides the ski trip," she added quickly. "That doesn't count since I had nothing to do with setting the date."

"You took me out for sushi after I made it back from Germany and made me wait to take you to bed."

Her cheeks bloomed pink. "I thought we were talking about surprises."

"That was a big one," he told her. "I was expecting to be ravished in the airport."

"Then that doesn't count either." She dipped her spoon into her miso soup, kept her gaze cast down. "Sex isn't a surprise or a gift."

Oh, but she was so very wrong. "Sex with you is a gift I will never tire of waiting to receive."

A grin quirked at the corner of her mouth. "And if this was the time or the place, I'd thank you properly for that, but since it's not . . ."

"Since it's not," he repeated, making sure he had her attention. "It's the perfect time to name the bakery."

"What?" she asked, her gaze coming up.

He pulled a small spiral notebook from the back pocket of his jeans, and a pen from the pocket of his shirt. He laid both on the table, but since he wasn't sure which one of them would be doing the writing, he didn't push them toward her. Pushing her toward this step was already close to presumptuous.

"It's like saving a computer file. Or an author titling a book. Or parents picking out baby names while pregnant. We can't keep calling it the bakery or the business. It needs a name to make it real. Like Sprinkles. Or Crumbs. Or Babycakes. And it has to be something that says Michelle Snow."

He stopped then because he knew he was rambling and Michelle was saying nothing at all. She hadn't touched her salad or her yellowtail rolls. Her eyes were big and filled with something he couldn't define. Uncertainty, maybe? Had he crossed a line? Been too insistent while making his case?

Or maybe not, he decided, as she came to whatever decision she'd been weighing and reached for the pen and paper, opening the blank notebook to the first page, clicking the barrel of the pen. "I've thought about a play on my name. Snow. Snowflakes. Snow Angels. Not Snowballs because of the Hostess snacks. But the whole snow thing may be too cold."

"Especially since you're going for warm and inviting," he said, picking up his unagi roll. She hadn't yet written down anything, but at least she was talking. That had to be a good sign. "So what's warm and inviting? Hot cocoa and marshmallows? A roaring fire? Socks?"

She arched a brow at him. "Socks?"

Her expression had him grinning. "Okay, instead of Snow, use Michelle. Or Chelle. Filled Chelles. Mama Michelle's."

"Too narcissistic," she said, scrapping his idea. "And too Italian."

"Then think ingredients. Sugar and Spice. Cocoa and cream. Butter and Rum."

She lost the battle with a smile. "Did you add booze cakes to my menu when I wasn't looking?"

"I tried," he teased because it was so good to see her having fun.

She sat back, tapped the pen on the table. "Tops and Bottoms. Except that sounds like a clothing store."

"Or a *Seinfeld* episode."

They spent the next thirty minutes batting around more ideas. Some based on flavors. Some on her cupcakes' names. He was a fan of Joe-n-Dough; it said it all. Coffee, dessert—or at least soon to be dessert.

He also liked Campfire. They were his favorite thing on the menu, and he'd never forget baking them with her the night he'd left for Germany. Besides, a campfire was warm and inviting. She wasn't convinced, and shook her head.

All out of ideas, he gave it one final shot. "I'd go with Sweets and Breads but that sounds too . . . brainy."

She groaned at that, closed up the notebook, handed him his pen. "We may need to table this for tonight. I'm not sure I've got anything else in me."

He nodded toward her barely touched food. "Bakery names or sushi."

"I know, right?" She reached for her drink. "It's just been so tense at work this week. My stomach's in such a knot I don't have room for an appetite."

"Then c'mon," he said, standing and holding out his hand. "Before we go home, I want to show you something."

"Part two of the surprise?" she asked, reaching for her purse, then allowing him to guide her outside.

They left the restaurant and drove through the city, parking near the FDR Memorial, Todd's favorite monument. The summer evening was warm, and they walked together through the outdoor galleries, holding hands, reading the inscriptions on the sculptures as they strolled, mist rising above the Potomac behind them.

Todd knew the moment had to be right before he spoke to Michelle. He'd waited too long already. He wasn't sure why. He'd known for months of his feelings. He didn't know what had kept him from putting them into words before now except normal fear of rejection. That wasn't a worry any longer.

They made their way to the edge of the Tidal Basin, the cherry trees standing like sentries, the Jefferson Memorial in the near distance. Across the water, a huge dinner-plate moon hung in the sky next to the Washington Monument. The view was humbling, inspiring. Such beauty made it easy to speak the words he'd come here to say.

Holding Michelle in front of him, he leaned close. They'd stood like this together so many times. He knew the way she fit, the way she felt. Knew to anticipate the way she snuggled against him. He rubbed his cheek to hers, breathing her in, moving his mouth to her ear, and finally, *finally* whispering, "I love you."

He heard her swift intake of breath, felt her body begin to shake. He wrapped his arms tighter around her, uncertain if she wasn't feeling well or on the verge of flight. He couldn't imagine it was the latter, but she hadn't said a word.

And he needed to be sure . . . "Did you hear me, baby? I love you so much. You're my world, my everything. Our future couldn't be any brighter. I can't wait to experience every moment it brings us."

"Oh, Todd. I love you, too!" She turned in his arms, threw herself against him, hugging him to her with everything she had. He held the back of her head, burying his face in her hair, breathing in the evening's scents and those he would recognize as hers were he blindfolded.

At last she pulled back, looking up at him with tears in her eyes. He felt his own threatening, and so he lowered his mouth to hers, telling her again with his kiss that he loved her, that she was his life, that now that he'd found her, he was never going to let her go.

Twenty-Four

*Peanut Brothers & Chocolate:
chocolate bottom with peanut butter buttercream top

THE MINUTE TODD WALKED INTO THE CONDO, he knew something was wrong. Most of the time Michelle beat him home, and by the time he arrived she was either changing for their evening run or throwing together a quick dinner that wouldn't be too heavy in the August heat.

But she wasn't in the kitchen or in the bedroom. He saw her the minute he walked inside, curled up in her big brown chair, the lights and TV off, her eyes closed. For a very long few seconds he just stood there, not moving, not speaking, denying that anything was wrong, that he wasn't going to lose her after having her for only a year.

That thought galvanized him, and heart in his throat, he dropped his computer bag, flicked on one of the living room lamps, and perched on the ottoman in front of her. "Michelle? What's wrong? Are you okay?"

She shook her head, but said nothing, so he reached a hand to her forehead. "Are you sick?"

He didn't think she had a temperature, and moved his hand to cup her cheek. "Talk to me, baby. What's going on?"

"Nothing," she said, her voice choked with emotion. "Absolutely nothing. Not anymore."

He didn't even know what that meant. "Your mom and dad are okay? Your brothers? Did something happen to Woodsie? Or Eileen?"

"As far as I know, they're all fine."

Meaning . . . "And you're not sick?"

"I want to throw up. I can barely breathe. But sick? No."

If she was nauseous . . . but why would she be crying? "Are you pregnant?"

Her head came up off the chair at that, and she opened her eyes. "Why would you think I'm pregnant?"

"You said you wanted to throw up."

"Being sick to my stomach does not mean I'm pregnant."

"Then what does it mean?" He was tired of his questions getting no real answers.

"It means I'm not going to have a bakery and pretty soon I won't even have health insurance because today I lost my job."

Lost her job? "What?"

"I was laid off. A statistic. One more victim of the economy."

Oh. That. He took a deep breath, sat straighter. He knew she hadn't seen this coming. Or if she had, she hadn't said a word, and since there was nothing they didn't talk about . . .

Damn. He didn't know whether to offer consolation or advice, to try to fix what she was feeling or to let her work it out on her own. But he didn't want her to look out and see her future falling apart when a layoff, as bad as it seemed, was not the end of the world.

"You said nothing's going on. Not anymore. Do you mean the bakery? You're giving up on it?"

"What do you want me to do, Todd?" She pulled her legs under her, moved farther away. "Use my severance to finance a business that might see me going broke faster than the lack of a job?"

He told himself to tread carefully. He knew how independent she was, how self-sufficient. She'd proven herself over the years and climbed from entry level to management. Losing that was a blow. Of course it was a blow.

But it was not a reflection on who she was, her skills, her acumen. "I don't want you to go broke, no, but you've got your parents in your corner. It's not like you'd be using all of your severance. You'd still have enough to live on while you got the bakery off the ground."

"I need to get another job," was all she said.

That was her thinking now, in the heat of the moment. He reminded her that days ago she'd thought differently. "You were going to quit when the bakery opened anyway. Why would you get another job if you're going forward?"

She remained silent, refused to meet his gaze. He reached for her one foot he could see and pulled it into his lap, massaging her toes, her heel, her arch. He didn't speak again until he felt the tightness ease, saw the worst of the stress lines on her face vanish.

"Do you realize how much time you'll have now to work on getting the business off the ground? No more ten-hour days at the office. No more stress headaches and spending the weekends prepping for Mondays."

"You act like me losing my job is a good thing," she said, shifting to prop her other foot in his lap.

"Who's to say it won't turn out to be just that?"

"My mortgage company? My credit card companies? Not to mention my checking account."

"So you cut back on the outlet malls and boutiques. We'll eat in or the tabs will all be on me when we go out."

"How's that fair to you?"

She knew better than to go there. He knew that she did; he knew, too, this wasn't the time or place for making life decisions. "This is a relationship. It's not about fifty-fifty. I pick up the slack when you're in a bind, you do the same for me."

"You know there won't be any weekends if I go ahead with this. And there will still be a lot of stress headaches."

"Yeah, but wouldn't you rather have your head hurt because of cupcakes than real estate?"

She lifted a hand, rubbed at her temple. "I'd rather my head not hurt at all."

"Then get up. Change clothes. We'll go for a run."

"What if I don't want to run?"

He had never known her to not want to run. "I do. And it's not as much fun if you're not there."

"You're just trying to get me out of this chair."

"Out of that chair and into a better mood."

"I like this chair."

"Then you can curl up and sleep in it when we get back."

"I used to, you know. Before you."

"What? Slept in your chair?" He barely remembered her sitting in it. She always sat next to him on the couch.

"I ate here, slept here, paid bills here, watched TV here. I sat here for hours one night searching Match.com profiles."

"Then we'll have to have it bronzed. Or save it for our grand-children."

"Are we going to have grandchildren?"

Not a conversation he wanted to have now even though he was the one who had opened the door. He reached for her hands, got to his feet then pulled her to hers. "Not if you don't get out of that chair, change your clothes, and make me a happy man by running with me."

"Running's not how you get grandchildren," she told him as she trudged to her room.

Ah, if she only knew, but how could she? She wasn't the one watching her body in motion as she ran.

"You go get showered," Todd said as soon as they were back at the condo. "I'm going to make dinner."

She'd been following him through the main room but stopped at that. "You're going to cook? When have you ever cooked?"

"One of the skills I've been keeping a secret."

"You have more?"

"Oh, the surprises you're in for," he said, patting her on her bottom and shooing her on her way.

It was such a sexist gesture, and she loved it, laughing to herself all the way to the bathroom where she ditched her shoes and clothes and climbed beneath the stinging spray. What a day. What a day. She was exhausted, and though she was feeling better after her run with Todd, she still felt as if ten years of her life had been flushed down the drain.

He was right about one thing. Losing her job would give her that much more time to spend on her business. And if she was careful with the money, her severance would go a long way. Since she had always been careful, her living expenses were low.

She could cut out completely any shopping that didn't involve the bakery. She had clothes, shoes, jewelry. She could buy cards instead of the small gifts she loved picking up for friends. And if she and Todd gave up all but the occasional pizza night and sushi at Raku to eat at home . . .

Speaking of eating, what was that smell? Even over the soap

and shampoo she could smell something spicy. Tangy. Garlicky. Tomato and peppery. Like barbecue? Her stomach rumbling, she hurried through the rest of her shower, dressing in comfy shorts and clipping her wet hair in a twist on the back of her head on her way to the kitchen.

She reached it in time to see Todd toasting hamburger buns, a skillet of yummy smelling sloppy joe filling simmering. "That smells so good. I'm starving."

"Glad to hear it," he said, directing her to a barstool. "Just about done. I know how much you love barbecue. This isn't the same, but it's the best I could do on short notice."

"Your best looks amazing." She leaned over the bar, breathed in all the aromas she'd picked out earlier. "I might just have to hand over all future cooking duties to you."

"As long as you don't mind a lot of sloppy joes. Though I do make a mean chicken pot pie."

"Don't tease me unless you mean it. I could so get used to being spoiled."

He came around the bar then, set her plate in front of her, spun her chair to face him, and stepped between her knees. "Then get used to it. Let me spoil you. You bake your cupcakes and let me worry about everything else."

"I love you, sweet Todd. I don't know what I would do without you."

"Trust me, babe. You're never going to have to find out."

Twenty-Five

*Daddy's Joy: chocolate bottom with
almond coconut buttercream top

IN LINE AT THE DUNKIN' DONUTS drive-through, Todd gave
Michelle a quick call, and was uncharacteristically relieved to get
her voice mail. In all the months they'd been together, he'd never
once told her a lie. Lying to her now was not going to be easy, but
not having to hold a conversation while he did would make it
less hard.

"Hey, babe, I'm running late," he said once the beep sounded.
"I've got to help a guy with some stuff, a couple of errands, so I'll
be there when I can. Love you."

That done, he turned off his phone and placed his order. When
she got the message, she'd call him back. He knew that without
question. Michelle checked up on those she loved. It was one of
the things he adored about her.

But when she called, she would want to know what errands he
was running, who he was running them with, or for, and he
didn't want to expand the lie that—for now—was small and white
and turn it into something huge and ugly. His meeting with her

233

father wouldn't take long, and before he saw her, he'd figure out a way to cover his tracks.

He parked at Jack Snow's office, grabbed the coffees and sack of apple fritters. The pastries were Jack's favorite, and Todd loved the man like a father. This was hardly a conversation he needed to bribe his way into or one he needed Jack sweetened up to have. The talk would be cause for celebration, the coffee and fritters a way to toast the good news.

"Todd."

"Jack. Thanks for meeting me."

"Anytime," he said, and glancing at the goodies Todd held, smiled and added, "Let's take this into the conference room. Give ourselves some space."

Once settled at the table, Jack tore open the bag to use as a plate while Todd searched for the words he'd come to say. He wrapped both hands around his cup of coffee, but he was pretty sure the acid would eat up his stomach if he drank. This was a heavy conversation. He wanted to do it right.

"How's Michelle? I haven't talked to her in a couple of days."

Todd nodded while Jack bit into his fritter. "She's good. A bit crazy with all the bakery plans, but good."

"I'm glad she's got the new business to keep her busy. I was worried when she got laid off she'd be at loose ends. Though—" Jack reached for his coffee "—knowing my girl, that was a pretty stupid worry."

Todd knew the love Jack had for his daughter, and that worrying was what fathers did. Rolling his own cup back and forth in his hands, he cleared his throat. "You're probably wondering why I wanted to see you in person instead of picking up the phone."

Slowly, Jack sat back, one hand gripping the arm of his chair, the other braced on the table. "Since you mentioned it was personal, I've got an idea. Might as well get it out in the open before you pop."

Still staring at his hands and his cup, Todd grinned. If he'd gone shopping, he couldn't have found a better man for a father-in-law. And this man deserved his full attention, so Todd took a deep breath and faced him.

"If you've got an idea of why I'm here, then you've got an idea as to how I feel about your daughter."

"I do, but go on," Jack said, rubbing his forefinger and thumb over his mustache as if trying to hide a smile.

Todd had just about as much trouble hiding his. "I love Michelle, sir. I think I fell in love with her the first night we met. And if what I was feeling that night wasn't love, it was definitely the sort of like that leads there."

"Go on."

"Except for the week I was in Germany, and the week she was in the U.K., not a day has gone by that we haven't talked. She's been on my mind constantly. But more importantly, she's been in my heart." Todd paused, his chest tight, his pulse racing as if he'd run a 10K. Something about acknowledging Michelle as a vital piece of his life left him struggling to breathe.

What if he'd never found her? What if he'd blown off her e-mailed appreciation of his smile as shallow flirtation instead of writing her back? What if he'd never suggested they skip the business of e-mail and take things to a more personal level?

He closed his eyes, swallowed the lump of emotion lodged in his throat like a ball. Once that was cleared and he was pretty sure he could do more than squeak, he looked Jack in the eyes and said, "Sir, I would like very much to have your permission to marry your daughter."

Jack was the first to look away, swiveling forward in his chair and mirroring Todd's pose as he wrapped his hands around his coffee cup. He pursed his lips as if thinking, frowned as if thinking more, gave a little shake of his head as if the things he was thinking weren't going to go Todd's way.

Then he arched a brow, glanced over the rim of his glasses and winked. "Sorry. Just had to make you sweat there for a minute."

"A minute was probably all I was going to be able to stand," Todd admitted, though knowing Jack Snow as he did, he should've expected the other man would yank his chain.

"I've probably been thinking of you as my son-in-law since last Thanksgiving when Michelle brought you to dinner. In her entire life, my daughter has never been as happy as she's been since finding you. And I'm pretty sure her mother has been planning your wedding behind both of your backs for months. Of course once my daughter gets wind of what my wife's been up to, the fur's going to fly, but it's good to know I won't have to suffer the fallout alone."

He reached over, slapped Todd on the back. "Welcome to the family, Todd. Welcome, welcome, welcome."

Michelle was beginning to wonder if she'd be eating sushi alone. Rather than sitting at the bar where she and Todd liked to watch the chef prep their orders, she'd chosen to wait for him at a table.

She'd never expected she'd be waiting this long or that he wouldn't have checked in by now. It wasn't that she kept him on a leash, but he always, always, let her know when he was running late and why.

Their trips abroad aside, she didn't think they'd been out of touch for more than a few hours at a time since meeting. If they weren't talking, they were texting, even if they had nothing more than, "I love you," to say.

That constant contact was one of her favorite things about their relationship. He was always there for her. She was always there for him. The bond they shared was exactly what she'd craved, even if she hadn't known it till she met him.

What errands was he running? Who was he helping and what were they doing? Why was it taking so long?

Eyes closed, she dropped her head against the back of her chair and breathed deep. She was being ridiculous, worrying like this, but she couldn't help it. He wasn't picking up his messages. He wasn't responding to her texts. Something was wrong, and if she lost him now . . .

Okay, enough with the melodrama. They'd agreed to meet at seven-thirty. It wasn't yet seven-forty-five. She had her Day-Timer in her bag and tons of notes on the bakery to organize.

This was the perfect time to make sense of those she needed to keep, set aside the maybes, and toss the ones that weren't worth her bother. Getting the task out of the way now would give her more time later for follow through.

She'd opened her organizer and was sorting the scraps of paper she'd stuffed inside when Todd dropped into the seat beside her. She jumped, surprised, expecting him but her mind elsewhere. "Todd, you scared me to death. Don't do that."

"I figured you'd be forming a posse to send out and hunt me down." He leaned over, smacked her with a kiss that she knew was meant to distract her.

It didn't work. "Where have you been? I've been worried sick."

He took in the paperwork on the table. "So worried you were working?"

"I was trying to keep my mind off the billion things that could've happened to you."

"Like I fell asleep at my desk and Vikram and Guoming locked up the office behind me?" he asked, reminding her of the cut-ups his coworkers were.

"More like you fell asleep behind the wheel of your car and drove into the Potomac," she said, wondering what errands had inspired this good mood. He was acting as if he'd been right on time, as if she hadn't left him a dozen messages. As if he didn't know she'd been sitting here going nuts.

"So whatcha been doing?"

Obviously he knew nothing of the kind. "Just looking at a lot of notes I've been making."

He picked up one of the paper scraps. "'Cost of air-tight containers? What kind of freshness guarantee?' Are you thinking of offering shipping?"

"I'd love to, but I doubt it's going to be feasible the first year. I'd rather get the bakery off the ground, make sure we can handle the business locally before offering to ship."

The grin he gave her was slow to come and was awash in an humble satisfaction. "We?"

She nodded. Didn't he know she'd never have made it this far without him? "We."

"Have you decided on the name?" he asked, watching as she stacked the notes and filed them in a zippered pocket.

A store name was the last big thing. Signage, personalized boxes and bags, a logo, all the advertising—everything was on hold until it was settled. They'd tossed around so many, found out everything they'd liked had been used on a bakery somewhere in the country.

Not that she'd counted on being completely original, but anything too kitschy or overly precious would be confusing.

She wanted simple and clear, just not boring.

"Frosting. A Cupcakery."

His eyes widened. "Chelle! I like it! I really really like it!"

At his enthusiasm, the worry haunting the back of her mind all day vanished. "We've been calling it a cupcakery all this time, I figured, why not make it part of the name."

"It's perfect. Truly. And Frosting just says it all. Sweet and inviting and everything you wanted."

"I think so, too. I think it'll work. I can see the signage and the lettering." She bobbed her head, thinking, liking, pleased. At least she was pleased until she realized the look on Todd's face had changed.

He was serious now, contemplative, had something really big on his mind. "Todd? What's up? What aren't you telling me?"

"I've told you everything," he said, his voice low and even, his tone measured, as if he didn't want to step wrongly. "I love you, Michelle. And I would love it if you would let your dream be my dream."

He inspired her. He strengthened her. But he had to know how much was on the line. "You know if this falls through, the debt's going to kill me. Even if it succeeds, the debt's going to be hanging over my head for years."

A soft shake of his head told her she needn't worry. "If it were hanging over mine, too, it wouldn't hurt you so badly if it fell."

"Todd, I don't want to ask you to do that."

"You didn't ask me. I made the offer." He reached for both of her hands, so small in his, so strong yet fragile. Her strength amazed him, her courage. She had to know that. "I want to be a part of your life. I want to be with you forever. I want to mourn your losses as well as celebrate your wins. I want all of them, every single one of them, to be ours."

She dropped her gaze to their joined hands as he rubbed his thumbs over her knuckles, her wrists. But he didn't know she was crying until the first of her tears fell to wet his skin.

"What is it, babe? Tell me what's wrong, what you're thinking."

She shook her head, sniffed, her hair a fall of waves, in golds and browns. "I've done everything on my own for so long. For years. For my entire adult life. Part of me fears if I can't do this alone, I'm nothing but a big fat failure."

"And the other part?"

"The other part wants so badly to have a shoulder to lean on."

"I have a shoulder. I have two."

"But not just a shoulder. I want a brain to pick—"

"Got one—"

"And arms to hold me—"

"Got two—"

"And a strong back to pick me up when I crash from the crazy and the stress and the sugar overdose from all the test tasting I'll have to do."

"I'm good at test tasting. Also good at getting the both of us into our running shoes to burn off all those calories."

"Then you don't think I need to put on a couple of pounds to be hot?"

"Michelle Snow. If you don't know by now how hot you are."

"How hot you think I am, you mean."

"No. I don't mean." And he waited for her to look up. Only when she had, when her eyes that were so deep and so blue met his, did he continue. "You are an amazing woman, Michelle Snow. I get that this bakery is making you nuts, but that doesn't change anything about who you are.

"You're loving and giving. Your friends know that. Your family knows that. I probably know it more than any of them. I've never met anyone with your generous heart." He took a breath, letting that sink in. He wasn't going to blow smoke up her skirt, but neither was he going to sit back while she gave up on her dream. "You're so smart, Michelle. You're driven. You know what you want and you go after it. That's a huge turn on."

"Really?"

"Really. You've also got a sense of style, like you're King Midas or something, that turns everything you touch into gold. The tables you set, the parties you throw, not to mention the way you always look like a million bucks. And whoever said you needed to put on a couple of pounds to be sexy?" He really wanted to kick that jerk's ass. "Point me in their direction."

The corner of her mouth lifted. "So you can go all Krav Maga on his butt?"

"That, too. You're the whole package, and seeing you so torn up over this bakery business makes me want to hurt someone. Or punch a wall, or something."

She laughed at that, a soft sound of tension being released that made it a whole lot easier to breathe. "If you want to punch a wall, do it at your place where you've already got the tools to fix it. As far as the something . . . you could kiss me."

That he could do. Oh, that he could do. He leaned forward, caught the corner of her mouth with his and kissed her sweetly, a tender expression of all the feelings he couldn't let go with a table in the way and an audience. But when her lips parted and he tasted her, he decided what the hell.

He pushed back his chair, came around to where she was sitting, scooped her up, and dropped into her seat with her in his lap. She reached for him wildly, wrapping her arms around his neck to keep from tumbling to the floor, and then she smiled. A big, wide smile that reached her still watery eyes and had his own stinging.

She made him ache, this woman. She made him want things he'd thought impossible to achieve. She made him desire to be better, to strive for more, to take risks and walk through the fire of every one. But most of all she made him want to have her at his side, his partner, his better half.

He cupped the back of her head, brought her mouth to his. Around them, Raku's patrons clapped and cheered. Beneath him, Michelle sighed and smiled. He smiled, too, but he didn't release her. Instead, he slanted his head just so and opened his mouth. She returned the delicious favor, her tongue finding his, her surrender not meek at all but demanding, insistent. Equal to his.

Her mouth was sweet, giving. Her hands at his nape squeezed with possessive intent. He thought of the way they felt on his skin, teasing, tempting, torturing, and knew he could never get what he wanted, go where he wanted, in the middle of a restaurant with the world looking on.

With a reluctance that bit deep, he pulled away, but only far enough that he could see his reflection in her eyes. "Will you let your dream be my dream?"

She bobbed her head, a crazy frenzied nod of excited hope. "I will. Oh, Todd, yes. Sharing the bakery with you is like the last piece of the puzzle finally falling into place."

It wasn't quite the last, but that one could wait till next week.

Twenty-Six

*Pumpkin Pie: pumpkin spice bottom with
vanilla cream cheese buttercream top

MICHELLE COULDN'T THINK OF ANYTHING that sounded
less appealing than running in this morning's 10K Turkey Chase.
The cause was a good one, benefiting charities supported by the
Rotary Club, and she'd feel like a scrooge if she bailed. But she
was thinking about it. She had all the energy of warmed-over
crap, Todd was on the verge of a full-blown cold, and for the first
time she could remember, they were both running late.

She dropped to sit on the ottoman in front of her cushy brown
chair, the chair she hadn't used in months since curling up on the
sofa to watch TV, Todd's arms around her, had become her ritual
at the end of the day. Spending the morning there, or even crawl-
ing back into bed, sounded so much better than heading out into
the abysmal weather.

"Are you sure you're up to this?"

"It's Thanksgiving, babe. It's tradition. The turkeys are counting on us."

He said it through the stuffiest nose ever. He wasn't up to running in the damp and the cold any more than she did. Her hero,

such a brave front. She wasn't half as sick as Todd, and yet she was
the one looking for a reason not to go.

At least she'd finished baking the cupcakes last night. All that
was left to do before taking them to her parents' for dinner was
frosting them. Doing so sounded much better than running, and
as an excuse, it wasn't much of a stretch. "I should probably stay
and frost the cupcakes."

"You'll have time when we get back," he told her, checking that
he had both of his gloves.

What had she done with hers? "Assuming we can work up the
energy to make the run in our usual time."

"We'll be fine."

"Or we'll come home feverish with pneumonia."

"No pneumonia. No fever. I promise." He reached for her
hands and tugged her to her feet. "We'll take the car and park
near check-in. Save our strength for the race."

Fine. But she wasn't going to make it easy for him to get her to
the door. "I need to get my gloves."

"Hurry up, babe. Time's a ticking."

What was with him today? He was feeling way too bad to be
acting so cheery, though she supposed the thought of her
mother's Thanksgiving dinner was enough to lift anyone's mood.
And if she would put her own butt in gear, the run would be over
and done with, and they'd be on their way to enjoying the feast of
food, family, and friends.

That was the only thought that got her out the door and into the
car. The drive was short, and Todd found a spot to park in a neighborhood near the check-in at the Bethesda YMCA. The walk over,
however, was miserable, the cold seeping through all of Michelle's
clothes, turning her skin into gooseflesh. She was shivering when

they picked up their numbers and shoe timers, making her feel a gazillion times worse. All she wanted to do was go home.

Due to running so late, they had only a couple of minutes to warm up before the runners were called to the starting line. And it was a mob scene. Great. Six miles spent running like packed sardines on tight city streets was not her idea of a good time. It was only Todd's strangely good mood keeping her from heading back to the car to nap while she waited for him to finish the race.

Not wanting to ruin his day, she pressed forward, one step after another, Todd just in front of her doing the same. She thought of her cupcakes as she ran, her body moving of its own volition, but even running with the man she loved, her mind focused on the business she loved, she was not having fun.

Fun would be hanging out with her mother and Colleen and Eileen in her parents' kitchen. Fun would be listening to her dad and Brian and Michael and Todd cheering on whatever football team they were rooting for.

Fun would be sitting around the table after dessert, drinking coffee or wine, talking the rest of the day away and noshing on leftovers until it was time to go home.

Then there was the fun of having a clean bathroom, because with a mile and a half left, she had to stop. "Todd. I've got to find a restroom. You go on. I'll catch up."

"No, I'll wait," he said, just as a gas station on Old Georgetown Road came into view. "Make it quick. We're almost done."

Knowing they had but a short distance left made it a whole lot easier to get in and get out and get back on the road. She flew through the rest of the race, running her hardest and crossing the finish line at the same time as Todd. After a celebratory high-five, they headed for the sideline folding chairs to remove the timing chips from their shoes.

She was so ready to get home. She still had to shower, dress, and frost her cupcakes, but they'd be to her parents' house in plenty of time. Todd knelt on the road in front of her to untie the timer from her shoe, pulling off his gloves . . . then taking a diamond ring from his pinky.

Offering it to her, he said, "Michelle, will you run with me forever?"

Oh, God! Oh, God! Was this real? she thought, but what she said was, "Oh, Baby," leaning forward to throw her arms around him. He was giving her a ring, a gorgeous, perfect, really big ring. She couldn't push any words past the lump of emotion choking her. All she could do was hold him.

But Todd pulled away, to look into her eyes, and ask her, "Will you marry me, Michelle?"

Hadn't she just said that she would? No! She hadn't said anything at all! Oh, gosh. She was such a moron, making him wait. "Oh, yes, yes. Yes, Todd, I'll marry you," she said, holding out her hand for him to slip the ring on her finger.

And though they'd just run a 10K, they ran all the way to their car, kissing and laughing and rejoicing as they did. Life was good, how could they not celebrate? They called Todd's mother once back at the condo, then spent a long, long, really long time getting ready for Thanksgiving dinner.

Of course since she was never late to her parents for the holiday, through the years often sleeping over the Wednesday night before to help with the preparations the next morning, Michelle knew she'd be in for a load of grief.

Her big brother Brian was the first to deliver it. "Thanks for being late and holding things up, Chelle. Some of us here are starving, you know."

"Oh, I'm sorry, Brian. I just couldn't make myself hurry because I was too busy getting engaged!" She nearly shrieked the last word, jumping up and down as she showed off her ring.

"What?" Brian asked, his eyes wide, his smiled wider as he pulled her into a hug. He let her go but only to reach for Todd and do the same. Her mother and Colleen descended, laughing, nearly crying, admiring her ring and offering their best wishes with a whole lot of kisses and hugs.

She met Todd's gaze over the crowd, watched him accept just as many handshakes and slaps to the back. The moment was glorious, surreal, her family sharing in the most important day of her life, her favorite holiday made extra special by the event.

As everyone moved to the table to eat, her eyes misted, and she reached for Todd to hold him just a minute more. Their embrace brought out more laughter and calls of, "Save it for the bedroom," and "You've got a lifetime of that ahead of you. Don't burn yourselves out now," and "Enough already, I want to eat."

Her mother put a stop to it all. "Sit down, sit down. I want to hear all about the proposal."

Todd helped Michelle tell the tale as the turkey was carved, dishes of stuffing and mashed potatoes and peas and cranberries passed around, gravy poured, hot rolls buttered, all of it pounced on as if Brian wasn't the only one starving.

Her mother asked about the wedding. Her father asked about the honeymoon. Her brothers teased about becoming uncles. Colleen talked wedding dresses, then as dessert was served, asked, "At the reception, are you going to serve cupcakes?"

That prompted Jack to get to his feet, lifting his pumpkin spice cupcake. "I'd like to make a toast."

Everyone at the table lifted their cupcake, following her father's lead as he peeled away the baking paper, releasing the fragrances of cinnamon and cloves and sweet pumpkin around the table like a cloud.

"To Michelle and Todd. May their lives together be a plentiful feast, and their love the icing on the cake."

Epilogue

*Fluffer Nutter: vanilla bottom filled with
marshmallow with peanut butter buttercream
and topped with a honey drizzle

"I THINK WE DID IT," Michelle said, hooking her arm through
Todd's, her head against his shoulder. It had been a very, very, very
long day, and he knew she had to be beat. "I was beginning to
wonder if we could pull it off, but look at this place, will you? I
really, really think we did it."

They had, but Todd wasn't looking at *this place*—Frosting A
Cupcakery. The name fit their Chevy Chase bakeshop like no
other. He was too busy looking at Michelle, his wife of five
months, his life from the moment he'd met her almost three
years before.

He pulled his arm from her to hug her close, finally taking in
the dream they'd created together, partners every step of the way.
The bakery was an inviting oasis of soothing colors, cream and
tan and soft white, and enough sweet sugary scents to make lettuce leaves tremble.

Todd wondered how many diets had fallen prey to the day's
rich creamy espressos and *Raspberry Zzzurbert* cupcakes, among

others. They'd sold even more than they'd given away, their clientele mad for the treats, every person he spoke with swearing to come back, to buy more, to bring friends. Pretty damn successful day.

Planning their New Year's Eve wedding and their bakery at the same time had proved both Todd and Michelle insane. But if anything, sharing the insanity had gotten them through all of it—including the hours they'd spent together in her kitchen the day of their nuptials, baking the cupcakes they'd served to guests at the reception that night.

Now those same flavors of cupcakes, along with dozens of others, were sold in the bakeshop they'd opened late in April. Today, June 5, 2010, had been their official grand opening, and by any set of standards, an overwhelming success. And to think, they owed it all to Match.com.

Beside him, Michelle frowned, looked up. "Todd? Are you listening to me?"

She was tired, he could tell, but he loved how the sparkle never went out of her eyes. He dropped a quick kiss to her forehead. "How many people do you think came through here today? Five hundred?"

"At least. Oh, and a little bird told me that you're making a name for yourself as a marketing expert."

"Who knew, huh?" Todd had certainly never considered himself an advertising guru, but the work he and Michelle had done to get the word out about Frosting had paid off better than either anticipated.

And then there were the blog reviews that were worth their weight in bulk sugar. "Did you hear that several customers think we out bake some of the same spots we visited during our New York tour?"

"I loved that tour. That you thought of it and surprised me with it. That I got to take it with you." She sighed, swatted at a balloon that had lost its helium and was drifting, tired, to the floor. "I love even more that you're here with me now. I could never have done this alone."

As much as she'd wanted it, he was pretty sure she'd have found a way, but contributing his own blood, sweat, and tears made him appreciate her efforts tenfold.

"I'm sorry you had to handle most of the crowd," she told him.

"I'm sorry you had to spend so much time baking," he replied.

"Are you kidding me? Loving to bake got me here. I wouldn't want to be anywhere else." She moved to stand in front of him, looping her arms around his neck, smiling the smile that had stolen his heart. "Except wherever you are."

She had said it best in her wedding toast. *I am complete. I am more than content. I have been given an unexpected gift in life and I am truly grateful . . . for you . . . for us . . . and for everything we will always share. From the top, middle, and bottom of my heart, I love you.*

Todd returned every bit of the sentiment. And he would for the rest of his life. It was time to go, to climb into bed and as they did every night as husband and wife, say, "I love you, and I'll miss you while you sleep."

"Let's go home."

Submit Your Own True Romance Story

"The marriage of real-life stories with classic, fictional romance—an amazing concept."

—**Peggy Webb**, award-winning author of sixty romance novels

Do you have the greatest love story never told? A sexy, steamy, bigger-than-life or just plain worthwhile love story to tell?

If so, then here's your chance to share it with us. Your true romance may possibly be selected as the basis for the next book in the TRUE VOWS series, the first-ever Reality-Based Romance™ series.

- Did you meet the love of your life under unusual circumstances that defy the laws of nature and/or have a relationship that flourished against all odds of making it to the altar?

- Did your parents tell you a story so remarkable about themselves that it makes you feel lucky to have ever been born?

- Are you a military wife who stood by her man while he was oceans away, held down the fort at home, then had to rediscover each other upon his return?

- Did you lose a great love and think you would never survive, only for fate to deliver an embarrassment of riches a second or even third time around?

Story submissions are reviewed by TRUE VOWS editors, who are always on the lookout for the next TRUE VOWS Romance.

**Visit www.truevowsbooks.com
to tell us your true romance.**

TRUE VOWS. It's Life . . . Romanticized